LAST RESORT

EMMA LAST SERIES: BOOK NINE

MARY STONE

Copyright © 2024 by Mary Stone Publishing

All rights reserved.

No part of this book may be reproduced in any form or by any electronic or mechanical means, including information storage and retrieval systems, without written permission from the author, except for the use of brief quotations in a book review.

❋ Created with Vellum

This book is dedicated to the memory of my mom, who would shudder and ask, "How can you watch/read such things?" whenever she found me engrossed in scary stories or movies as a child. I'm still at it, Mom. Some things never change. Miss you terribly. Love you always.

DESCRIPTION

He's checking his list, checking it twice. Which agent's fate will be sealed tonight?

Haunted by the whispers of the Other, a chilling real-world threat has Special Agent Emma Last and the Violent Crimes Unit on high alert. Their recent victory against D.C.'s gangs is overshadowed by a sinister promise of vengeance that materializes swiftly, claiming the life of a young FBI recruit.

"I'll spell it out in the blood of one of your agents."

This brutal act marks the beginning of a deadly game, drawing Emma and her team into a dark web of danger, where every clue leads them deeper into the mystery and closer to the monster stalking them from the unseen.

And that's just the beginning. When the body of a cop working the dead agent's crime scene surfaces the next day, the VCU team comes to the chilling realization that the killer isn't just watching. He's one step ahead of them.

Even worse...

He knows where they live. And he's not just coming for

one of them. He's coming for them all. And they may not get out of this one alive.

Last Resort is the ninth book in the Emma Last series by bestselling author Mary Stone, where no one is safe when they're on a madman's list.

1

Newly minted FBI Agent Valerie Lundgren silently willed the intersection light to change in her favor. Her fingers drummed the steering wheel, and she couldn't help but look at the ring finger on her left hand.

Currently, that digit was bare. But in the space of the next couple hours, she anticipated that changing.

Though he won't ever get the chance to pop the damn question if this stinking light doesn't change.

She had one stop to make on the way home—the liquor store that served as the cornerstone of the tiny commercial center.

After years of hard work, everything—personally and professionally—seemed to be paying off at once.

She had a lot to celebrate.

Only forty-five days into her employment with the FBI's Cybersecurity Division, Valerie had already uncovered and helped dismantle two major fraud and phishing operations. The perpetrators had been sentenced over a week ago, and just this morning, she'd been awarded recognition as the principal investigator on both cases.

And Will, her longtime boyfriend, was planning to transform into her fiancé tonight.

That's two wins in one day. What better way to celebrate than with a bottle of bubbly?

The light changed, finally, and Valerie accelerated across the intersection, flinching as the car behind her whipped around on the left and sped onward to the freeway.

"Somebody wants to get home. Drive safe, buddy, and we'll all get there too. Ya jerk."

She pulled into the liquor store parking lot and aimed for the perpendicular parking spaces by the entrance. Only one other car sat in the lot—a gray Toyota minivan parked in the first space by the door.

A car that had followed Valerie into the lot headed over to the noodle house to park beside a white sedan. Valerie'd eaten there a few times, but Will's cooking kept her from grabbing takeout too often.

That man knows his way around every pot and pan in the kitchen.

Thinking of Will and wanting nothing more than to be home with him, she snagged a spot next to the van. Easy in, easy out.

Grabbing her shoulder bag with her laptop from the passenger seat, Valerie got out. She double-clicked her key fob to lock the doors and got the confirming *chirp* from her Hyundai Elantra. Holding her bag against her chest, she stepped through the space between the vehicles, past the van's front bumper, and into the store.

Rows and racks of bottles awaited her inside. The clerk, a young man with a head of scraggly blond hair, waved from behind the bulletproof partition that closed in the cash register area.

Lingering in the aisle between the blanc de blancs and rosé, Valerie wondered if a red wine would be a better choice. Will had said he was going to cook prime rib tonight. She swiveled back and forth until she landed on a bottle of Merlot that promised to pair well.

Then she also grabbed the blanc de blancs—for dessert.

At the counter, the clerk checked her driver's license, and Valerie endured his excessive scrutiny as he looked from her face to the card she held out. It was all she could do not to snatch it from him. She had places to be.

"I'm older than I look, I promise. Do you need to see another form of ID?" Without waiting for an answer, Valerie flipped open her other wallet, the one that held her federal ID and badge.

The clerk's eyes went wide, and he flicked his gaze from the ID to her face and back again. "Yeah, okay. You're good."

She paid and headed for the door with her purchases in a brown paper bag, the annoying clerk forgotten. All she could think about was being home with Will and his cooking and the expectation that her ring finger wouldn't be bare in the morning.

Valerie stepped into the late evening air, happy to hear the rush of cars moving beyond the parking lot as traffic spilled effortlessly from the intersection onto the waiting on-ramp. Soon she would be on that ramp and headed to Will. She held the paper bag filled with her celebratory bottles close to her chest.

The last rays of the sun were below the horizon and the night was cooling off. Yellowish parking lot lights did little more than create tiny, dim pools, and in her hurry to get the bubbly and leave, she hadn't thought to park beneath one of them, like she usually did. Even though there was traffic nearby, the parking lot felt like a dark island among the city lights.

She paused after stepping out of the store, her quick gait slowing. If anyone asked her why, she wouldn't be able to articulate the reasons behind her decision to slow down. Something in the air felt different.

Isolated. Exposed.

A crunch of gravel nearby startled her, and she scanned the lot.

Check your environment.

The parking lot was still empty except for her car and the minivan, which she assumed belonged to the clerk inside. It had been there when she pulled up.

But the crunch of gravel had sounded like a footstep.

Headlights streaked past the lot entrance, heading toward the freeway on-ramp. Each passing car stirred up bits of trash that settled against the meridian strip, only to be picked up again by the next car.

She'd probably heard a car's tire grinding over something in the road. Still, Valerie knew better than to assume safety. The cadre of trainers at Quantico had drilled that into everyone's heads.

Since she'd only been an FBI agent for forty-five days, she was still honing her skills, but they were becoming more automatic.

Valerie scanned down the way toward the storefronts trailing from the liquor store to the other end of the parking lot. The car that had followed her into the lot and headed to the noodle house was gone. There were no new vehicles.

Whatever illumination came from the liquor store itself was dimmed by all the advertisements and displays crowding the windows.

When she reached her car, she checked the minivan beside her. The front seats were empty, but she couldn't see through the tinted windows in the back.

As she'd done on her way in, Valerie slid around the front bumper of the minivan and into the space between it and her sedan.

Shifting the wine and champagne to her left arm, she tucked her right hand into her jacket, around the handle of her service weapon, ready to draw as she stepped slowly to her driver's side door and checked the back seat.

Empty. Okay, so there's nobody waiting for me in there.

"Girl, catching bad guys has made you paranoid."

The sound of her own voice broke the spell of isolation she'd been feeling. Relaxing a bit, Valerie let go of her gun and reached into her shoulder bag for her key fob. She thumbed the button and opened the door.

Stepping in and settling into the driver's seat, Valerie looked at her left hand again.

I can already see the band around my finger. With a simple stone, modest and understated, just like Will.

Leaning over, she set the wine and her shoulder bag on the floor of the passenger seat. She turned back, then leaned out to grab her door and pull it closed, but froze with her hand on the door. The dashboard light showed the right rear door was also open. A weight settling into the back seat and the rear door snapping shut were the only precursors of warning.

An arm snaked from the back seat, around her throat, pulling her flush against the headrest. Her back arched as she fought the pressure on her larynx. Reactively, she tried to hook one hand around her assailant's arm to yank it free while reaching for her gun with the other. She couldn't twist to reach it though.

A sharp point pierced the skin of her neck.

A needle.

Panicked, she grabbed at his arms, trying to pry them apart, to get the needle away from her neck. But her assailant yanked back harder, choking her, and drove the point into her skin.

"Stop! Stop, you're—"

"Let's not and say we didn't, eh, Valerie?"

He knew her name. She tried to take a breath, tried to calm herself down, but lack of oxygen from his grip made her dizzy.

"The syringe is filled with a chemical of my own making, and I have no problem injecting it straight into your neck. I don't think you want me to do that. Now, very slowly, because I saw you go for your Glock, take out the service weapon and toss it onto the floor by your bag. Do it."

Not knowing what was in the syringe was more terrifying than knowing for certain. It could be anything. Bleach. Lye. Some kind of drug.

Even though her body trembled—she couldn't seem to stop—Valerie didn't want this man, whoever he was, to know she was scared.

For a moment, she contemplated how fast she would have to move to draw her gun and fire. But no mental scenario resulted in her getting off a shot before he injected her. Plus, his other arm remained tightly wrapped around her throat, choking her.

One wrong move, and she was dead.

Gold and white spots appearing in her vision wavered as she struggled to breathe, and it became harder to maintain her grip on his arm.

You have to get back to Will.

The thought of Will helped calm Valerie a little. Picturing his smile, she tried to use that to refocus. She needed to take advantage of any opening this asshole gave her. For Will.

He tugged back again, closing her airway. Valerie's lungs began to burn.

"Clock is ticking, Val. You have about a minute left, maybe, but my patience is already at its end. I guess this is goodbye."

The needle at her throat moved, tugging at her skin, and

for a second, Valerie feared he was pushing on the plunger. She dropped her hands into her lap, and the pressure eased up. He even released his hold on her throat enough so that she could take a breath.

"Good move. Now...gun on the floor."

She did as he commanded, using only one hand, and dropped it to the floor between her feet.

"Well done. You get to live a little longer, maybe even to see Will again."

Feeling her airway open up, Valerie swallowed. But even though this man had managed to sneak up on her, drive a needle into her throat, choke her, and disarm her, his actions were nowhere near as terrifying as the fact he knew Will's name.

How does he know about us?

But the pressure he'd put on her neck made her words come out in a wheezy croak. "How do you know about Will?"

He tightened his arm around her throat again. "Now close the driver's door. Slowly, left hand only. Right hand goes on the wheel. Got it?"

In the rearview mirror, she saw a mask of some type across the attacker's face. It was dark outside, and the interior car light overhead mostly created shadows. His arm was too tight on her throat for her to do more than choke out a reply. "Okay. If you'll just—"

"Shut the door." His arm tightened on her throat again, cutting off her oxygen. Again. Her lungs felt like they'd explode this time. She hadn't pulled in a full breath in minutes.

But he hadn't pushed the needle in deeper. "Put your right hand on the wheel. *Now.* Then shut the door, and you'll get to breathe."

Just do what he says. If you're alive, you can negotiate with him.

Every instinct in her screamed to fight back, but he held the needle in her throat, ready to inject whatever it contained into her system. She cautiously lifted her right hand and gripped the wheel.

Her left hand shook as she reached for the door and pulled it closed.

She let it settle into the frame, but didn't fully latch it, hoping she might be able to scream for help.

"Nice try, Val." The needle stayed where it was. "If you open your mouth, I'll inject you with enough of this to shred your veins while you squirm and scream for mercy. Nod slowly if you understand."

She lowered her chin and lifted it again in a smooth motion, never taking her eyes from his shadowy form in her rearview mirror. Her expression she kept carefully blank. Beneath the surface, however, she was ready to kill him if she got the chance.

"Good girl." He loosened his arm on her throat. "You're going to put your cybersecurity skills to use for me. If you refuse, Will dies. I'll make you watch, and then you'll join him. Now close that door all the way. We have something to discuss, and I don't want to be interrupted."

Heart pounding, Valerie considered what she knew of this man. Compliance, for the moment, was probably her best option. Grappling him and wrenching his hand off the syringe might work, but that would require her hands be free.

She'd already made the mistake of giving in to her fear once. If she was going to get out of this, she'd need to be smarter.

Quantico trained you better, Valerie. You know how to get out of situations like this.

She opened her door again, just enough to pull it closed with a slam.

Maybe that'll get someone's attention. If not, I'll just have to wait for him to give me an opening.

"The door's closed. You said you wanted to discuss something."

"Indeed, I do. Get your laptop out. Slowly."

"How will my laptop help?"

He flexed his left arm, tightening the grip and choking her again. He held on long enough that she almost blacked out. When he released her enough to take in a breath, she felt his mouth hovering beside her ear. She glanced in the rearview mirror again. He kept his face turned away so that all she could make out was part of his profile.

Square jaw. Thick head of hair maybe but sticking out from under a watch cap pulled down low.

"Val, I know you're trying to size me up, gauge how much of a chance you have of surviving this. I'm going to be honest with you. I just need you to do one thing, and this will all be over. Now, are you ready to talk, or are you still thinking you might fight your way free?"

"I'm ready to talk."

"Good. I've been watching you and your Fed buddies for a while now. You've been quite the rising star, netting those scammers last month."

"How do—"

He pulled harder against her neck. "The FBI, in its infinite arrogance, announces when an agent does something particularly well. Like taking down a phishing ring."

The pieces clicked into place. Her department had released an article on her work. That was how he'd found her name. Then it would've been a matter of doing some simple computer research. As a member of Cyber, she knew how fragile personal data could be exposed.

"Or taking down two of the biggest gangs in the D.C. area."

Valerie had heard about that incident too. The whole country had. Watching the footage and knowing how those agents had handled the situation, Valerie admired the VCU team. After her own success at the phishing scam, Valerie had debated whether she should approach SSA Jacinda Hollingsworth and offer her services on future cases.

"I had nothing to do with the Drivers and Powders situation."

"Maybe not, but I did. And those VCU assholes in your organization made a lot of trouble for me, disrupting my operations in a big way. I don't take kindly to that."

"Ah, you're involved with criminal operations. And the VCU stopped you. Sounds like they did their jobs."

The man scoffed, and she felt the needle jiggle in her neck.

"I'm guessing you were involved with drugs?" Valerie couldn't quite believe her own boldness. Calling out a criminal for his crimes was a risky maneuver. But she needed to get back to Will. "Do you have something to do with that crystal clear stuff?"

He ignored her efforts. "Be a good girl and move the seat back as far as it'll go. Give yourself some room to work."

"What kind of work do I need to do?"

"Okay. I guess I have to play hardball."

His arm left her throat, and she thought that meant she had to get her laptop. She reached over, carefully, for his one hand was still holding the syringe in her neck. As she leaned forward for her computer bag, something sharp prodded at her back.

"That's a knife. I have it right behind your kidney. If you want to die bleeding out while burning up from the inside when I flood your bloodstream with that *crystal clear stuff*, by all means, keep being a stupid bitch and thinking you can negotiate your way out of this."

The pressure of the knife against her back let up. Valerie heard him digging in a pocket, which meant he'd let go of the knife, but the needle wiggled in her neck with every move she made. Before she could jerk away from the needle, he stuck a phone into her field of vision over her left shoulder.

"Get with the program, Val, or Will dies. See?"

She slid her gaze to the side, taking in the smudged phone screen. But she was able to read the message.

Bitch isn't cooperating. Kill him. Make it messy.

Valerie felt like she might vomit all over that phone screen. If he was working with the gangs, then he definitely had lackeys.

The thought that someone could be watching Will or even threatening him at this very moment created knots of anxiety behind her solar plexus.

His thumb hovered over the send button. "Nice and slow now. Move the seat back."

The phone vanished from her view.

Gingerly, with a surge of terror for Will's safety coursing through her, Valerie reached down and pressed the controls to move the seat backward, the knife pressing just behind her kidney again, forcing her to strain against the seat belt so it wouldn't puncture her skin.

"Take out your laptop. I want the home addresses of the Bureau's Violent Crime Unit agents."

Fucking hell.

She froze with her right hand on her shoulder bag. She could grab the laptop, or she could grab her key fob and hit the panic button.

As she debated her next move, the sharp prod of the knife vanished from her back and was at the left side of her throat in a flash. And still, the needle's pressure on the right reminded her how close she was to an agonizing death.

"Valerie, honey," his growl came closer to her ear, "I'm waiting."

The knife pressed in, and a warm wetness saturated the cotton of her collar, along with a sting that spoke of a deeper threat.

She gritted her teeth. There was no way she could give up the VCU members. Exposing them would make her a traitor.

"Does Will deserve to be carved apart, his limbs left scattered over his students' papers, just because you wanted to show loyalty to agents who don't even know your name?"

Oh, god, he knows Will's a teacher. Shit, shit, shit.

"You're evil." Valerie choked on the word. She'd thought she understood criminals, how they thought, what their processes were. In her time at Cyber, she'd seen people save horrid photographs of their crimes, steal social security from their grandmothers, and launder millions. This guy was different.

Her fingers clutched her laptop. She could see her key fob at the bottom of her bag, but the thought of Will being butchered…

She made her decision.

"Just stop. I'll do it, okay? Just stop."

They'll be okay. They're FBI. They're one of the best teams in the country. And this guy's already got my address, so he'll get theirs somehow, even if I don't help him. Plus, I'll warn them. Soon as I get away, I'll warn them.

She drew her computer from its case and brought it onto her lap.

"Good girl. Let's get started, then. And no sending messages for help or any warnings. I'll see you do it, and you and Will won't survive it. I'm going to take the syringe out now, so you can work fast, but the knife stays where it is. If you make one move for that gun, you'll be spraying arterial blood across your dashboard." His voice turned sickly sweet and mocking. "We 'crystal clear,' Val?"

She gave another gentle nod, just as she'd done when he first attacked. The pressure from the syringe remained until she had her computer booted up. Then he drew the needle out.

Valerie ignored the impulse to wipe at the blood trailing down the other side of her neck into her collar, and she typed as fast as she ever had. Her laptop gave her a direct line into the FBI's database of personnel, and finding the files for the agents on the VCU squad was the work of only a few minutes.

Supervisory Special Agent Jacinda Hollingsworth.
Special Agent Leo Ambrose.
Special Agent Emma Last.
Special Agent Vance Jessup.
Special Agent Mia Logan.
Special Agent Denae Monroe.

When the man behind her passed her a USB drive, she took it without comment.

A strange numbness overtook her. It was like she watched her own actions from a distance.

"I'm watching you save every one of those files on this drive, Valerie. Don't even think of disappointing me."

"What are you going to do with these files?"

Her whisper hung in the air, but he only twitched the knife down to the USB in answer. She took it out and passed it back to him. The quiet hiss of a zipper told her he'd tucked it away.

"You'll let me go now? Please. It would cost me my job if I told anyone what I gave you. I won't speak of this to—"

The prick of a needle entered her neck on the right again, and the words died in her throat.

Warmth spread from the pinprick, burning her skin, a fiery heat like nothing she'd ever experienced.

Throat drying, and terror racing through her chest, even as an odd, comforting sensation began to envelope her, Valerie let one hand drift to her neck, to where the needle had just left her skin.

Fighting against the effects of the drug, she shot her left hand for the door handle, but his knife came down, slashing it open from her thumb to her wrist. Her hand fell to her side, slack. Blood welled up and poured down her fingers just as an intense sensation overwhelmed her.

She'd expected pain, terrifying agony, like something tight and stabbing in her guts or throat. Instead, she met with euphoria.

In a million ways, the euphoria was worse.

She gasped, shutting her eyes and pressing her head back into the seat, deep and heavy. Never had she felt this powerful or this strong. She'd kill this man in a moment. Just as soon as she finished enjoying this feeling, she'd rip his limbs apart. Drop his head into one seat and leave his body in the other.

Her lungs burned, her heart pounding with a strength she felt was suddenly overtaking her, controlling her. Every muscle contracted, ready to burst. She pressed her feet into the floorboard, gasping for air and whining like a frightened dog.

Her whimpers grew louder, more desperate, but she couldn't stop herself from trying to release the pain with a wheezing whine, and the man in the back laughed. She raised a hand and pressed it hard into her neck, trembling, as the temperature in her body increased with each beat of her heart.

A shiver ran through her—or was it the car that was

shivering around her? Violent but warm? And then the weight of anxiety fell in on her.

Something's coming. Something worse than him. I'm going to die. There are monsters everywhere, and they're going to kill us, and we're going to die. We're all going to die. My body's going to explode and be taken away by monsters.

Valerie knew her brain was spiraling, but all she could do was stare at the liquor store's glowing window displays. Lottery numbers strobed in her vision, taunting her with promises of fortunes she would never enjoy.

And through it all, the man chuckled, deep in his throat like a predator that had just killed its prey.

Terror built in Valerie, feeding off her nerves as her heart pounded faster.

"Chest. Hurts." The gasped words didn't sound like words at all, so she tried again.

The man laughed and patted her arm. "You're a government puppet, Valerie. But you did good for me, didn't you? And now you get to die, just like you deserve."

She pressed her hands to her chest, pulling at her shirt, wishing she could relieve the pressure, but it only built tighter. She couldn't breathe. Not even a little, not anymore.

And then the monsters closed in.

2

Eyes. Eyes through the trees.

A mist, seeping through stands of evergreens, surrounded Emma, but she could only watch the eyes appear and vanish.

Then the silhouettes of two women drifted out of the mist. Maybe they were made of the mist itself. One woman stared at Emma, her eyes an icy blue. A chill, like a cold wind, surrounded Emma, but she moved toward the woman. The mossy grass squelched beneath her feet.

But another woman's misty arm reached through and held Emma's arm, pulling her to a stop. This woman had brown eyes that seemed to smile.

And all around them, a wolf howled and howled.

Panting, FBI Special Agent Emma Last jerked awake and pressed one hand to her chest, staring into the dark of her bedroom. She jerked the covers of her comforter away, freeing her legs to swing over the side of the bed. Weak light from the street filtered through the blinds as the first tendrils of sunrise approached. When she'd caught her breath, Emma pushed herself to sitting and reached out to silence her alarm.

She rubbed her eyes and blinked them clear of sleep's grip. But she barely saw the room around her.

Even though Emma didn't know who those two women were, she recognized them. They were in a photograph with her mother, but she didn't know how the three were connected.

Emma glanced at the framed picture of her mother she kept on the nightstand. A cold sweat wet her tank top as she thought of the dream. If she'd set her alarm to go off a bit later, maybe she'd have stayed in it and learned something more.

Or maybe you'd have gotten lost in those woods of the Other forever, Emma girl.

The thought stilled her, and she shoved it away by rising from her bed. Without bothering to dress, she made a fast circuit of the apartment. She checked every door and window—all locked, even the tiny one in the bathroom that a child couldn't have fit through—before breathing deeply.

The dream now forgotten, Emma refocused around the very real and present threats that had come in against her team. Their last case saw the dissolution of D.C.'s two largest gangs and more violence than Emma had witnessed in a long time. The team had also been forced to accept that their work lives and personal lives could end up being more closely linked than any of them had previously imagined.

Denae Monroe's youngest brother—an active member of the Drivers gang who was being hunted by a member of the rival Powders gang—had been central to their case.

Just when we thought that whole mess was behind us, some maniac called Jacinda to threaten us all.

"I'll spell it out in the blood of one of your agents."

Emma no longer felt nauseated by the memory, but tension ate at her. The man had sounded serious.

Supervisory Special Agent Jacinda Hollingsworth laughed

when they last talked about it, forcing humor into her voice when she said the man was too dramatic to be dangerous. But Emma had heard the edge, however subtle.

Jacinda often tried to keep additional burdens and stresses off of the team. But there was no way to mitigate all the sometimes-terrifying aspects of their work. Emma had seen the anxiety around Jacinda's eyes.

Their SSA was shook, just like Emma was. Nobody believed this guy was a joke, despite wishful thinking. At some point, probably soon, he would come for at least one of them.

I hope it's me and not the others. I'll take him down for all of us.

Hurrying through a shower, Emma let herself be spurred on by that promise. And by the faith her boyfriend Oren had in her. When he'd still lived, Oren had been a source of confidence Emma hadn't known she needed. And now, in death, his ghost provided no less a measure of support.

If he believed she could use her talent as a gift to protect her team, she would do it. She glanced around her room after dressing, hoping, but no sign of him appeared. And she wouldn't call him to her again so soon.

Not when he'd made it clear that coming to her wasn't exactly safe.

Stop thinking about him, Emma girl. Get dressed and get the day going already.

She'd let herself sleep late, right through the possibility of yoga or a run, but had done it on purpose when she set her alarm last night. As on edge as she was, she needed the extra time to fall asleep and stay asleep.

In her kitchen, the coffee tasted bitter, but at least her Keurig had behaved. Across the island from her, the ghost of Mrs. Kellerly patted her white hair and prattled on about how handsome Oren was, but Emma barely heard her.

Barely even shivered at the cold of the Other that had intruded with the ghost's presence.

Eating her bagel, she let her mind circle back to the woods she'd seen in the dreams. She told herself they were of the Other, no reality she really knew, but they seemed familiar now. More so than before. Like seeing a person who you recognized from the past, even though you couldn't place them.

But woods were woods. Didn't they all pretty much look the same?

Perhaps Oren, who'd spent so much time hiking, could differentiate, but she certainly couldn't.

If there was one thing she couldn't claim to be, it was a tree expert.

"Do you know anything about trees, Mrs. Kellerly?" Emma half joked, but still watched the old woman for a response.

"Me?" The woman fluttered her hands around her poofy white hair some more. "I should think not. The forest is no place for a lady, Emma Last. I never understood why Oren would want to drag you out to march around the woods like a couple of children."

Emma smiled, but the buzz of her phone stole away any further time for conversation. Jacinda's name beckoned from the screen.

Grabbing the device, Emma jumped to her feet, speaking even before she'd raised it to her lips. "Jacinda, what's going on?"

"Our mystery caller made a move. He—"

"Is everyone okay?" Emma stood rigid beside her counter, crumbling the remains of her bagel in her fist. "Have you talked to everyone? Who—"

"Stop, Emma, everyone's okay. Breathe!" Jacinda sighed through the line, taking a minute before she continued.

Emma lowered herself back onto the stool at her island. Though her mind kept cycling through the images of her team members around the briefing table where they'd all last been gathered, she told her body to relax.

"Everyone on our team is okay."

Emma forced a breath from her lungs. "Okay. But you're calling because he made a move?"

"He did. So MPD has a vehicle downstairs waiting to escort you in."

Emma's heart pounded faster. An escort from the police department? "What's going—"

"Uh-uh, Emma. I'll fill you in when you get into the office. I have other calls to make. For now, eyes up."

Before Emma could respond, the SSA had hung up on her, and Emma was left staring at her silent phone.

"But everyone's okay." She dropped her phone and hurried off to get dressed. "Everyone's okay."

She didn't allow herself to say the words banging at the corner of her mind, the words Jacinda had spoken.

"Everyone on our team is okay."

That meant someone else wasn't.

3

Leo enjoyed the last few sips of his coffee, one hand resting idly on Denae's bare knee. Ahead of them, the sun inched up over Leo's backyard, and his little patio offered the perfect spot for a relaxing morning.

Denae's head rested against his shoulder. They'd pressed the patio chairs together so they could be closer. He smelled her lotion and the fragrant coffee she special ordered. Neither one of them said a word. They had fallen into a comfortable knowledge of each other where they didn't have to speak every minute of the day. For the moment, it was just them, the rising sun, and peace. He wished the moment could stretch on and on.

After the hellish ordeal of their last case, he committed to spending as much quality time with her as he could. Thankfully, the disciplinary review Denae had been subjected to only left her with the two days of suspension Jacinda had implemented during their previous case.

It hadn't even been referred up to the Office of Professional Responsibility, which meant the team could effectively act as if nothing had happened.

She could've told us her brother was a member of one of the gangs that took to the streets in open warfare with their biggest rival. But if I'd been in her shoes, protecting my brothers would've come first too.

Denae rested her hand on his, playing her fingers across his knuckles. "This has been a really nice morning. I'm tempted to call in sick and keep it going."

Smiling at how closely her thoughts echoed his, Leo turned over his hand and gripped hers. "Sounds tempting. Also doesn't sound like you."

She shrugged. "My head's just so full. I'm worried about Jamaal. He has his art and his skill with spray paint, but not much in the way of goals or aspirations."

"Maybe being around your parents again will give him the push he needs."

"I don't think Mom and Dad are going to push him anywhere, unless it's into college."

Without knowing what else to tell her, Leo could only watch as Denae finally sighed and pushed herself up from the patio chair.

"I'm gonna hop in the shower real quick. See you inside."

She bent and gave him a quick kiss, and he caught her arm to keep her against him. Laughing into the kiss, she pulled away with a little skip, and he grinned at her before she turned and flounced away with a bit more of a spring in her step. At least he'd gotten her smiling again.

Following her inside after another few minutes of quiet, Leo poured himself a second cup of coffee. He'd gotten up before Denae, as usual, and all he'd need to do was pull on his suit jacket before heading out the door. No need to do that yet.

He took his coffee to the couch and flipped on the television, but the sight of the news soured his stomach. Every damn station was talking about their previous case.

The crazed murderer with her bladed brass knuckles who'd killed one of their task force leaders and set off a gang war that left more than a dozen people dead, including eight MPD cops.

A memorial service and procession were being planned, and would include comments from the mayor and the MPD chief. Maryland's and Virginia's senators would attend, as well, because the fallen officers had lived in those states.

Flipping the channel again, Leo was met by the spectacle of his own face as he ushered a gang member into the back of a cop car. Perfect. All he needed was to be going about his day and have people recognize him and want to chat about the week's violence.

Couple days, it'll blow over. Maybe Denae had the right idea about calling in sick after all.

His phone buzzed.

But he couldn't find his phone. He heard it clear as day. Leo set his coffee cup down and listened. The phone died.

Then it buzzed again. This time he figured out where it was hiding and fished the phone from between the couch cushions where it had fallen last night. Jacinda's name flashed at him, and he answered.

"Ambrose."

"Decided to answer your phone this morning?" Jacinda Hollingsworth sounded drily amused.

"It was…never mind. What's—"

"Our guy made a move. MPD has an escort en route to your place."

Taking a second to find a response, Leo glanced toward the hallway. At least he knew Denae was safe. "Is Emma—"

"She's fine, and so are Mia and Vance. I'll fill everyone in when we're in the office. I'm guessing Denae's with you?"

"Yeah, I'll tell her."

"Thanks. See you soon. And wait for the escort to arrive before stepping out your door."

Leo nodded into the silent phone. Jacinda had already ended the call. He turned off the television and rose.

His gut churning, he pocketed his phone and headed back toward the sound of the shower, needing to get the news to Denae as soon as possible, before she could daydream any further about taking a day off. He only wished, but this wasn't the time.

On the way, he touched his fingertips to the portrait of Yaya and Papu, which he'd hung in the hallway. He'd been in danger plenty of times, but whoever this new perpetrator was, they were targeting the FBI specifically.

He could only feel grateful his grandmother didn't know that.

At the bathroom door, he took a quick breath before knocking, treasuring this last bit of calm before another case came crashing down on them. Giving Denae one last little breath of calm too.

This was the life they'd chosen, he knew, and it was the life he wanted.

He only wished it left a little more time for everything else that mattered.

4

Emma followed Mia and Vance into the conference room, Denae and Leo coming in right behind her. Jacinda greeted them with a silent nod and gestured to the chairs around the table. Once they'd taken their seats, the SSA stood up straight and closed her eyes. She drew in a deep breath and released it before speaking.

"There's no sugarcoating this. Our victim is one of our own, a relatively new addition to the Cybersecurity Division. Agent Valerie Lundgren, twenty-five years old. I'm assuming none of you knew her personally?"

Emma shook her head along with the others, her throat feeling tight. She remembered just what it had been like to be fresh out of Quantico and new to the Bureau, anxious to make an impression and start the career she'd fought for. "She was brand new?"

The SSA nodded. "Started here a month ago. Last night, she was seen leaving work as expected. She never made it home. She was found in her car in the parking lot of Freeman's Liquor Store this morning. MPD identified her, realized she was a federal agent, and handed the case to us this morning. They've left a perimeter at the scene so we can lead the investigation."

"So a federal agent was targeted." Until now, Emma'd felt a sliver of hope this wasn't their guy at all. Jacinda's gaze met hers and softened. She'd seen the hope die in her, Emma guessed. "It's him, isn't it? The guy who called you."

"Affirmative. He called again this morning. Same voice Emma and I heard. Same encryption, also untraceable. He said, and I quote, 'Valerie is only the beginning.'" Jacinda paused there, allowing the threat to sink in. "Valerie's team is looking into her current casework, in the event there's a tie-in somewhere. We'll be first to hear if they come up with anything."

A picture flashed up on the overhead screen. A Bureau ID badge showed a slender, young woman with auburn hair and thin, frameless glasses. Her lips were pursed, as if she were trying to hide a smile at having her picture taken for the ID.

The expression made Emma's heart hurt.

"And she was fine at work?" Eyes on the picture, Mia spoke quietly. With Valerie's image up on the screen, an extra solemnity had taken over the air. "Nothing happened yesterday to make her act outside the norm or get upset?"

Jacinda referred to her notes. "Her colleagues reported nothing out of the ordinary in her behavior or productivity. She'd worked longer hours since she started, but Cyber often attracts night owls."

"I think the FBI attracts night owls." Denae waved at the coffee cups in everyone's hands, then hoisted her own cup in a toast.

Emma raised her mug in answer, appreciating Denae lightening the mood a bit.

"Valerie came into the parking garage at half past seven yesterday morning, and her car remained where she'd parked it until near eight last night. In full view of security footage, too, so it's highly unlikely that her vehicle had been tampered with over the course of the day. Security's already gone over the footage, and nobody but her touched the car."

Vance leaned forward, shifting a touch closer to Mia as he did. "Wasn't the initial threat against us? The VCU specifically?"

Jacinda took a seat at the head of the table. "Yes, it was. But we have very little to go on. Forming this perpetrator's psychological profile is going to be a challenge. It's possible he doesn't even understand the difference between FBI departments. For all we know, he says he's targeting the VCU, but in his mind, that's just the D.C. Bureau. We simply don't know."

Emma grimaced. "Great. So everyone in the FBI is a potential target. That makes things more complicated."

Nodding, Jacinda checked her phone before looking back up. "I'll keep you abreast of updates. Meanwhile, Emma, Denae, and Mia, check out Valerie's apartment complex and talk with her boyfriend, William Butler. Leo and Vance, you two head out to the scene. I'll be here, working with a BAU specialist to create a profile."

Jacinda tapped a few buttons on her laptop, and a security still of a little blue sedan came up on the screen.

"That a Hyundai Elantra?" Vance squinted at the picture. "With a William and Mary decorative cover over the front license plate?"

"Good eye, Vance." Jacinda consulted her notes and then continued. "It's a 2021 Elantra, blue in color. Maryland license plate. Cyber have tried to trace her phone with no luck. It's possible our perpetrator turned it off or destroyed it."

Leo stood up and stretched, practically vibrating with nerves. Denae rose beside him. He met Jacinda's eyes. "I'm ready to go if that's it, Boss."

Jacinda's lips tightened, worry tugging at her expression, but she looked around the table and met everyone's gaze in turn. "Be extra careful while you're out there investigating. Keep GPS on at all times and wear your bulletproof gear. Nobody, and I mean *nobody*, for any reason, works alone."

Nodding, Emma turned toward the door. She saw Leo staring at her in particular and knew he worried about her going rogue most.

She mouthed, *I promise*.

And this time, she meant it.

5

Leo led the way down to the parking garage, Vance right behind him. Neither spoke, and the stairwell echoed with their footsteps.

Holding the door to their parking level open for Vance, Leo thumbed the key fob for the SUV they'd checked out. Its lights blinked, signaling them forward.

"Let's take the Beltway, yeah?"

Vance yanked open the passenger door. "You're driving, but I'm thinking Parkinson Street is better. Avoid the Mall and Beltway. That's what I'd do after a long day of work, and we may want to follow as close to her route as we can."

"Good point," Leo climbed into the driver's seat, "even though I doubt our perpetrator's going to be standing on the sidewalk with a sign."

"Can't hurt to see what she saw."

He snapped his seat belt in place as Leo did the same. Vance checked his phone four times before Leo finally exited the garage and got them into traffic.

"Expecting a call?"

After a pause, Vance scoffed. "I understand the assignments. I just wish we were all together on this one."

Leo ran his tongue against his teeth, trying to lock down his nerves. It wasn't working. "I'm with you on that. I know everyone can take care of themselves—"

"But it doesn't change wanting to be there with them, just in case." Vance knocked the back of his head against the headrest and groaned. "I'm such an idiot. All these years, I bent over backward to avoid even looking at a colleague like *that*. Then Mia Logan walks in the office door, and I roll over with my belly up and tongue hanging out. I'm lucky she doesn't know she's got me wrapped around her finger."

A stoplight allowed Leo to glance over and laugh. "Oh, she knows it. She's just too good to take advantage of it."

Vance grunted in agreement.

"I get it." Leo spoke toward the window, not particularly wanting to face Vance at the moment. "Denae and I have a great thing right now. Kills me to think of her being in danger and me not being there to help."

"Or of losing her?"

Leo's foot nearly came down on the gas and shot them into the next car, the words hit him so hard. He looked sideways and met Vance's hard gaze. *"Excuse me?"*

"You've gotta be thinking it. I know I am." Vance shook his head and stared out his window. "They can take care of themselves, yeah, but shit still happens. I'm not worried about Mia being in danger. I'm worried about *losing her*. Period."

Vance's flat voice crackled with tension. Leo stared at him wordlessly for another second, then focused back on his driving.

He couldn't think like that about Denae. *Wouldn't* think like that.

When Leo finally spoke, his voice was barely above a murmur. "We're in the same place. But I can't let my mind go there. I'll be paralyzed if I do. We just have to remember our women are damn fine agents."

So was Valerie.

Vance craned his neck as they passed a drugstore, and Leo slowed to accommodate him, but he gestured them forward. "And keep our own heads down and safe too."

"Right." Leo coughed, hating that he could hear emotion in his own voice even in the one simple word. Denae would've been laughing at him, telling him, "Get your head on straight, Scruffy." He focused on that. "Nice to be with someone who understands all this shit."

The car fell into silence and remained there. Leo drove as fast as traffic would allow, which was still below the speed limit. A few minutes later, they pulled up to the parking lot outside the liquor store. The whole area was swarming with cops.

A uniformed officer stepped back from blocking the lot entrance, waving them in on seeing Leo's identification. Leo pulled the SUV to a stop just inside the lot, facing toward a planting strip that bordered the back of the paved area. They got out and headed toward the shop's front door, where Valerie's blue sedan was surrounded by a team of uniformed officers.

Peering past the cop nearest the driver's seat, Leo glimpsed Valerie's still form. Wide-eyed and open-mouthed, she sat upright in the seat with her head turned to the left.

Leo's gut twisted at how young she seemed. To him, it was like looking at the face of a teenager. Someone not old enough to understand the dangers of the world.

An open laptop was lying half on her leg and half on the center console.

Her shoulder bag and bottles of wine and champagne sat on the floor in front of the passenger seat.

"Looks like someone was planning a party." He was heartbroken this young woman never got to celebrate whatever she had planned.

Valerie's left hand was smeared with blood from a slice that ran from her thumb to her wrist. It looked like a knife wound, and Leo checked the interior for any sign of the weapon. Seeing nothing apparent, he went back to examining Valerie's corpse.

A small trickle of blood originated just below and to the left of her larynx and disappeared into her blouse, as if she'd been pierced by the tip of a blade.

Vance was standing on the passenger side of the car, examining her from that angle. He waved and called for Leo's attention. "Really small puncture wound to the right side of her neck and some slight bruising."

"Same just above her collar, right here." Leo motioned to his throat. "Could be what killed her." He moved around the rear of the vehicle, carefully examining each door he passed, and the trunk, for signs of forced entry. When he spotted nothing, he came to stand beside Vance.

A uniformed officer by the front bumper motioned to them and spoke quietly, his voice soft with sympathy. "The morning clerk found her when she came to open up." He pointed across the lot where another uniform spoke to the clerk. The middle-aged blond woman seemed shaken, even from a distance.

"What time did she come in?"

"She says she pulled up at eight thirty and immediately thought the car had been stolen for a joyride and dumped here."

Vance huffed. "Was she on shift last night?"

"No, it was some other guy. She gave us a name and says

he isn't too attentive, so it shouldn't surprise us if he didn't see the car when he left. We're getting a full statement and will send that over to you guys ASAP. We sent a unit around to the victim's place of residence. Her boyfriend called around ten last night to report her missing."

"Nobody followed up?"

The cop spread his hands in front of him.

Leo nodded, the unsaid words clearly ringing in his mind. *She was an adult and an FBI agent. Plus, it hadn't even been twelve hours when he started calling.*

He let his gaze roam around the interior of the vehicle and pointed to her feet, limp on the floorboard. "Where she's positioned, she couldn't reach the pedals if she tried. She had the seat pulled way back from the wheel."

Vance eyed the car, then walked around it and glanced at the cop. "Any indication our car was moved here by someone else?"

He shrugged. "Not that I can see, but your guess is as good as mine."

"How'd he get in? Do we think he was hiding in the vehicle or got in with her? Did she know him maybe?"

"There's a camera over the door," Vance pointed, "that might give us some answers."

Taking a last look at Valerie where she lay limp in the driver's seat, Leo did one more pass around the car. He noted a puncture or rip in the back of the driver's seat and a slight dent in the driver's side rear panel, but there was no telling if either had anything to do with the murder or their perpetrator. Nevertheless, he pointed them out and marked them down.

The clerk's employee polo shirt was tucked in tight and clean, but the mascara rubbed into raccoon markings around her eyes betrayed the stress of finding their victim. Softening his expression, Leo flashed his ID. "Special Agent Leo

Ambrose. This is my partner, Special Agent Vance Jessup. We understand you found the victim?"

"Yeah, I did. My name's Daisy Kirk, in case you need it." She frowned, plucking a stray thread from her polo shirt. Her gaze shifted past them, back to the car. "I hear she's FBI?"

There goes that part not making the daily news.

Ignoring the question, Leo forced a sympathetic smile. He'd heard what the cops had to say but needed to hear it from the witness herself too. "It looks like she stopped to buy two bottles of wine last night and didn't leave. Any reason your night clerk wouldn't have noticed the car?"

"Our new guy, Pete something or other, was working last night. He handles the job well enough but doesn't pay attention to anything that isn't right under his nose. He probably just locked up, climbed into his van, and took off. He always parks right here in front by the door, so he might not have even seen her car."

Vance had his notebook out and clicked his pen. "Got a last name and address for Pete the Unobservant?"

Nodding, Daisy motioned at the store. "I think one of the cops put a call in to the owner, but she didn't pick up. If she calls back, she might be able to give you Pete's info or give me the okay to look at his employee file."

Leo held up his iPad so Daisy could approve his spelling of her name, then pointed up at the security camera mounted above the front door. "You mind showing us the footage, whatever's there?"

"Yeah, but I doubt it'll help. Pete's van probably blocked her car from view."

"Any reason you haven't told him not to park like that? If he's blocking the camera from capturing part of the lot, he could be setting you guys up to get robbed."

"I have told him. Twice. Like I said, he's not that alert. I'll tell him again, you can bet on that."

Leo made a note to dig into Pete's background before anyone on the team interviewed the man, then nodded to Daisy. "Let's see that footage?"

She brushed off her jeans and led the way inside.

They passed by liquor and wine displays taller than any of them and moved on toward a back office where a little security station sat beside a tower of soda fridge packs and Pringles cans. "Owner's always got the munchies for both, but she'd tell you to help yourself to either. I'll check with the cops to see if she's called back yet while you're figuring out the security stuff."

The little monitor was dark with static, and she glanced at it doubtfully, but the setup looked just like a million others Leo had seen. He only hoped everything had been hooked up to record properly.

Vance waved her off, and she backed out of the little office, promising to be back with Pete's information.

They were able to rewind back to the night before, and there was Valerie, entering a few minutes after eight o'clock. She dithered a bit, turning from side to side and examining the racks of wine. A small, self-satisfied grin lit her young face when she finally selected a couple bottles and approached the counter. The scraggly-haired clerk, Pete the Unobservant, triple checked her ID.

Watching, Vance grimaced. "Can't blame him for being doubtful. She could pass for eighteen easy if she weren't wearing that suit."

"Looks like she was prepared for that. She showed him her federal ID too."

Daisy came back and handed them a slip of note paper with Pete's name and contact details. "Owner just called and said I could give you the info. She's on her way, but she lives across town. It'll be an hour before she gets here."

Thanking her, Leo turned back to the screen.

Valerie finished making her purchase and headed for the door. She appeared on the exterior view a moment later, hesitating with one hand holding it open.

Leo paused the playback. "Did she forget something? It doesn't look like she sees anyone, just stopped moving."

"Keep it rolling. Maybe we'll get a look at whoever killed her. He could be off camera and holding a gun on her."

As unlikely as that seemed, given the public and visible location of the liquor store lot, Leo keyed the video to start playing again.

Valerie stayed paused by the door, eventually letting it swing shut behind her. She seemed to be scanning the lot, then turned to look in the direction of the other storefronts that ran alongside the liquor store before turning back to the minivan.

"She's checking the van, look."

He and Vance watched as Valerie peered into the van from the driver's side, then edged her way into the narrow space between the van's front bumper and the store.

"Goes for her gun there." Vance pointed.

Leo paused the video again.

"She's sensing a threat. But why? What set off her alarm bells, and why did they stop ringing?"

Vance reached out and restarted the video. "Hand's still inside her jacket as she steps around the van's bumper."

"Does she relax right there?" Leo stopped the video, backed it up, and they rewatched Valerie's movements around the van. "She gets around the van, hand on her gun, but she doesn't draw. Why not?"

They watched as Valerie moved toward her driver's side door, where she disappeared from view. Only the front bumper and top of her windshield could be seen with the minivan concealing the rest of her vehicle. Her head was momentarily visible as she opened the door.

"She didn't see anything to be afraid of." Leo paused the footage again. "Two bottles of wine mean she had plans. She's nervous, maybe, or exhausted and wants to get home."

"Something put her on alert, then she chalks it up to nerves? Or, like you said, she's beat and wants to get home."

Leo drew in a breath and restarted the video, waiting for some sign of the attacker. Valerie got in. The sedan shook and jostled briefly, the bumper rocking up and down before going still. Vance let out a groan of disgust.

"He already got in the car at this point. How'd she let him get the drop on her like that?"

"She had to have checked, though. You saw the way she was scoping out the van and going for her gun. She was being careful."

"Until she wasn't. This guy waited for her to unlock the car and slid in behind her. Dude's lightning fast."

They watched a while longer, Leo hoping against hope that the attacker would reveal himself. But he'd obviously taken care to avoid being caught by the camera so far.

As he was about to shut off the feed, a shadowy figure emerged from what had to have been Valerie's back seat.

Vance stabbed a finger to pause the playback. "Son of a bitch. That's our guy."

It was a bulky figure, apparently male, broad shouldered, and with a watch cap pulled down over his ears, concealing his hairstyle.

Leo restarted the feed, and they watched the person move off camera, disappearing in the direction of the trees and lawn at the back of the lot.

"We should make sure to check over there, see if there's any indication he headed across that planting area."

They left the office, waving at Daisy as they headed back outside. At the car, Leo bypassed the cops still gathered around Valerie's body by the driver's side door. He walked around the parking lot, toward the grass at the edge opposite the roadway, and squatted. It hadn't rained lately, but footsteps had trampled down the grass in places. He called to Vance and pointed. "No telling if this is related to the murder, but we saw him move in this direction."

Vance motioned at another cop. "Do me a favor and square off this bit of grass with tape, all right? Looks like someone passed this way."

The cop nodded and went to one of the three nearby police cruisers, popping the back open and digging into a kit for a roll of crime scene tape.

Leo stood and began making a slow, careful survey of the lawn and plantings that bordered the parking lot. A chain-link fence overgrown with ivy stood behind several bushes and small trees.

He didn't see anything other than landscaping and trash and was about to give up when his gaze flagged on a flash of metal at the base of a small tree. He made his way over to it and knelt.

A bloody knife sat half covered over by grass. The blade was a standard hunting knife, straight-edged but not rusted, and the blood had long since dried. Vance, hovering over Leo's shoulder, pulled out his phone and snapped a picture.

"Could be our weapon here, even if that cut on her hand wasn't fatal." Leo stood up.

A Bureau SUV turned into the lot's entrance, and Leo headed over to meet Jacinda with Vance on his heels.

If someone was threatening FBI agents, he could at least be thankful that the team would soon all be together again this morning. Nobody would come after them like this, assuming they'd dare to do it at all. Once Denae and the others arrived, he'd breathe a lot easier, but Jacinda being there was a start.

Yet, as he headed her way, Leo could've sworn he felt their dead agent staring at his back.

Accusing him, warning him.

6

Emma pulled the SUV into Valerie's apartment complex a little after nine o'clock. Denae and Mia were both a little wide-eyed, but Emma ignored their silent commentary on her driving. They'd made good time in traffic. And, anyway, it was important they talk to Valerie's boyfriend immediately.

The three of them got out, with Denae and Mia taking the lead as they headed into the complex. Six two-story blocks stood among winding walkways and plantings. The first building had a large letter *A* on the wall facing the parking lot.

Emma checked her tablet for the notes she'd made during the briefing.

"Valerie Lundgren shared unit A12 with her boyfriend. Should be around the backside of this building."

They followed a walkway around to apartment A12. Mia was about to knock when the door opened on a tall man in jeans and a button-down. His brown hair and beard sprouted in every direction. Between that and the bags beneath his eyes, he came off like a wild-eyed man who hadn't slept a wink.

He stared at them. "You're from the FBI? Did you find who killed her?"

"I'm sorry. Not yet." Emma flashed her ID, and he barely glanced at it before stepping back to wave them in, not even pretending to look at Denae's or Mia's credentials before they tucked them away. "You're her boyfriend? Fiancé?"

He choked on air hard, and Denae patted him on the back when it seemed he might need it. Once he'd caught his breath, he shut the door behind them and waved them to a sectional that took up most of the living space. "Boyfriend. Will Butler."

The apartment was neat and bright, with the only sign of clutter being a scattering of student papers laid on the table in front of the couch. "You teach?"

He nodded as he sat across from them, folding himself down into the sectional so that he suddenly appeared half the man he had a moment ago. "Fifth grade. Called out sick today."

Emma almost wanted to give him a hug. A fifth-grade teacher seemed like such an innocent career. So wholesome.

Anyone can be a murderer, Emma girl.

He sighed, eyes on the papers without really focusing on them. "How did you all know I was going to propose? That an FBI trick?"

Mia gave a little murmur of surprise. "I'm sorry. We thought—"

Will waved her off with one giant paw of a hand. "I was going to propose last night. It was our one-year anniversary." He glanced up, and Emma saw moisture welling in his eyes. The guy really seemed like a big teddy bear. "I made prime rib and sautéed asparagus and mushrooms. Baked fresh bread. She was supposed to come home."

Emma glanced to Denae helplessly, but the other woman looked as uncomfortable as she did.

"I already asked her parents for their blessing." Will leaned his head back over the sectional's back, staring at the ceiling and visibly working to get ahold of himself. "They said yes. I haven't called them yet."

Mia leaned forward, clearing her throat for his attention, and only spoke when he looked back at her. "Will, I know you've already spoken with the police and have told them what you know. Can we ask you to repeat it for us? Sometimes a retelling sparks a memory or some fact that gets missed the first time."

Will nodded, covering a cough with his fist before he sat straighter and looked back and forth among them. "I was cooking, and she was supposed to be on her way home. She came home late a lot since she started working for you guys, but she promised she'd be here by eight thirty." He shrugged, frowning. "I think she meant it. It sounded like she left on time."

Emma nodded, thankful his voice seemed steadier now.

He ran one hand through his beard, tugging at it. "When it got to be eight forty, and she wasn't here, I called. Then I called again at nine. No answer. When it got to be near ten, I broke down and called the cops. They were ready to brush me off because Valerie's an adult. Especially when I mentioned she was FBI. The dispatcher said she was probably working a case and couldn't answer for security reasons or something like that."

"There's always the threat of work taking a sudden turn in law enforcement," Emma spoke gently, "and MPD has to respond to so many calls for emergency assistance—"

"I know! I'm sorry. I know. And I understand they can't go looking for every missing person who gets reported, especially not when it's only been a few hours."

"We know you want answers, Will." She used his name because it would often create a sense of rapport and comfort. "I promise you we're covering all angles. As soon as we have answers, you'll hear."

Emma shifted on the sectional, glancing around the space for any signs of a ghost that might provide her the information she desperately wanted, namely who killed Valerie and why. No constricting chills occurred, and no white-eyed denizens from the Other showed themselves.

Based on his reactions and the timeline of events, Emma thought it was highly unlikely Will himself had killed Valerie. Even so, Emma knew they couldn't leave without asking him the question every bereaved survivor dreaded hearing.

"Will, just to confirm, you were here cooking dinner until eight thirty last night and placed your first call to Valerie about ten minutes later?"

"That's right. And then at nine, and again and again. I called five times, I think, maybe six or seven. I don't know. I finally passed out around three in the morning. Woke up with my phone in my lap, and it was ringing."

If he'd picked up on Emma checking his alibi, he didn't show it. They'd confirm his phone records later, just to be sure.

Denae pointed to a picture on the mantel. It showed Will and Valerie, her auburn hair shining in the sun. They looked happy. "Tell us about Valerie, okay? Whatever you can tell us might help, and then we'll get out of your way."

Taking the cue and running with it, Will began telling them everything from Valerie's favorite foods and songs to where they'd met and how he'd planned to propose. He spoke fast, and Mia dutifully tapped everything into her iPad.

Will was memorializing Valerie with his words. Emma's gaze went back to the photo of the two of them smiling, practically glowing. If not for the very real need that she and her colleagues stay together, she would've excused herself to talk to security at the complex.

When Will rambled to a halt, Denae was the first to rise from the sectional and make their excuses.

She was mid-sentence when Will rose, too, and pulled her into a hug. "Find who did this to her, okay? Please?"

Emma nodded as she allowed him to crush her in a bear hug, as well, before she joined Mia and Denae on the step.

Seeming reluctant to close the door, Will stared outside at them.

Emma gestured at the two closest buildings behind them, mirror images of each other. "Where's the office?"

Will pointed down the walkway, in the direction they'd come from the lot. "Just follow the sidewalk. It'll take you around building B. The manager's office has a black door there instead of a white door."

※

The security office was just where Will had promised, and the door stood open. Inside, a heavyset man sat behind a desk looking at a dozen monitors sprawled across the wall beside him.

In his fifties, he appeared to be enjoying middle age with a few too many beers and barbecues, but his eyes were sharp when he rose and stuck out his hand to greet them. "Stan Peralta. You're here about Valerie Lundgren. Sweet girl."

Nodding, Emma offered her badge for his review and was pleased to see that he took his time examining it, as well as those of her colleagues. When he looked back up, she gestured for him to sit back down. "What can you tell us about surveillance footage around here?"

He shrugged. "That we've got plenty of it, but it won't help you. I know Valerie's car. We keep a record of all residents' vehicles coming and going. Hers left, with her at the wheel, yesterday morning. I looked back two days in the history and didn't see anybody tampering with it either. I've been over the footage twice. Yesterday, you can see her leave, but she never comes back."

Mia sighed. "Thanks for letting us know. We'll still need copies of that footage, if you can send them to us?"

"Sure thing. You got an email I should send it to?"

Emma handed him her business card and waited while Stan typed at his keyboard and cued the video files to upload.

The air chilled, going heavy around them.

Emma froze where she stood. Working at being casual about it, she stretched her shoulders and glanced around. Across the little office, a young-seeming woman with auburn air stared at Emma with white eyes. Valerie's ghost.

Dammit.

As Denae continued speaking to Stan, Emma leaned toward Mia with a whisper. "Keep them distracted for a second, okay?"

Mia darted her gaze around the room, then gave Emma a quick nod of understanding.

Making a show of stretching a nonexistent kink from her shoulder, Emma headed toward the window where Valerie stood. The air grew colder as she approached, but the thick atmosphere of the Other no longer offered any shock.

Emma ran her eyes up and down Valerie's form, searching for signs of a wound, but didn't see much. Some bruising around the neck—it reminded Emma of the bruising that could happen when a nurse didn't know how to insert an IV. A nick above her collar on the left side, like she'd been poked with something sharp, but not enough to do more than cause a trickle of blood down her collar.

Another cut showed on her left hand.

Outside, the courtyard shined in the sun, perfectly

maintained and ripe with blossoming flowers. Benches framed the outskirts, and Emma recognized it from the picture of Valerie and Will that had sat on their mantel. That explained Valerie's attachment, then.

Emma looked out the window—leaning toward the glass so that anyone looking their way from Stan's desk wouldn't see her mouth moving—and spoke as softly as she could without being heard by her colleagues. "What happened to you? Can you tell me?"

The ghost gave a visible shiver. "It felt so good before I died. So very good. And then monsters came, and it didn't."

Well, that's clear as mud.

But it was never easy with the Other. Emma should've known that by now. She pressed forward anyway. "What felt good? What did the monsters look like?"

The ghost stared at her, then turned away from the courtyard and faced the middle of the office. She shook where she stood, and it seemed as if the very air trembled around them as Valerie covered her ears tightly, her eyes clenched shut as if in pain. "Monsters are coming. They're in the needles. They hurt! They burn!"

And then she was gone, leaving Emma staring into thin air that warmed slowly in the absence of the Other.

Mia glanced back at her, but Emma could only shake her head. Whatever Valerie's ghost had tried to tell her, she hadn't understood.

7

Freeman's Liquor Store was crawling with law enforcement. MPD uniform officers, crime scene technicians, and the blue of FBI windbreakers swarmed the place. Nothing like the death of a fellow LEO to mobilize teams.

Emma pulled the SUV into the lot, bringing the vehicle to a stop beside another of the Bureau's Explorers. Denae shot out of the car even before the engine had gone silent. She raced across the lot to where Leo, Vance, and Jacinda stood near the store entrance beside a deep-blue Hyundai sedan.

Mia waved at Vance as she opened the door, and he set off in their direction.

Climbing from the SUV, Emma stayed put while Mia and Vance shared a quiet moment. Just from his posture, Emma could tell he was barely holding back from embracing her, and Mia seemed to be doing the same. Emma didn't particularly blame either of them. A dead agent wasn't an average day's work by any means, and she imagined it had shaken every one of them at least a touch.

Especially considering it was their own SSA who'd received the threatening phone calls.

Denae had caught up to Leo and Jacinda where they stood near Valerie's car beside a huddle of cops. A forensic team was already at work around the driver's side door.

The SSA waved as Emma approached with Mia and Vance at her back. "Welcome to the action. Leo, will you bring everyone up to speed?"

He pointed toward a patch of grass on the other side of Valerie's car. "There's some trampled grass, and Vance and I found a bloodied knife over there. The killer might've hidden over there before attacking or fled that way after he—"

"Was the knife the murder weapon?" Emma glanced around for wherever the blade was sealed up for forensics.

Leo shook his head. "Blood on the tip, and she's got a wound below her neckline and on her left hand. But neither killed her. Looks like it was used to threaten her, maybe. Jacinda was able to get them to put a rush on processing the fingerprints."

Though grim-faced, the SSA barely reacted as she watched the techs working over Valerie's body.

"I hope that means this'll be over quickly." Emma stopped speaking as a skinny, dark-haired man in his thirties separated himself from the techs near the car and headed over to their small grouping.

Jacinda introduced him. "Team, this is Medical Examiner Derek Winthrop. Derek, what can you tell us?"

The M.E. offered a tight smile around the group of agents as he tugged his latex gloves off. "We found a syringe between Valerie's body and the armrest. Looks like the killer either got lazy and left it behind or lost track of where it fell. And there're two punctures in the right side of her neck. One much deeper than the other and probably the ultimate injection site."

Mia grimaced. "So poison?"

He pursed his lips, a row of wrinkles appearing on his forehead and aging him a few years. "It's possible, but I doubt it. It looks like she bit her tongue badly right before dying, which suggests a seizure. If you're asking me for my best guess, which I know you are, I'd say we're looking at a lethal injection of a street drug overdose. Likely a methamphetamine, though I won't be sure until I've done a more thorough toxicology screening."

"We understand." Jacinda's focus returned to the car as some techs began pulling Valerie from the front seat. "And what about wounds that might've come from that knife?"

"Ah, right. She has a slight puncture wound above her collarbone, left side of her body. Not deep, but it did break the skin." He shook his head, a flash of sorrow showing up in his expression before he went back to being a more flat-faced professional. "Definitely not the cause of death, but he…well, he could've been torturing her or threatening her with worse if she didn't comply. We don't see any signs of sexual assault, thankfully."

Emma flinched at the words even though she'd expected them. "That's good to know, but it leaves us wondering what she was being forced to do."

"Hard to say. We might never know." With that, the M.E. offered all of them an apologetic goodbye and headed back to his vehicle, preparing to move the body off scene.

Watching Valerie's face being covered over by a body bag, Emma couldn't help going back to their caller's words once again. And to what he'd said about the bad actors in their last case being "nothing" compared to him. She could only hope he was wrong.

Leo and Denae hung back while Emma wandered closer to Valerie's car.

An older cop with gray hair and a neatly trimmed salt-

and-pepper beard waved her toward the back seat. Emma eyed his name tag. *Reinhart.* "Forensics is about done, and then you can take her bag, laptop, all that."

Emma forced a smile. "Thanks. We can use all the evidence we can get."

"Nasty business." The cop shoved his hands into his pockets, shaking his head. "That agent didn't look old enough to be buying liquor, let alone getting killed, and here she ends up like this. It's a damn shame."

Emma dug a card out of her pocket and passed it his way. "You all find anything else after we leave today, make sure to call us. Or anything else about Valerie. This is our top priority."

The man eyed the card, then went to hand it back. "This is my last day on the job, Agent Last. Better off giving it to someone else."

"Last day, huh?" She waved off the card. "Keep it. I've got plenty. Congrats on the retirement?"

He chuckled sadly. "Never been so glad as I am this morning. I swear, I barely recognize this city sometimes. I hadn't planned on moving, but stuff like this happens...I can't help considering it."

"Wouldn't have expected you to be out here on crime scene duty, Officer Reinhart. Don't soon-to-be retirees get desk duty?"

His grin appeared wilted after the morning he'd had. "I told 'em to put me somewhere I could help this week. Didn't want my last memories on the job to be deskbound. Rethinking that now, I gotta say."

"Well, one way or another, just enjoy your retirement, okay? You've earned it, and we'll take things from here." Emma patted him on the shoulder before stepping away, wondering whether she'd ever be able to imagine retiring herself.

Probably not until you've drawn your last breath, Emma girl. Not as long as innocent people are at risk.

8

I held in a laugh as I watched the cops and Feds swarm Valerie's car like ants at a picnic.

Wouldn't it have been something if I could've bombed that parking lot and liquor store, igniting all that alcohol with them trapped inside? I'd seen a lab go up before, seen what happened when dumb people played with things they didn't know how to control.

The roof comes off, the walls fall down, and you're left standing in the flames. Until you die, of course.

Though I wasn't ready to drop the VCU team into the hot seat just yet, laughing while those idiots danced around on fire wasn't out of my wheelhouse.

I dropped the binoculars in my lap and rubbed my eyes before plucking another strawberry whip from the bag tucked in at my side as a reward. Letting it hang out of my mouth like a cigarette, I grinned.

I'd keep taking the government's puppets as my own, pulling their strings and watching them trip over themselves to follow my orders.

Another cop car pulled up outside along the street beside

the parking lot, making for a total of five cruisers to go along with the forensic vans and flashy FBI vehicles. They stood out like the rats they carried.

I sucked on the rope, more aware than they were of what was happening. "Come and get your candy, boys. See what I'm about to do to you and your ladies next."

The little liquor store was surrounded by the chaos I'd started, all of them intent on finding me to avenge their dead cybersecurity puppet.

And still, every one of them was a worthless waste of space—inept and struggling to put the pieces together.

I raised my binoculars again, roving back and forth across the mess of agents. I'd already selected my target from among them.

The really fun part would be the torture, but preparing for that element of the game was an art. Just like a meth cook, you had to take your time and choose your ingredients before you got to have your fun. But I was ready for it.

Little Valerie helped me prepare too.

With the Feds announcing Valerie's work, all I had to do was search up her name, find a photograph on social media, and do a little extra digging. It was amazing how easy it was to dox someone, even a Fed.

I almost feel bad for killing Valerie, since she gave me all the VCU agents' names. But you gotta break eggs to make an omelet.

With all that information at my fingertips, I could set about fixing the mess this team of federal parasites had made for me. I was so close to finally getting out from under the government's thumb.

My meth'd be lining the streets all over D.C. right now if it weren't for the VCU agents in that parking lot fucking everything up. First, somebody started killing Drivers, then the VCU went on a rampage, staking out the gang's territory like they were there to "stop the killing" or some shit.

Funny how that worked out, because the guy who led the Powders got whacked pretty soon after that, and the whole thing turned into a street war.

My meth wasn't going anywhere without the distribution the Driver promised. None of the smaller D.C. gangs could cover enough territory to move my product, not without getting snapped up by the cops. And I knew I couldn't trust anybody but Marcus "Rails" Foster to keep my name out of their mouth.

With him dead, too, I had nobody to lean on in D.C., so I was right back where I started. Owing back taxes to the county for land my family owned outright. And owing blood money to the federal government. They called it property tax and income tax, but I knew what it really was.

Just another way to bleed the people dry so they can't ever get enough of a foothold to rise up and throw off the yoke.

Two agents stood near the back of Valerie's car, and others were side by side in the grass where I'd dumped the knife. They were really close together.

Based on the files I got from Valerie, I knew the white man was Leo Ambrose. The Black woman beside him was Denae Monroe. Neither of them had my eye, though. I'd be taking little ole Mia Logan, unless something I spotted today changed my mind.

Ultimately, it wouldn't matter which of them was the most central to the team or would be the easiest to take down.

The choice would come down to their addresses. Based on the info Valerie had been so kind to provide, my choice had been made before I got out of bed this morning.

Looks like it's you and me for a date with destiny, Mia.

Maybe the pretty bitch would even get some Stockholm syndrome going for me. Wouldn't that just make the team hurt even more, when they realized she'd come around to my way of seeing things?

Doubtful, but hell, it wasn't like she'd really have much time to enjoy my company. Once the team was taken out, she'd only be useful to me as a plaything.

I finished up my strawberry whip and stared at Agent Mia Logan.

Her apartment placed her more remote than any of the others, more distant from aid and support in the form of cops and other Feds.

The other male agent, Vance Jessup, sidled up to her. I tightened my sighting on the two of them, leaning forward in my seat. Their bodies were close together, leaning toward one another.

And then Jessup's hand came down, brushing Logan's lower back.

Familiar. Comfortable. And she wore a smile on her face, so this wasn't a jerk of a colleague making moves, but a welcome advance.

Hot damn, but they are a couple.

I slammed my hand against the steering wheel, just refraining from letting out a yell that might've caught some nearby ears. The triumph of what was coming solidified in me, hard and sweet.

If Jessup and Logan were a thing, then she was even more perfect than I'd realized. Once I took her, the team would have a suffering lover in their midst, adding to the chaos, tripping them up at every turn with his demands that they do something, anything, to get his woman back.

I could almost cry with joy, it was so perfect.

I pulled one more sweet treat from the pack and hung it between my lips to chew on, breathing in the sweet, fruity scent.

Here we go, just like we planned.

I had some calls to make before I grabbed Mia. The morning's surveillance had whetted my taste buds just right, and Agent Logan would keep fine in the meantime.

My hand went for my key in the ignition, but I waited to start the engine. An old cop over there was getting into his car. He had been talking with the mousy-haired chick standing beside Mia. I knew she was Emma Last, another of the VCU's rock star agents.

Wouldn't it just be something to find out that the same cop she'd been shooting the shit with ended up dead later that day?

I almost busted up laughing as I imagined the look on Last's face when she heard the news.

Poor Emma. It seems you're the only one of your little gang who doesn't have a lover. That means you'll be harder to fuck with, but I think I might have found a way to drive the point home.

By the time I'd tucked the binoculars safely into their carrying case, I was just about vibrating with excitement for what was to come. I had to get going. The start of my car's engine was like the revving of a weapon instead of a vehicle, the way it signaled blood to come.

Not only did I have to set things up for tonight's kill—the old, gray-haired cop, but—I also had a holding room to prepare for Mia Logan. Plenty to keep me busy.

By this time tomorrow, Emma Last would be twisted up with worry about a dead cop I was about to follow away from the scene. Then, when it came time for me to steal Logan away and put the whole team on notice, I'd have them all right where I needed them.

9

After spending the entire day around the crime scene at Freeman's Liquor Store, Emma was ready for a drink or three herself. From across the parking lot, Mia offered a tired wave as she stood and stretched. She and Vance had been busy bagging potential evidence—or trash, if they were out of luck—from the lot.

The night clerk had shown up a few minutes ago and was being cleared by MPD to park his minivan farther down the line of shops. Emma watched as a muscular officer directed the clerk to a parking space, then escorted him in her direction.

"Agent Last, I'm Officer Murdock, MPD. This gentleman is Pete Falstaff." Murdock turned to the night clerk. "She has some questions for you before you begin your shift."

Emma acknowledged Murdock's assistance with a nod and motioned with her eyes for him to stand just a few steps away, in case Pete made a break for it. Then she turned her attention to Pete the Unobservant, as Leo had taken to referencing the man.

I sure hope you're mistaken about him, Leo, because we really need a break. Fast.

"Mr. Falstaff, what can you tell me about last night, between eight and nine o'clock?"

He swiveled his head before answering. "Am I in trouble or something?"

This guy was truly unobservant. Only a space cadet could look at the number of cops around here and question whether they might be in trouble. Even innocent people felt guilty surrounded by this many officers.

"Like, I just sell booze, and I always check ID. Always, I'm serious. It's on the security cameras, you know?"

"I'm sure you do, Mr. Falstaff. That's not why we're all here." Emma gestured at the officers and her colleagues still gathered around the parking lot. She made a point of indicating Officer Murdock. The officer lifted a hand and waved, then set it back on his belt.

Pete flinched and waved back. "This is a lot of cops for selling to a minor. I'm not saying I do that. I swear." His hand flew back up in surrender.

Her patience wearing damnably thin, Emma got to the point. "Mr. Falstaff, last night, a woman was murdered in this parking lot. Her car was parked right next to your van. Did you notice anything before leaving for the night? Anything at all."

"Um, not really. I mean, I take my time closing up, make sure the right lights stay on, check the bathroom in case someone's hiding out back there."

"You didn't notice the car still parked there beside your van?"

"I mean, yeah. I saw it, but I figured it was somebody sleeping it off, so they wouldn't get a DUI. We get people doing that in the parking lot sometimes."

Working at holding back an eye roll, Emma dutifully

jotted down all the "odd things" that their night clerk Pete had heard as he'd left the store and got into his van. She continued to probe for any indication that Pete had seen more than his own shoes last night.

"I was more worried about backing into somebody coming into the lot. Sometimes, we get people flying in here right around closing, trying to buy a bottle or a six-pack. I had a dude push me back inside once after I was already shut down. Guy was, like, spun out, you know? Needed his sauce bad, and I was all, 'Hey, man, we are closed', and I spelled it for him. C-L-O, and so on, you know?"

Emma eyed Officer Murdock and shook her head.

He gave her a sympathetic nod and headed back to his cruiser while Pete finished rambling.

When Emma handed Pete her card, the young man stared at it. "You think I'm in danger? Maybe I need protection?"

She forced a smile that, with any luck, appeared more comforting than annoyed. "This is more about you being able to get in touch with us. In the event you remember anything else."

Here's hoping he doesn't start calling you up with theories about alien abduction, Emma girl.

Pete didn't seem convinced, but he hummed to himself and stuffed the card in a pocket before turning away.

Please let that be today's last interview.

The manager, Daisy, had been easier but no more helpful than Pete. From the look Leo had shot her earlier, Emma doubted he'd garnered anything from the people he'd interviewed either.

Denae and Jacinda were the only ones to score a hit. In reviewing security footage of the nearby businesses, they got an image of an older model Chrysler sedan pulling into the lot behind Valerie's car and driving down to the Asian restaurant nestled among the storefronts beside the liquor store. At approximately four minutes after eight, the sedan reversed and drove farther down the line of shops, turning at the end to presumably drive down the delivery lane along the back of the building.

But they never got sight of the perpetrator, or his vehicle, in any of the camera feeds that covered the delivery lane.

After an entire day of searching and scouring, their best leads still came down to the weapons they'd found that morning. The knife Leo and Vance found in the bushes at the back of the lot and the syringe left inside the car.

Jacinda stood near one of the SUVs, speaking on her phone while jotting down notes on her iPad. Emma headed in her direction. The SSA raised a hand in greeting, and mouthed, *Forensics*, as Denae approached with Leo at her side.

After a few monosyllabic grunts of agreement or confirmation, and one fairly loud shout of surprise—"What?"—Jacinda ended the call. She met Emma's gaze and acknowledged Denae and Leo as well. "We got a hit on the prints found on the knife. They belong to Marcus 'Rails' Foster."

Emma blinked. "I'm sorry. As in the recently deceased gang leader of the Drivers?"

The SSA nodded, already waving Mia and Vance over so she could include them in the briefing.

Letting out a snort of frustration, Leo leaned back against the SUV. "Well, that's fantastic. Anyone want to conduct a séance?"

Oh, if only you knew, Leo.

Emma held her reaction to his comment in, though. She *did* plan on getting around to telling Leo about the Other, but now was definitely not the time.

Jacinda shot him an unamused frown as Denae gave him a light punch to the arm. Once everyone was gathered,

Jacinda took a deep breath and continued. "The prints don't give us our perp—"

Vance held up a hand to stop her. "They do a lot less than that. The phone call you got named Marcus 'Rails' Foster and Tyler 'the Professor' Michaels. This is just our perpetrator pointing us in the wrong direction or reminding us of his initial threat."

"Yes, he's playing games. We have another connection to the Drivers, though. The syringe has been confirmed to contain trace remains of methamphetamine, and we already know that gang's involved in the meth trade."

Emma glanced at Denae, whose face had tightened with every word spoken about the gang her brother had been a part of.

Mia stepped closer to Denae and hesitated before she spoke. "Maybe if the knife was a red herring, the syringe was too. Trying to send us to the Drivers when they have nothing to do with it."

"Our guy would still be using the Drivers as a red herring for a reason." Leo shifted his glance to Denae and softened his tone. "And he couldn't have pulled that syringe and knife out of a hat. Not with Marcus Foster's prints on the knife. That had to come from a direct connection."

"But," Emma eyed the liquor store, "they're our primary pieces of evidence at this stage. They're what we have to go on, so there's no choice but to follow them. Even if we suspect they might both be red herrings or some stupid game our perpetrator's playing."

Vance huffed annoyance but didn't disagree.

Leo shifted to glance over Jacinda's shoulder at the forensic report. "Do we have another contact on the Safe Streets Task Force? Someone who might be able to tell us how Foster's prints could have ended up on our weapon?"

"Maybe." Jacinda frowned, and Emma could read her

thoughts without asking. Their last liaison to the task force had just been killed three days ago, and that whole team deserved some time to grieve their lost colleague. "I can put a call in, but Max had the most experience with the Drivers, and with his informant in the Powders dead as a result of the violence earlier this week, I'm not sure there's anything they know that could help us."

"Is there anyone else we can trust to tell us what they can about the Drivers?" Vance's question hung in the air, pointed but without singling Denae out. Still, Emma couldn't help looking at her.

Stress lined her face, and she kept her arms crossed tight, but finally, she nodded. "We can trust my brother." She sighed, seeming to wilt beside Leo as she also leaned back against the vehicle behind them.

The sun had set, leaving them standing in the shadows between streetlamps, but Emma guessed she would've seen pain there if there'd been more light.

"After everything that happened this week, Jamaal's severed ties with all of them. He's been staying with Mom and Dad. I don't know if that will last. God, I hope it does, but I know he'll help us however he can."

"Thank you, Denae." Jacinda reached out and patted her shoulder, her hand lingering on the other woman's arm for an extra moment of support. "I'm sorry about how everything went down with that case, and I know it's a big ask to involve family."

Emma met Denae's gaze with a small nod. "I can go along with Denae to interview him, since he's been around me more than anyone else on the team."

"Thanks, Emma. Make that the plan for first thing tomorrow, okay?" Jacinda reactivated her iPad, reviewing some notes as she spoke again. "Mia and I should be able to check in on the results of Valerie Lundgren's autopsy tomorrow morning. Vance and Leo, I want the two of you to do another round of patrolling Drivers' territory. You're familiar with it already, but see if anything stands out as new or suspicious."

A round of murmured assent came from the gathered agents.

With assignments doled out, Jacinda gave a last glance around the liquor store's lot. "We'll have uniforms sit on the crime scene just in case our perpetrator returns, but I think we're done here. You all go home, get some sleep, and get back on the case tomorrow morning. Weekend's canceled, if you hadn't guessed."

Saw that one coming.

Heading back toward the SUV she'd driven over with Mia and Denae, Emma slowed as Leo came trotting up. Behind him, Vance and Mia were still speaking with Jacinda. "Mind if I catch a ride back to the Bureau? Mia's gonna ride with Vance."

Emma raised an eyebrow. "Ah, I get it. You don't want to be a third wheel, so it gets to be my job?" Leo's face went slack so quickly that she couldn't help letting out a laugh that even forced a grin to Denae's face. "Relax, I'm joking. Get in the back."

Once they got on the road, Denae seemed to wilt in the passenger seat. Leo's hand rested on her shoulder.

Emma allowed the silence of the drive to sink in around them, figuring Denae would speak when she was ready. The day had been heavy with the weight of a fellow agent's death, but at the prospect of involving Denae's brother again, and more gang violence, the atmosphere had become stiff with dread.

"Jamaal going to prison would break my parents' hearts." Denae spoke softly and reached up to take Leo's hand on her shoulder. "He can't be involved in this."

Emma darted a glance her friend's way, frowning at the pain in her colleague's voice. "I'm sure he isn't. How could he be?"

"He's not. I know it." Denae shook her head, frowning. "Like I said before, though, we've never been close. He's my kid brother. I was almost out of the house by the time he was running around the yard with his friends. I feel like I hardly know him, and I almost lost him this week."

Leo leaned toward her from the back seat, his hand gently squeezing her shoulder. She settled into the touch, enough so that Emma was suddenly thankful he'd run to catch up with them. "You're going to be there for him, Denae, and so are your parents. We're just looking to him for information, remember? Nobody suspects him of anything."

She coughed into her arm, and Emma stared forward into the night. This was the hard part of having family, loved ones you cared about. The concern she'd seen in the expressions of Denae's parents had been haunting her all day, making her think of how close Denae had come to losing Jamaal. And Mia had lost her own brother to violence, as well, that grief still fresh.

"I know you didn't want to involve your brother." Leo's quiet words hung in the air, echoing Emma's own thoughts. "If we need to find another way—"

"No." Denae shook her head, reaching one hand up to rub at her eyes. The exhaustion was showing through for all of them. "We don't have a choice. Jamaal will understand, and it'll be fine. I'm just tired. Lives are at stake, and I know he'll want to help if he can."

Leo and Denae's hands seemed to form a lifeline between them. The warmth of the exchange settled the air some.

This wouldn't be an easy case, but they'd find their bad guy.

They always did.

10

Agent Valerie Lundgren's face had haunted Officer Chuck Reinhart—now officially retired—all damn day. That had been a hell of a case to end his career on. From the time when he'd arrived on scene that morning, throughout the comings and goings of techs and officers, and on through the end of the evening when he'd been released from duty.

Forever.

But that was a good thing, right? Even if forever was a long damn time.

When he arrived home to his little bungalow, he stood in the front doorway and just thought about that. He'd never imagined a day when he wouldn't have to put on the uniform and head into work.

He was supposed to have a retirement party at the precinct's favorite watering hole.

That was the plan before the last few days happened.

The chief had to arrange a memorial procession for the officers killed during that gang shootout. Then the funeral services had to happen.

Celebration of any kind would have to wait, and Chuck

honestly had no complaints there. He'd had his share of close calls and injuries since joining the force. But nothing like what happened in the past seventy-two hours.

So Chuck departed the precinct without much fanfare. He got plenty of pats on the back, though, and promises to buy him a round next time.

Whenever next time is. Might be I've had my last beer among friends for a good long while. At my age, maybe that's a good thing.

He turned on the light in his living room, took off his belt, and left his service weapon on the stand by the front door, just for now. Tucking it away into its case felt like too final a step. He'd bought one of those frames for it and his badge, and he planned to hang it on the wall someday. For now, just having it where he could see it was good enough.

Not like anyone else was gonna be coming into his house.

His latest ex-wife, Marissa, was long gone, and his kids lived out of state.

Maybe I'll get a dog. After I do some traveling, that wouldn't be a bad thing.

Hell, maybe I'll even get a third wife if the dog works out.

But there were other matters to enjoy before trying that old routine on again.

He had that new car in the garage just waiting to go cruising. It was a beauty, painted in metallic carbonized gray with orange Shelby stripes. The insides were like a gosh-darn space shuttle, what with all the buttons and computer whatsits.

A pooch with his head stuck out the window might be just the thing to attract some nice widow who wanted only a weekend fling. Nothing more than that, but he wouldn't mind having someone to wander out on a few dates with. Now that the job wouldn't be following him home anymore.

For tonight, however, traveling would wait. So would cleaning up the house. Sitting down in front of the tube and relaxing into those old couch cushions sounded pretty darn heavenly. He had a few beers in the fridge, and the night and the television were his alone.

Chuck changed into jeans and an old team sweatshirt before he collapsed onto his couch with a sigh.

He had plenty of time to figure out how to enjoy his pension. The job had cost him two marriages, he'd been so addicted to it, and he'd earned this break from reality.

From the reality that had left the image of that young agent in his mind. *Still.*

Grimacing, he flipped on the television, first going to ESPN. This time of year, their focus was on basketball, hockey, and major league spring training. But the announcers were some of the annoying ones, always spouting opinions Chuck disagreed with. He flipped to another channel and kept surfing.

One good thing about no longer having Marissa or any other woman around. Nobody was there to complain about what he watched, or how much he watched it, or if he just wandered between all the options, never staying on one long enough to get invested.

He paused on a commercial for a local golf course. Golfing and woodworking had both been hobbies he'd tried to get into but failed because he simply hadn't had the time.

Things were different now. He had the time. Maybe he'd take up both.

A clang sounded in the garage. Something high pitched and odd.

The thought of his brand-new car being in jeopardy had Chuck on his feet so fast that he nearly tripped over the coffee table.

The garage door branching off the kitchen was unlocked, just like always, and he yanked it open and flicked the light on in one motion. His gaze darted around, searching for the source of the noise, but he didn't see anything.

A while ago, a few pigeons had found a way in through the gable vent and nested on top of the electrical box on the other side of the garage.

Chuck stalked across the space and looked behind the box. Nothing.

He checked the side garage door. It was unlocked, which was weird. He always locked the door, especially with his new car in there now.

Better go get that gun. If someone's in here, all it'll take is one look at my Glock, and they'll think twice about stealing my ride.

Chuck backed out of the garage, watching the shadows for any sign of motion. He stepped into the kitchen with an eye on his car. Thinking about his gun, and keeping a close watch on the garage door, in case someone in there was waiting for him to turn his back, Chuck retreated into the living room.

Just as he was about to pivot to head to his gun, an arm wrapped around his throat and yanked him backward. Whoever had him was moving fast enough that Chuck stumbled over his own feet while he tried to claw the attacker's arm off his neck.

He threw a foot back and planted it so he could twist with his hip, trying to throw the guy off him. He got about halfway around and staggered as he took a series of hard punches to his kidneys.

"Dammit!" Chuck fought for control, trying his hardest to get his feet under him and turn so the guy wouldn't have as easy a time slugging him in the back. With a shout, he slammed his head backward, hoping to catch the guy in the face, maybe bust his nose.

He hit something hard, probably his attacker's forehead. An angry grunt behind him gave Chuck a boost of confidence. He slammed his head back again, and the arm around his neck loosened up.

Chuck rotated on his right foot, ready to lift his arms and shove the man off him. He got halfway around when a sharp sting pierced his neck. "What'd you—"

A raging pressure exploded, racing up his head and down into his heart.

The image of the dead FBI agent, the bruising marring her neck, flashed through his mind like a siren. The needle was yanked from his neck, and his attacker stepped away, releasing him fully. Chuck caught a flash of the man's angry glare, his thick jaw, and a shock of brownish hair tucked into a watch cap pulled down around his ears.

"Who the hell are you? What'd you put in me?"

The man stepped back and laughed as Chuck crumpled to his knees.

The peace of his dreams and cruising in his new car all faded beneath the blazing heat sweeping through his body. His blood was warm, pulsing beneath his skin, rolling in waves and flooding his arms with each breath.

A drift of enlightenment, buzzing and warm, filled him. Euphoria, sweet and blessed, wrapped its ribbons of peace around him and lifted him up even as he slumped forward, catching himself with one hand on the carpet.

He fought to stay upright, but his strength left him as a blissful ease flooded his body, sending him forward. He rolled to the side, ending up on his back in front of his television.

Chuck's eyes felt stuck in their sockets, unable to move. But so focused, so intensely alert to what was happening on his ceiling.

Ain't nothing up there but cobwebs and old paint. But it's so cool, so intricate and pretty. I could paint like that. Another hobby I'll pick up.

He could see himself lying on the living room floor, floating above it all. Thrilled for the life he had. Thrilled for the retirement ahead of him. It'd work out, after all. He could feel it.

A man's voice from somewhere behind him chuckled, and the sensation tickled Chuck's ears. But the retired officer was lost to his sense of pleasure, running hot and sweet through his blood.

"This is your punishment for profiting off corruption."

Words kept washing over Chuck, sinking in through the euphoria of the heat.

"And you'll make such a nice surprise for those federal scumbags you were hanging out with this morning."

Chuck coughed, feeling a protest building in his throat. "I'm retired. Last day today. Supposed to be a good day."

"Oh, it's a good day. Bet your ass it is. Best day of my life, and the last day of yours."

Chuck barely blinked as the man gripped both his wrists and pulled him across his floor toward the front door. He wasn't a small man. Near on six feet and heavyset, with a paunch that his last wife had tried hard to get him to lose.

Whoever had a grip on him must've been a body builder. Chuck struggled and squirmed, but the best he could do was twist one hand to the side in the guy's grip.

She was a good woman. I should call her up. It couldn't hurt. Bet she'd like a good old hound dog to keep us company too.

Chuck opened his mouth to protest, but only groaned.

The man pulling him laughed out loud between heavy breaths as he struggled to haul Chuck across the room.

"Too many doughnuts or too much beer, Chucky my boy? What was it that did you in at the end? Oh, I know." He heaved in a breath and yanked Chuck a few feet closer to the front door. "You got fat by being a fucking slug, a parasitic organism making a living off good people's money."

Though the man dropped his arms, Chuck found he couldn't move.

"I know you call it taxpayer money, but let's be honest with each other for a moment. It's blood money, and it's time somebody else did the bleeding for a change."

Chuck thought about reaching up for his gun. It was right there above his head, within reach. His front door squealed open. He'd been meaning to oil up those hinges for months.

Or was it years? No matter, he'd get it. First, Chuck needed to grab his gun and take care of this asshole who thought he could just yank him around his own front room. He lifted his arm and could almost feel the cold metal of the pistol molding to his hand when the man grabbed him again.

Chuck was tugged over the threshold of his own house. His ribs and back sawed across the metal sill. The pleasure that had run through his blood gave way entirely to weight and heat when he was pulled down his front step, then again down to the concrete walk, and onto the grass of his front yard.

Heat overtook him, weighing him down into the grass. Heating him, heavier and heavier. Like he was a sealed pot on a stove full of bubbling sauce, getting hotter with no valve available for release.

The man kicked at him, and Chuck felt his arms move, but he couldn't do more than gurgle in protest. He wished he could ask for water or help. Help would be good.

Still laughing from time to time, the man moved away until his laughter receded toward the street. An engine turned over, roaring with some of the exuberance Chuck had felt filling his blood up earlier, and then the vehicle zoomed away.

Had to be the guy who killed me.
Killed me. Huh. Yeah. That's what he did. This is it.

Chuck opened his mouth as he stared up at the dark sky.

He aimed to call for help, but little more than a groan came out.

Everyone was in their homes. Tucked away safe, watching television on this Friday night. Just like he was supposed to be.

He coughed and swallowed his own spit, gasping with the heated pressure building inside him.

Across the yard, his garage door stood like a wall between him and his new baby, right off the dealership floor. He'd only ever gotten to drive her home just the one time.

The pressure in Chuck's lungs and heart built up, getting hotter and hotter, and he closed his eyes. A power swelled in his chest, pushing and shoving at his lungs, tearing them apart. His head might explode. He knew it was next.

He tried to picture his Mustang. She was quite the beauty. He got in. The engine revved.

And then everything got blazing hot, and he couldn't see anything at all.

11

Emma had just picked up Denae from her apartment when her phone buzzed. She sent the call to Bluetooth, and Jacinda's voice rang through the speaker a moment later. "You already pick up Denae?"

"Yeah." Emma glanced sideways at the other woman's pinched face. Her curls were pulled back, not bouncing free like usual, and she looked older because of it. "Figured we'd get a head start and told Jamaal we'd be there around eight. We were just gonna pick up coffee and go."

"Well, change of plans." Jacinda's voice was muffled for a moment, directed elsewhere, and then she came back. "Another body's been found. A cop this time. I'm sending Denae the address now. Coordinate the scene, see what you find, and then check in. Questioning Jamaal can wait until after."

"Understood." Emma nodded to Denae as the other woman held up the phone and then began typing something into the GPS. "We have the address. We'll check in once we have an update."

"Very good. And please, remember, MPD has just lost a

ninth officer. They're hurting, and angry." The other woman hung up, her voice replaced by the refrain of a popular rock song about ten times too upbeat for the moment.

Emma reached out and flicked off the radio. "You wanna text Jamaal? Tell him we'll be by later?"

"Yeah, will do." After a few exchanged texts, Denae tucked her phone away again. "Says he'll be home whenever. He was visiting Hope earlier. She's recovering slowly, but it sounds like she'll be okay."

Emma shivered as she remembered holding the young woman while she bled from the stab wounds to her abdomen. Hope's sister, Grace, had been so hell-bent on killing Jamaal that she wasn't prepared for how deeply Hope loved him. She'd thrown herself between them as Grace was delivering what she'd no doubt intended as a killing blow, aimed at Jamaal's midsection.

She struck Hope instead and could only hold back enough to avoid sinking the blades fully into her sister's body.

"Two-inch puncture wounds are going to take a long time to heal. Do you think she'll ever speak to Grace again?"

"You mean if Grace is allowed to have visitors? She killed two cops and five other people. D.A.'s gotta push for max security and a life sentence."

"I wish I could say you were wrong." Emma waited for Denae to respond, but the other woman remained quiet.

The neighborhood they'd been sent to turned out to be a suburb on the very edge of D.C. Small homes on tiny lots of land dotted the landscape in a grid-like pattern, not quite cookie-cutter enough to pass for having been built in the last few decades. Other than a few mailboxes tilted at odd angles, the suburb was well-maintained and had all the earmarks of an area catering to retired folks. Older cars, carefully trimmed lawns, and gardens that suggested they got more attention than the average worker bee could've spared.

Emma pulled up behind a line of cop cruisers, still two blocks away from the address Jacinda had sent them to. Two more black-and-whites buzzed by and parked facing the wrong way on the other side of the street.

Denae frowned as she unbuckled. "This is more cops than we had at the liquor store. Here's hoping the scene's protected."

Emma winced. The last thing they needed was a scene messed up by endless footprints. Even the most professional of cops couldn't necessarily be expected to retain objectivity when it was a friend on the ground.

And she already counted more than a dozen cruisers. They'd had about six at the liquor store, even at the height of activity.

Walking down the sidewalk with Denae tight by her side, she saw small groupings of cops everywhere. Some were scattered around the house in question, but others just huddled together as if conferencing. Had the whole force known this guy?

When they finally made it beyond the inner rim of cops and police tape, Emma suddenly realized why.

"Shit."

Denae shot her a look. "What?"

Emma paced forward and came to a stop beside the prone body of the cop who she'd spoken to just the day before. "I talked to him at the scene yesterday." She squatted beside him, noting the same tortured expression that Valerie Lundgren had worn when found in her car. "It was his last day on the job. Retired as of last night."

Above her, Denae cursed under her breath. Emma stood straight and glanced around. The little home with forest-green siding was old but well-maintained, if in need of a power wash. Pretty maroon shutters looked like they'd recently been painted.

Moving back, Emma let a tech come in closer to the body, bagging little fibers and hairs as she watched.

When a detective stepped down from the front porch with a bag in hand, it was all she could do to tear her focus away from the dead cop. The little bag glinted in the morning sunlight as he offered half a wave in greeting. "Agent Last? I'm Detective Barrett. SSA Hollingsworth told us to expect you."

Emma forced a thin-lipped smile and flashed her ID as Denae did the same. "That's me. What do you have for us?"

Barrett held up the baggie between them. A lone syringe sat empty inside, a copied image of the one found in Valerie Lundgren's car. "Just like the one from yesterday, from what I hear, but this one was inside. Lab'll have to tell you if the contents match up."

His phone buzzed and he stepped away to answer it. Emma eyed the baggie in his hand as he walked to a cruiser parked on the street.

More evidence left lying around. This asshole's really playing with us.

Denae gave the syringe a closer look and then crouched by the body just as Medical Examiner Derek Winthrop appeared from inside the house. He nodded at them as he came to stand across from Denae, dismissing the tech.

"Agents. Sorry to see you again so soon." The man sighed, running one hand through his dark hair, then donning a new pair of gloves. "I believe you met Chuck Reinhart yesterday?"

Emma forced a nod. "Yeah. And I guess we're looking at the same perpetrator, but I don't see any stab wounds this time, or defensive ones."

"No punctures through his clothes. Some slight abrasions to the lower back and torso where he looks to have been dragged. I can't be sure, but we might have mild contusions to the back of the skull. It's possible he was grabbed from behind and tried to get free by slamming his head into the attacker's face."

"Any chance we'll get trace DNA from that?"

Winthrop wiggled a hand side to side. "Iffy. Saliva and blood could be present, assuming he struck the attacker in the mouth or nose. But I haven't seen anything inside to suggest that. There's no biological evidence of their fight, just the crumpled-up area rug and some drag marks through the carpet."

The M.E. knelt and pointed to the victim's feet. "Marks through the grass indicate he was brought here by someone else. Blood and skin on the front porch, plus abrasions to the lower back, support that theory. We have a needle mark in his neck I assume came from the syringe, which was found inside the house in the middle of the living room floor."

Denae circled the body, taking careful steps until she stood beside Winthrop.

"Other than that, we have signs of a slight scuffle. My guess is they fought briefly, but after your victim was taken by surprise. Hell, his service weapon was sitting on the table inside the house, still in its holster."

"But he was older, and it was nighttime, so it wouldn't surprise me if he was taken unawares. You thinking another overdose?"

The M.E. sighed, pointing to the veins at Chuck's neck. "Constricted blood vessels make me think so, and because we found a syringe here that's similar to the one found with Valerie Lundgren yesterday."

Emma didn't need to kneel and look any closer.

It wasn't a matter of trusting the medical examiner. It was a matter of instinct.

Their perpetrator had dropped another body, and they

hadn't even known the retired officer might be in danger. He wasn't even a member of their team. He'd just completed his final day of wearing a badge.

The perpetrator has more people than us in his sights. Or he's playing with us.

She glanced around the yard, hoping for a clue from Chuck in the Other, but saw only cops and defeat. There was no point in making a spectacle of glancing over a shoulder either. The Other always announced itself with that dangerous cold it carried, and all she felt now was the ironically warm breeze of April teasing her skin.

Refreshing. Easy. The opposite of everything on the ground at her feet and in her memories of yesterday.

Denae stepped in closer to Emma, speaking low enough that only she'd hear. "You know what this means. About yesterday."

Emma nodded, as she could have said the same to Denae in another instant. Her brain already felt numb with the awareness. "The killer was watching us when we were at the crime scene. We need to warn the others."

"Yeah, this feels like a warning." Denae sighed, her gaze shifting around the area to the various groupings of cops. "I'm gonna find Barrett and let him know. Make sure he warns his people to keep their eyes up, heads down."

"I'm sure they're already doing that. This makes number nine, like Jacinda said. MPD's on red alert."

"Good point. Can't hurt to show them we understand that, though."

"Yeah, good call. I'll take a look inside." Emma swallowed down the emotion in her voice. She'd met this man and admired his devotion to the job, to what his badge represented.

Chuck was a cop's cop. He went to work for a reason and only came home when the job was done. Retiring may have been the hardest decision he ever made.

Plenty of people burned out of law enforcement from the relentless hours, the constant reminder that the job was never truly "done." Chuck had put in a full career, devoted the bulk of his life to doing that job.

And the day he chose to call his last ended up being exactly that.

Emma hesitated before heading toward his front door. She felt her stomach rolling at the thought of seeing Chuck's house and his possessions, what he'd hoped to enjoy and never would.

Wandering away from the body, Emma stepped across the threshold and made a circuit of the house and scene. Techs and cops created their own perimeter, respecting the need to limit the number of people spread over the scene itself while also wanting to stay close. Emma couldn't blame them, but she did little more than return a tight-lipped nod as she walked around.

Still, she could see that Denae's message had spread. Cops were stiffening. Looking around the neighborhood outside the scene, from where they stood, as if suddenly realizing that they, too, might be under surveillance.

To her delight, they'd also begun moving off in teams of two, hands resting on weapons as they shined flashlights under parked vehicles and peered around bushes and overgrown landscaping.

Score one for our team, Emma girl. Maybe we'll catch this guy just because he's a lurker.

She doubted it, though. The guy *felt* smart so far, even if she couldn't put her finger on exactly why, beyond the fact that he'd been brazen enough to not only make threats but also follow through by taking down an agent, newbie or not.

When Denae came back around to meet her, Emma

gestured around them at the hubbub and the M.E. bent over Chuck's body. "Think they need us here at this point?"

"I don't know." Denae frowned. "But we've got more than enough manpower, and with no stab wounds on the officer, it doesn't seem likely we're looking for a weapon beyond the syringe. Wanna call Jacinda?"

By way of reply, Emma pulled out her phone and dialed. "Hey, Jacinda. Update time. Chuck was jabbed in the neck just like Valerie Lundgren, and the syringe was found inside. No other wounds to the body beyond superficial ones, so I doubt we're looking for another weapon. Seems to be the one divergence in M.O., aside from location. With the victim being a retired cop, though, it feels like we have half the force keeping an eye on the scene. You still want us here anyway?"

Jacinda sighed. "I was hoping you'd tell me the murder was unconnected, to be honest."

"Wishful thinking?" Emma waited until Jacinda huffed agreement before going on. "Denae and I agree that this feels like an extra warning. The killer had to be watching the scene yesterday to know that Chuck Reinhart was involved. I was talking to the man while I was there, right by Valerie's car. If our perpetrator was there at that point, he might have appeared on footage from nearby businesses."

Her blood chilled with the realization, but Jacinda picked up the thought for her.

"We'll canvass those shops immediately, you can bet on it. He knew Chuck's death would feel personal because he had contact with our team." Jacinda paused there, conferring with someone else on her end. "Get over to Jamaal's and question him like you planned. MPD can take care of their own and will gather that footage. We need to learn what we can about the Drivers ASAP."

Denae went over to check in with Winthrop while Emma

alerted the lead detective on scene that they were heading out. Officers watched from every side, grim-faced.

Everyone felt under fire, and Emma could only hope that speaking to Denae's kid brother might make a difference before more of them fell.

12

Leo's hands clenched the wheel even as he eyed Vance's phone when it buzzed, antsy for news. But he brought his focus back to the road almost immediately.

"You good?" He coughed when Vance didn't answer and prodded him again. "Vance, you good? That Mia who buzzed?"

Vance knocked his phone against his knee, bouncing his foot over and over again. "That was Emma. She and Denae are on scene at another murder with a shit ton of cops. Victim just retired, guy named Chuck Reinhart. He was there yesterday, in the parking lot guarding Valerie's car."

"You're kidding. Did Emma say if the M.O. was a match?"

"Yeah, same deal. Single victim. Needle in the neck and syringe found at the scene."

They drove in silence for a while. Leo wanted so badly to find the perpetrator, to lay hands on him and physically haul him into a jail cell. He imagined every cop on the force felt the same way. It was never easy to know a fellow officer had been killed.

"Wait, Reinhart was retired. So what was he doing on scene yesterday?"

"Last day on the job. Emma says she talked with him for a while. He didn't want his last day to be spent sitting at a desk."

Leo had nothing to say in response. Anything that came to mind felt vapid and pointless. A man had stepped out his front door to perform his final day of duty and got maybe a few hours afterward to spend pondering what the rest of his life would be like before some asshole murdered him.

Both his and Vance's phones buzzed, and Leo resisted the urge to reach for his device. Vance swiped at his screen and filled him in.

"Mia, finally. She and Jacinda are still at the morgue. Want to check yours? Might be Denae."

"Once we're off the road, yeah."

She's fine. Not to mention that she can take care of herself. But so can cops, even retired ones. And Chuck Reinhart is still dead.

He slowed to examine a large group of teenagers playing pickup basketball on cracked asphalt. The hoop had long since lost its net. A few of the teens watched them pass, every one of them sporting blue and red, Drivers' colors. But nobody made a move toward the car.

Vance cursed under his breath, and his knocking foot got louder. "This is absurd. We oughta have the team all together when we're under threat like this. Surveying Drivers' territory without an exact target in mind? Where did that get us last time? Nowhere! We might as well be spinning our wheels."

"I'm right there with you, man, but maybe calm down—"

"Fuck off." Vance shifted uncomfortably.

Leo thought for a second that his partner might apologize, but he tightened his lips and stared out the window instead.

No matter. They were both on edge.

"This is bullshit work," Vance jabbed at his phone, then put it down again, "and you know it. Hell, put us at the new crime scene, at least."

Leo's throat tightened. He liked even less the idea of facing a crime scene that already had more than enough police presence. And there wasn't any point in adding his own fears and nerves to Vance's. Not out loud, where they'd just fester in the vehicle and give the worry more weight.

Denae's with Emma. Mia's with Jacinda. We each have backup, and it sounds like the victims were taken when they were alone. We're safe.

He jumped when Vance slammed his foot into the floor. "I hate this shit. Spinning our fucking wheels when there's someone out there threatening us. I can think of a million useful things we could be doing instead of this."

"We're building a geographic profile of the gang. You know that." Leo turned left off the street they'd been following, beginning a circle back toward where the gang war had erupted between the Drivers and Powders a few days ago. "The Drivers are involved somehow. Or the killer wants us to believe that, at least. But anything we learn is potentially valuable. The killer could be nearby, right here in this neighborhood. A little patience isn't gonna kill you."

Vance's expression thinned. "I hope you're right."

Leo was passing an alley when the other man's hand clamped down on the door lever. "What are you—"

"Stop." Vance pushed open the door before Leo had responded, which was enough for him to slam on the brakes as Vance released his belt. "There, look! Pull over!"

Vance was already out of the SUV, trotting down the alley toward a Black man who was spray-painting a wall. A duffel bag sat by his feet, and he had what looked like a clipboard in his other hand. He kept glancing at it and then back to the wall.

The man's stance in front of the wall reminded Leo of Jamaal Monroe, but a little shorter and several years older.

"Vance!" Leo punched off the engine and hurried out of the SUV, sprinting to catch up with his partner. Down the alley, the man stopped painting and turned to face them, hands in the air. He'd dropped the spray paint can and held the clipboard over his head.

"FBI! Drop it!" Vance's scream echoed off the alley wall, and his hand hovered near his gun.

The man flung the clipboard to the side and thrust both hands high in the air. "I ain't armed. I swear." From ten feet away, Leo could already see the man was older than they were—in his late forties maybe—and all but trembling in terror.

Leo sprinted to catch up with his partner, heart in his mouth. This already felt like it was going wrong. "Vance, calm down." His whisper had no effect.

"What do you think you're doing?" Vance gestured at the painting coming into being on the alley wall. Black lines and white shapes made for an indecipherable image. No blue and red, Leo noted. "In broad daylight? You stupid? You want to get arrested? Maybe you're new to the Drivers?"

The man's arms shook as his arms went wide. "No. You don't understand. I got nothing to do with them! I was hired to paint a mural by the owner of the building. It begins here," he jerked his head backward toward the end of the alley, "and wraps forward around to the front of the bike shop, opening up there. I have my sketches on the clipboard there."

Leo moved over and collected the clipboard. It held a sketch of bikes racing forward through the alley to a finish beside the shop's entrance. Beneath the image was a letter explaining the desired date of completion and an agreed-upon payment. Two signatures at the bottom indicated an "Artist" and "Proprietor" had entered into agreement for the project.

"Vance, take a look." He extended the clipboard to his partner, but Vance wasn't paying attention. He just stared at the artist and gritted his teeth.

"You think we're stupid? You're in the Drivers! And you're gonna tell us everything you know about the meth—"

"Agent Jessup." Leo stepped past him, putting up his hands between Vance and the man. He stared at his partner, noting the wide-eyed look. The case was pulling Vance apart from the inside already, and their team hadn't even been directly attacked. *Yet.*

The artist hissed a curse under his breath, and Leo cast a look at him over his shoulder. "Sir, if you'll just stand by the wall there," he aimed his chin at the opposite side of the alley, "we'll have this figured out."

Vance took a step back, breathing deep, as Leo waved the man to ease.

"He's telling the truth." Leo lifted the clipboard and displayed the letter for Vance to read. Vance grunted in disgust and spun on his heel, marching back to the SUV without a single word of apology.

Turning to the artist, Leo held out the clipboard, then took out his ID and opened it. "Sorry for disturbing you."

The man eyed his badge while he accepted his clipboard back. "Agent Ambrose. Appreciate you stepping in like that. My name's Philip Morton."

Leo bent down to collect the spray paint can Philip had dropped and returned that to him. "I'll make sure our team knows your work here is all aboveboard, Mr. Morton. Sorry again about my partner's behavior. We're on edge right now. Maybe you were here earlier this week and heard about what happened?"

"Oh, yeah. I live a few blocks away. Third floor, so I was lucky. My downstairs neighbors didn't have it so good."

Leo's throat tightened. "I hope no one was injured."

"No, nothing like that, thankfully. Just broken windows and a lot of scared children."

"I'm sorry to hear that, but glad it wasn't worse. Can I ask if you've heard anything since, especially about the gangs retaliating against cops?"

The man shook his head. "No, can't say I have. I don't spend much time out here on the street unless I'm working," he gestured to the mural he'd begun, "and even then, I try to do my work in the daylight, well before the evening comes. Streets are usually pretty quiet around here, except for when kids with their loud cars and music come rolling through."

Leo dug out a business card and passed it over. "If you do hear anything, can I ask you to give me a call?"

The man took the card and stuck it under the pages on his clipboard. "I suppose I can, though like I said, I try to stay clear of all that. Mind if I get back to work? Want to take advantage of the daylight while I have it."

Leo nodded and offered the man another apology before returning to the SUV. Vance was in the passenger seat with the door open, and he was still fuming. He didn't acknowledge Leo as he got in.

"You gotta get it together, Vance, or we're all gonna end up in hot water. Cop-killing perpetrator aside, that is not how we get information out of anybody."

"I'm *fine*, Leo."

Vance remained stiffly focused out the window. He was unraveling with nerves. That was the last thing the team needed, particularly when they were under such a clear and evident threat.

If he doesn't get it together, I'll be doing the thinking for both of us.

Leo started the engine, and Vance slammed his door shut. He pulled out his phone, and Leo stole an extra second to calm his own breathing before putting the vehicle in gear. The day had just begun, and it already felt long.

Mia and Denae need us to be strong, not basket cases.

I just hope they're staying safe. And with their heads on straighter than ours.

13

Mia stared down at Valerie Lundgren. The M.E. had folded back the sheet to reveal the agent's face only. She looked even younger today, despite her grayish skin and her lips being blue with death.

Her mouth had been a rictus of pain the day before. Now Mia could almost pretend the slight part of her lips was the start of a smile.

Jacinda paced beside her, on her phone with someone from Cyber. "You confirmed Will Butler's phone never left his apartment? Okay, thank you." Turning back to Mia, she gave a shrug and pocketed her phone. "Not that we thought he was a likely candidate, but we can now write him off with certainty."

When the door opened behind them, M.E. Derek Winthrop's assistant, a younger Black man named Dante Levert, entered. He walked around the table to stand across from Mia and Jacinda. Valerie's slim, covered body served as a thin moat between them.

Dante removed his glasses and polished them with a

tissue. "Good thing Derek came in early to do the autopsy for you guys."

Jacinda sighed, pressing one hand down the line of her perfectly pressed suit jacket. Mia knew the secret, though. Jacinda was always put together, but the more she allowed herself to fidget over her clothing—even in casual gestures like that one—the more stressed she was.

"I'll thank him when I see him," Jacinda leaned in, peering at the puncture mark on Valerie's neck, "but I hate that he finished one autopsy only to rush out the door to gather another body. That certainly wasn't the goal of getting this done fast."

Dante replaced his glasses and pursed his lips. "Fast but done right."

Mia refocused on his face, as did Jacinda. "So you have more information?"

Dante passed Jacinda some folded paperwork but spoke as he did. "First, we discovered a shallow laceration at her lower back. It's really small, but it matched up with an incision in her car seat. The blade didn't really poke through and only just broke the skin. He may have used that to intimidate her or control her, with the threat of being stabbed."

Jacinda and Mia nodded, and the SSA motioned for him to continue.

He adjusted his glasses and pointed at the paperwork he'd handed over. "Derek was right about the cause of death being a methamphetamine OD. Chemical analysis suggests we're looking at a version of what's being called 'crystal clear' on the street, which I know you're familiar with."

Mia winced, despite herself. "The primary product for the Drivers."

Dante's brow lined. "It's the exact chemical makeup we've been seeing on the majority of overdoses coming in."

Jacinda glanced down at the paperwork, humming to herself, and Mia allowed her gaze to drift back to the dead agent before them.

Mia's phone buzzed in her pocket, jerking her out of her thought, and she glanced at the screen. *Nick Doerr.* She pursed her lips and looked to Jacinda. "Uh, this is my apartment complex manager, Jacinda. You mind if I answer?"

Jacinda waved her off, and Mia took her phone to the other side of the autopsy room for some privacy.

"Nick? What's up?"

"Hey, Mia." The man hesitated, nerves ringing out of his voice. "Look, I hate to be the bearer of bad news, but we have a gas leak in or around your apartment. We're trying to determine its source. I was gonna go inside with the utility guys, but you changed the locks already, and the locksmith is taking forever to get here. Any chance you can swing by and drop off the new key now?"

As if today couldn't get any messier.

Mia closed her eyes, sighing. Due to the current threat, she'd gotten permission to change her locks and had the locksmith out already. She'd planned to give Nick copies of the new key when she got home. "Sorry. Yeah, I think I can be there. You've evacuated the building, right? So if I can't get there soon, everyone should still be safe."

"Yeah, yeah. Everyone's out, it's just…the utility guys are already on the way." Nick sighed.

"Hold on." Mia moved back to Jacinda and offered an apologetic smile. "Jacinda, there's a situation at my complex. They're trying to hunt down a gas leak and need inside my apartment. You okay for me to duck out for, I don't know, an hour to let them in and get back?"

Jacinda's brow knit, but she nodded. "Okay, but you're not going alone. I'll have an officer escort you."

Mia smiled her thanks and gave Nick the good news. "I'll be over in a bit."

"That's great. Thanks, Mia. Just come to my place and drop off the key. I'll take care of everything else."

As Mia ended the call, Jacinda was putting her own phone back in her pocket. The SSA pointed toward the morgue exit. "MPD Officer Drake Murdock will escort you. Check his ID and stick to him at all times. Understood? When you get done at your apartment, call in to see where I am. Murdock'll get you back to me. Got it?"

Mia fought the urge to give her a quick hug. Jacinda was seriously embracing her mother hen role this week, but considering the situation, Mia didn't actually have any complaints. "Never alone, not until this case is through. Thanks, Jacinda."

14

Emma pulled into the Monroe family's driveway behind Hope's little car. Jamaal had been using it to visit her in the hospital. "Your parents glad to have Jamaal home for a while?"

Denae scoffed. "You have *no* idea. Their youngest in the house again? They're in seventh heaven."

Emma could only imagine.

The thought of such protective and loving parents offering a safe harbor sent a pang of regret shimmering through Emma's heart. She sped her step behind Denae and moved toward the patio at the side of the house.

Denae explained over her shoulder. "The front entrance is for strangers. We're family."

Emma forced a smile. *Family indeed.*

At the back door, Denae slipped a key into the lock and then waved for Emma to enter first. The kitchen looked just like before and smelled of bacon and eggs and toast. A platter of food sat on the kitchen table, unattended.

Jamaal appeared from the hall leading to the bathroom, wearing sweats and with a pair of heavy work gloves in his hands. "Y'all come for the excitement, or you here to help me out?"

Sarcasm rang in his voice—he knew why they were there—but Emma played along and hung back as Denae went over and hugged her brother. "What's going on?"

"Baked bread with Mom this morning, and now it's on to my new career in landscaping." Jamaal waved the gloves he held toward the back garden. "Mom and Dad's out buying whatever the hell you need for all that. They're taking full advantage of having me around. Bonding time."

Denae hugged him and tousled his hair. "It's sweet, and you know it. Enjoy it."

His face warmed, but he nodded. "You said you got some business to talk about?"

Denae smiled, the expression not quite reaching her eyes. "Nothing you have to worry about. Just some Drivers shit we're hoping you can help us figure out."

Jamaal wilted where he stood but lifted his hands as if in surrender. "Yeah, okay. Lemme just eat my breakfast before I lose my appetite." He turned to the kitchen and slouched his way over to the table.

Denae sat down across from her brother. Emma sat beside her, soaking in the warmth of the kitchen and the clear bond between the two siblings, even as they began to get serious.

Jamaal gazed out the window at the back garden. "Hope's gonna have a hard time. The Starlight's been generous about keeping her job for when she's ready to come back. Mom and Dad said she can come stay here whenever she wants, but I think she'll probably keep her apartment for now. You know what's going on with her sister? She keeps asking."

Emma glanced to Denae, then back to the young man in front of them as he started poking at his breakfast, taking a bite of eggs. "We don't have any word yet. I'm sorry, and please, tell her not to get wrapped up in speculating. Just be there for her."

Jamaal swallowed, took a sip of his coffee, and straightened where he sat, nodding. "So what'd y'all need to ask about? 'Drivers shit' can mean a lot of things." He went back to eating, apparently ready to discuss whatever they needed to.

"We need to talk about Marcus." Emma waited, and Jamaal nodded again as he forked in more of his eggs. And, with that, Denae filled him in while he finished his breakfast.

She told him about the threats, the dead federal agent and the dead cop, and, finally, the knife. She pulled her phone forth and brought up a picture of the weapon to display. "Is that Marcus's knife?"

Jerking his head in a nod, Jamaal lowered his voice in reply. "I remember when he got it. Rails...I mean Marcus...he showed it off. Real proud of it. Said it was a gift from a business partner."

"Business partner?" Emma echoed the phrasing, taking out her iPad to get down any details, but Jamaal only shrugged.

"That's what he said, but don't ask me who he was talking about. I don't have a clue. None of us ever heard about who Marcus did business with, where he got the drugs the gang was pushing, or guns, any of that. We'd get orders, and you know I stayed as clear of all that as I could."

He flashed a look at both of them, fear evident in his wide eyes. Denae reached across the table and gripped his hand. He flinched at first, but then gripped her back and nodded. "Jamaal, I know this isn't easy, talking about that life you only left behind four days ago. But you were cleared of direct involvement in any of the crimes that occurred. Except perhaps for several dozen counts of vandalism."

The young man barked a short laugh and shook his head.

"Probably got some community service hours in my future, huh?"

"That depends on if the property owners come forward and press charges. For now, you're in the clear, and I'm here for you, just like Mom and Dad. This'll pass."

"Yeah, I get it." He waved them on. "What else you need?"

"It looks," Emma spoke gently, "like the agent and cop both died by a forced meth overdose, and it matches the crystal clear stuff we know the Drivers were dealing."

Jamaal stiffened but nodded. "I wasn't involved in any of that, I swear. Marcus tried to get me to run for him, but I kept begging off. He knew my painting was all I cared about, and I think he kinda liked that. Like, having his own personal artist made him something more than a drug dealer, you know?"

Emma met his eyes. "But you knew he was a drug dealer."

"'Course I knew. Ain't that hard to figure it out when you see the man lifting stacks of cash out from under his bed."

"Do you know where they were getting the meth?"

He shook his head. "Not a clue. About a month ago, Marcus got access to a serious supply, but he wouldn't tell any of us where it was coming from. Acted real cagey about it. The shit was high quality, so we figured he just wanted to make sure nobody decided to take the contact and run with it. Other dudes would ask him, and he'd always play it off like he didn't hear the question, or he'd change the subject, you know? Making it clear the topic wasn't up for discussion."

"And you never asked him."

Jamaal looked Emma in the eye. "You were sitting right here a minute ago, right? When I said I didn't want to know. How I just kept my head down and painted."

His sister slapped a palm on the table. "Jamaal."

"Sorry. Just feel like I'm on the stand here and can't figure out for what."

Emma waited for him to continue but prodded him when he didn't. "You never asked Marcus about the meth he was bringing in, and you don't know anything more about it. That's the truth?"

He nodded and met her gaze. "Take it for what it is, but I never wanted to know about it, never touched it, and never wanted to touch it. I did hear Marcus and some other dudes call it crystal clear, but I swear that's the only thing I know."

Emma typed out what he said, word for word.

"Marcus always seemed real happy about how pure the meth was." Jamaal traced invisible patterns on the kitchen table. "Ask me, he mighta been smoking the shit himself."

Emma gave him a moment and traded a look with Denae. She coughed to get her brother's attention again. "And it's been around since they jumped you into the gang?"

"Huh? Oh, no." Jamaal refocused on them, mouthing something to himself as if thinking before speaking. "I mean, yeah, sure, there was a little before, up in B-more. Drivers have always been dealing meth, coke, all that shit. But it wasn't until they came down here that the new meth started showing up."

Emma was typing while he spoke. "What can you tell us about that day?"

"Marcus had a little baggie he was showing around. It was like little pieces of glass, it was so clear."

"When was this? Do you remember?"

"A few weeks after he got the knife, I think. And that was like a month ago, right before the meth hit hard. Everyone was talking about the new product, and the money was flowing. You remember Rux? One of the first dudes that Grace did." He mimed a stabbing motion.

Emma and Denae both nodded.

"Yeah, so Rux was big into renovating houses, right? Maybe a few weeks after Marcus came in with that little baggie, Rux is talking about buying up a whole city block down in South Islingtown, redoing all the houses and renting them out to folks. The money was crazy big."

With fingers stilled on the iPad, Emma glanced at Denae. *South Islingtown.*

Both the liquor store, where Valerie had been killed, and Chuck's home were in South Islingtown.

Edging up from the table, Emma gestured outside, and Denae nodded. Whatever else they might get from Jamaal, this was information they needed to get out to Jacinda as soon as possible. Denae could wrap the interview while Emma sent some texts to figure out their next steps.

One way or another, though, she could guess they were headed south.

15

"You work out?" Mia glanced sideways at the cop in the driver's seat, but he only shrugged in response to the question.

Shit, that sounded like a stupid come-on line.

The muscle-bound cop remained focused on the drive, frowning out at the traffic. His brown hair was regulation short, but his muscles probably could've used a uniform that was a size larger. Small talk was not his strong suit.

"I keep meaning to join a gym up here but haven't gotten around to it." Mia tucked some stray hair behind her ear. She was babbling, but the cop was so on edge that he was ramping *her* nerves up. "The job takes over, ya know? Time disappears."

The cop—Officer Drake Murdock—grunted in response.

It'd be easier to think of him by name if he'd act like a human instead of a uniform. Sheesh.

Her complex was up a few blocks on the right. Mia ran her hands up over her arms, pushing down a little shiver that had just risen. Murdock really was making her nervous.

Maybe it hadn't helped that she'd opened up conversation

by asking him if he knew of the nemesis who'd shared his name in the old *MacGyver* series, but how could she have known he'd be so untalkative? All business, no play.

Vance would probably appreciate that, she realized, especially when Murdock was around to keep her safe. She still would've preferred Vance by her side. His easy companionship compared to the stiff protection she had now.

"Agent, all due respect, we both have people down. I'd just as soon focus on what we're doing rather than sharing gym stories."

Mia's lips tightened. This was just a quick errand, but she understood. And she couldn't blame the man if her own nerves were feeding off his discomfort. "Understood, Officer Murdock. I get it. My place is the next parking lot on the right. Once you go into the complex, you'll want to make another quick right. The manager's unit is at the back."

His head jerked in acknowledgment as he drove them around the complex. Murdock parked the cruiser and glanced up and down the sidewalk pointedly. "I don't see anyone, Agent Logan. You don't think it's odd that we're not seeing any gas utility vehicles?"

Mia frowned out the window. Murdock was right. She'd expected to see Nick waiting for them outside. His front door couldn't be seen from the parking area, though.

She glanced around. "Maybe they found the leak. But Nick should've called me." She tapped out a text to his number.

Gas leak fixed? I don't see any utility trucks.

It took a moment before her message window pulsed with green dots to show Nick was typing his reply.

They're stuck in traffic. I'm watching the Final Four game, so just come on in.

"Not the most responsible guy, huh?"

"No, he's not. This happened when I had trouble with the toilet right after I moved in. I ended up having to call the plumber because he got distracted by a football game."

Murdock's shoulders tightened. "You know where he lives?"

"Yeah. It's that unit there." She pointed to a set of windows that could be seen behind hedges lining the parking lot. "His door's around the left side under that breezeway."

The officer frowned. "Let me call it in and take a look first." He thumbed his mic and got dispatch on the radio with an update on the situation.

"Good copy, unit four-oh-five-one. Keep us posted."

He got out before Mia could argue, but she quickly joined him. He lifted his eyebrows at her and gestured back to the SUV.

"We're both down a colleague, Murdock. Safety in numbers."

They moved in tandem toward Nick's apartment. At the door, Murdock stepped up to the hinge side, hand on his sidearm as Mia did the same and took position opposite. The cheers of a crowd watching a game were just detectable, and she shook her head. "That idiot." She relaxed and knocked.

"Nick, it's Mia Logan!"

"Yeah. Come on in!"

Mia opened the door and stepped into the entry hall, Murdock right behind her. A television hummed and roared in the living room straight ahead. The bathroom door to her left was wide open. Mia caught a glimpse of the kitchen and attached dining area to her right as Murdock shut the door behind them.

She leaned her head into the kitchen just enough to see into the dining area. Her hand flew to her gun when she saw Nick spread-eagle on the dining room floor. His torso was visible, the rest of him was obscured behind the kitchen counter.

"One body in the kitchen. It's Nick."

A syringe sprouted from Nick's thin neck. Murdock was calling in the scene as Mia stepped into the kitchen, gun at compressed ready. She quickly checked the space. Murdock stayed in the hall behind her.

Other than Nick on the floor, the space appeared empty.

"We should get outside, back to the cruiser and wait for backup."

A grunt from Murdock had her spinning around to see two men in black ski masks grappling with the officer from behind. One of the men already had a syringe in Murdock's throat, while the other held his arm to keep the officer's gun pointed at the floor.

"Let him go! Stand down and put your hands in the air!"

Whoever they were, the men didn't respond and continued to grapple with the struggling Murdock.

They are not getting away with this. Not again.

Mia's gun was up, tracking the assailants as she looked for a clear shot, when an arm in black came down across the kitchen doorway like an axe across her outstretched arms. The blow forced her aim down. She fought to redirect her weapon but couldn't risk shooting with Murdock directly in front of her shielding both of his attackers.

Stepping forward, hoping to get a line of sight on her attacker, Mia tripped as a foot came up and connected with her knee. She staggered forward, and her attacker wrapped an arm around her upper body, pinning her arms to her sides.

No, no, no. You do not get me that easily, not like this.

Mia called on her training, shifting her weight and sinking in her attacker's grasp, trying to throw him off balance. His other hand brought a rag up to cover her mouth.

Mia angled her wrist, hoping to get a shot off at her attacker's foot, but one of the two men grappling Murdock swung a foot and kicked her gun from her hands.

Holding her breath, Mia fought to get free of the man, but he was strong and felt even more muscle-bound than Murdock. The more she squirmed, the tighter he squeezed and the harder he pushed the rag into her mouth. Chemicals burned at her lips and beneath her nose, and she fought not to breathe even as her lungs screamed.

Ahead of her, Murdock now lay limp at the feet of the two men who'd attacked him. One of them kicked at his body and laughed.

Mia's lungs finally forced the issue, and she gasped in chemicals, a high-pitched whimper burning up and out her throat as the wretched stench of chloroform invaded her air passages.

Her head went light, her body limp against the man who held her.

The syringe in Murdock's neck blinked in her vision, then doubled, and a warm lightheadedness forced her eyes closed as she fell, limp and weightless, into the waiting darkness.

16

Emma had just about reached the halfway point between Denae's parents' house and the Bureau when both their phones lit up with notifications.

She frowned at her phone in the dashboard holder. "We just talked to Jacinda."

Denae answered with a swipe across the screen, putting the call on speaker. "Hey, Jacinda. Emma's driving. We're on the—"

"Detour to Mia's apartment complex. You've got to be closest."

Emma's whole body froze for just a second, but then she processed the command on instinct as much as anything.

"We're only a few blocks away. What's going on?" She took a fast left onto a thoroughfare that would take them to Mia's, half her focus on Jacinda's voice as the SSA kept talking.

"MPD received a distress call from an officer who was escorting Mia to her place. The dispatcher says it sounded like their man was choking. They haven't been able to raise him on the radio since, and we can't get ahold of Mia."

Emma's heart hammered in her chest as she swerved left and right again, narrowly making it around a Lexus, and stomped on the gas. She found an opening and surged them into the clear road ahead. She nearly choked on her next words. "I thought Mia was with you?"

"She got a call from her apartment manager. Something about a gas leak. She had an MPD escort. Hold on."

Denae gripped the door handle and cursed as Emma nearly ran up over the curb to pass a slow driver. Emma barely hit the brake when she took the next turn.

"Officer's name is Drake Murdock. Fifteen years on the force and plenty of commendations."

"I know him. He was at the liquor store crime scene."

Muttering came from Jacinda's end of the line, and Emma forced herself to remain quiet. Focused on the driving and not on what might be waiting for them. "His badge pic in the system matches the man who picked Mia up, and I told her to verify identification, so I have every reason to believe he's solid."

"He is. He helped me with that lame liquor store clerk. Pete the Useless."

Shit, shit, shit.

"You know her apartment location? I've sent the address." Jacinda's voice remained tense, quieter now that she'd said what she had to.

"Emma's on it." Denae breathed out, her face pinched. "GPS shows us two minutes out. Have you told Vance?"

"We'll be there in two, Jacinda." Emma touched the gas pedal a smidge harder, spurring the SUV on. "One if traffic agrees with me."

"Vance and Leo are farther out, but they're my next call. MPD have officers en route. I'll be right behind them, but you'll arrive first. And you two, remember, stay together, okay? Whatever you find there, you stay together."

Emma swallowed. That hint of fear in Jacinda's voice hadn't gone unnoticed. "Roger, Jacinda. See you there."

Denae ended the call. "He said he was coming after us, but I didn't believe him."

"I didn't want to believe him either." Emma clenched and unclenched her hands on the wheel, speeding through a yellow light and then cutting two lanes over to take the next right.

Denae grimaced. "He's already killed an agent and a cop. If Mia—"

"Uh-uh." Emma smashed a fist onto the wheel for emphasis. "Not going there, Denae. Not now."

Denae's lips formed a thin, tight line, but she nodded, and the two of them went silent.

As fast as the turns sped by and the roads blurred, Emma felt whole seconds dragging on like years, taunting her with Mia's separation from the group. She couldn't be blaming herself any more than Jacinda must be, but the truth was that Mia should have been safe. As capable as any of them, escorted by a cop, moving in familiar ground in broad daylight.

If the perpetrator got to Mia, he could get to any one of them.

Don't give up, Emma girl. Mia's okay. She wouldn't go down without a serious fight, and you know it.

Both their seat belts were unbuckled by the time Emma swerved into Mia's complex and nearly sideswiped a BMW as she sped toward her apartment.

An MPD cruiser sat outside the manager's building, doors closed and empty. No sign of either Mia or the officer assigned to escort her.

Emma jogged to the left, toward a breezeway that ran between the manager's building and the next set of apartments. Denae stayed right with her, hand hovering alongside her gun, eyes up.

"They've got to be here somewhere," Emma paused at the edge of the parking lot, hesitant to step into the shadows beneath the breezeway, "but we can't just go roaming around the complex without more backup."

"We can check these doors here," Denae motioned at the doors on opposite sides of the breezeway, "and if we don't find anything, we wait by that cruiser until MPD gets here."

Sirens were already cutting through the air from not too far away, but Emma wasn't going to wait. Not while Mia might be in trouble. She stepped onto the sidewalk, drew her weapon, and eyed both doors. One was the manager's unit, clearly marked with a sign. The other had a unit number.

"Manager's place first."

Denae was right beside her, gun in hand and held in front of her chest at sul position, muzzle to the floor. She flattened herself on the hinge side of the door, while Emma knocked from the other side.

"FBI! Please open the door now!"

Silence hung in the air, broken only by the growing wail of police sirens.

Emma wasn't waiting. Taking a step back, she lifted a leg and kicked next to the doorknob, slamming the door open. She and Denae moved inside as one but froze in their tracks in the entry hall.

The booted feet of an MPD officer—Drake Murdock, she assumed—extended from a bathroom door on the left side of the hall. They lay at odd angles, as if he'd been thrown or dragged inside the small room.

The chatter of a televised sports event came from deeper in the apartment, but she got nothing else. Stepping carefully, Emma eyed the kitchen doorway on the opposite side of the entry hall. She kept her weapon ready, muzzle up in case a threat appeared.

Another body awaited her there, lying spread-eagle. A syringe jutting from his neck. Emma and Denae entered the apartment, confirming the living area and bedroom were both empty, including the closets. They returned to the bathroom and kitchen to confirm what she feared to be true.

While Denae called Jacinda, Emma moved to examine the bodies, starting with the one in the bathroom. She crouched to search for a pulse, careful to avoid touching the syringe sticking out from his neck.

Denae had Jacinda on the phone and gave her the news. "Yes, it's Officer Drake Murdock and probably the apartment manager. No sign of Mia."

Emma hurried through the kitchen, weapon up and eyes alert for any movement, to confirm the man in there was also past the point of benefiting from medical attention.

She assumed he was the manager. Mia had talked about him from time to time, describing him as lazy and unkempt. His bristly whiskers and stained t-shirt matched the image Emma had formed of the man named Nick Doerr. His neck twisted at an odd angle from his body, and a syringe stuck out of it.

Emma checked for a pulse, knowing she was doing it only as a formality.

Behind her, Denae had ended the call with Jacinda and was now talking to Leo. Her voice carried all the anger that Emma felt burning inside her chest, along with a fierce injection of fear.

"We don't know. She's not here. Jacinda's on the way, and I hear MPD outside right now. Just get here."

He and Vance came storming in the door within minutes, hot on the heels of the first MPD units to respond.

Emma had to turn away from the look on Vance's face.

He was red with emotions—a whole storm of them, from the look of it—and pushed past her to search the apartment for himself. Yelling Mia's name the whole time.

In the narrow entryway, Leo stood beside Denae, a hand resting on her shoulder. They moved aside to make room for an MPD officer wearing sergeant's rank.

After she knelt beside Murdock's body, the officer stood and kicked a boot against the wall. "That's ten. Ten of our people in a matter of days."

Emma took a breath, darting a look toward Vance, who was pounding a fist against the wall in the living area. She called to him and included Leo and Denae with a glance. "You all ready to start searching the area?"

Denae's lips threaded tight as she nodded and led the way outside.

Two additional MPD units had arrived and were setting up a cordon around the manager's apartment and the abandoned police cruiser in the parking lot. Leo conferred with the sergeant inside the apartment before joining the team in the breezeway. "They have roadblocks going up around the area and will guard the scene. Sergeant Jameson says she'll establish Incident Command."

The officer he'd been speaking to turned at the sound of her name and raised a hand in confirmation. "We'll get drones up, too, looking for a sedan that matches the one you described. Older Chrysler, light in color?"

"That's correct. Thank you."

Waving his thanks, Leo turned to the team. "Mia would've had her phone, so we can start searching for her that way. Her GPS should still be active unless it's been turned off or destroyed."

Emma nodded. "Jacinda'll be here soon, but we should start searching the area. I'll text her. Denae and Leo, if you start on this side of the complex, between here and Mia's apartment, I'll go with Vance around the other side. Sound good?" She shifted on her feet, wishing there were anything else to say.

Leo and Denae nodded their agreement, but Vance was already off on a march in the direction Emma had indicated.

She moved to follow, and Leo caught her arm. "Let me go with him. You and Denae take this side."

He was already heading after Vance before Emma could protest, so she just called out to his back. "Tell him we'll find her. We will."

Leo turned back briefly, his lips as tight as Denae's had been all morning. Without offering a reply, he spun on his heel and headed after Vance.

He doesn't want to lie, but it's gotta be true, Emma girl. We will find her. We're not gonna lose a team member. Not today. Not like this.

Denae seemed even less inclined to speak, so Emma led the way back. When they got to the cruiser and their own vehicle, they found Leo's Bureau ride parked haphazardly nearby. MPD had three officers already providing security around the abandoned cruiser.

It was unlikely they'd find any evidence in Officer Murdock's SUV, but depending on how things had unraveled, it wasn't impossible.

Emma gestured left, and she and Denae moved to mirror each other's path along the sides of the parking lot, each taking one side. Carefully, without having to verbalize, they stayed within sight of each other and stayed on the pavement while covering as much ground as possible. Mia's apartment complex was on the small side, though, and it didn't take long to reach the property's wrought iron fence.

Beyond a few discarded soda cans by a tree and a plastic bag waving from a low branch, she and Denae didn't spot anything of obvious note. They left the cans and bag in place to be collected later. A deeper search would be conducted once forensics arrived, and Emma knew better than to start stepping all over the landscaping where trace evidence might be present.

They circled back, bypassing the cops guarding the fallen officer's vehicle. Jacinda's car was now parked beside Leo's ride, but she must have already headed to the crime scene.

Emma eyed Denae as they moved forward, but the other agent was more and more focused on the perimeter, leaning over hedges and stooping to peer underneath parked vehicles.

Which was good, because the ghost of Drake Murdock was up ahead, lingering near his abandoned cruiser. He drifted in her direction, and Emma moved to meet him halfway. She couldn't guess what he might have to share, but he angled closer as she approached.

The cold of the Other caught in her throat.

Emma kept her voice low but made no effort to hide that she was talking. Let the cops see her and think she was nuts. At this point, she'd deal with whatever people had to say about her being weird if it meant finding Mia.

"Officer Murdock? Can you tell me what happened?"

The well-built, stocky man wavered in place, his white eyes fixed on the cruiser he'd driven there not even an hour before. His hands shot up to his ears so suddenly that Emma almost pulled her gun in reaction. Then he cringed, turning away from her, eyes shut as if he were wincing in pain.

Could ghosts feel pain? Emma swallowed down the question and moved closer.

"Officer Murdock, please, tell me—"

"It's the howling! The howling! I can't go for it!" His voice bled into a whimper as he went to his knees, hands still shoved against his ears so tight that they pulled the skin of his cheeks and forehead taut.

Emma's breath caught as her steps faltered. She heard the howling, too, now that he mentioned it, but she'd gotten good at blocking it out lately. Only hearing it when she could afford the distraction.

She glanced into the breezeway between the nearest buildings, but she only saw the cops standing guard and multiple teams beginning to patrol the area and go door-to-door. The howls echoed, though, seemingly angered by her ability to ignore them. The cold of the Other spread around her, pressing on her will to remain standing upright.

I thought I was finally getting used to this. So much for that.

But she wouldn't cover her ears. Especially not with Denae circling back to her.

The other agent waved her phone. "Text from Jacinda. Security guard's office is up here on the left. Sounds like he just got back to the complex."

"Security guard? And he's just around now?"

Denae grimaced, planting her feet on the sidewalk as if she might stamp up some evidence to follow.

Up ahead, a man dressed in jeans and a black polo shirt waved them down. Heavyset and bald, he looked to be in his later fifties, maybe a former cop living a semiretirement lifestyle.

"Craig Lively?" Denae flashed her badge at him. "I understand you've been off premises for the last few hours?"

He gritted his teeth, rocking on his heels. Behind him, an open door offered a glimpse of a tiny office, a desk, and a number of blank-faced security cameras. "I was down at the station filling out a report."

Emma blinked. "The station? Sounds like you spend time there. Are you a cop working two jobs?"

"Huh?" He froze for a second, then crossed his arms, taking a defensive stance. "No. I've been a security guard here for twenty years. Usually an easy gig."

Waiting for him to continue, Emma finally stepped a hair closer when he didn't. Any other day, she might've had patience. "What happened today that made it not an 'easy gig'?"

He readjusted his arms over his chest, and she told herself to ease up on the interrogative tone. The man might become a suspect, but right now he was more likely a witness whose perspective they could use.

"We, uh, had an issue this morning. Someone spray-painted over some security cameras overnight. Black paint. Nobody noticed until the sun came up. Then I went around to check and found what I found." He shrugged, brow and bald head wrinkling with concern.

When he didn't offer anything else, Emma prompted him. "And what did you do next?"

"I combed the area for spray paint cans. Didn't find any. The cameras were ruined, so I gloved up and took them down. They're in my tool closet outside if you want to check them for fingerprints. I was gonna get new ones installed this afternoon."

"Seriously? You didn't know better than to tamper with potential evidence?"

"Hey, don't get mad at me!" The guard's face went a touch red. "You want to know how many times the cops have shown up for the half dozen calls I've made about vandalism? I've had high schoolers using these lots and part of the courtyard like skateboard parks."

Emma's fists clenched involuntarily, and she waited for him to lift a particular finger in her direction. When he didn't, she relaxed and was grateful that Denae was there to pick up the interview.

"You didn't see anything suspicious other than the paint on the cameras?" Denae gestured around the complex. "Any unusual vehicles? People you didn't recognize? Anything out of the ordinary?"

Lively took a deep breath, then leaned back against the frame of the security office door. "Just the ruined cameras. That's it."

Emma heaved a sigh of frustration, then turned on her heel. Behind her, she heard Denae passing on a card and then offering the usual niceties before rushing to catch up with her. "MPD can interview him again later."

Denae stepped closer, brushing her elbow with her own. "We're gonna find her, like you said."

Emma forced a nod. "Let's get back to Jacinda and the guys. See what the plan is."

Along the way, they passed cops interviewing residents. A swarm of uniforms had descended on the complex. Emma barely saw them and didn't allow herself to process the eerie howling in the distance. Even the ghost of Officer Murdock, rocking on his knees by the abandoned cruiser with his hands still pressed to his ears, failed to slow her steps.

Outside Nick's doorway, Jacinda and Leo and Vance stood in a tight circle. Vance's fists were clenched at his sides, and Leo had one hand gripping his shoulder. As they got closer, Emma heard Vance raving.

"Why the hell would you let a cop be her escort? A damn *uniform?*"

Jacinda was running damage control instantly, informing the assembled MPD officers, and anyone within earshot, that Vance had a tight bond with their missing colleague. "They've been partners for a long time."

That seemed to settle it for a few of the cops, but plenty others sent glares in Vance's direction.

Sergeant Jameson was standing just inside Nick's apartment. She stepped out to face him. "We lost one of ours in there. The tenth in the past few days. She's your partner, fine. I get it. But you need to fix your shit. Please."

Vance kicked his heel into the ground, clenching and unclenching his fists. "Who the fuck manages an apartment complex and doesn't have master keys to every unit? Why did she need to be here? She didn't. Fuck!"

He turned and paced away as if to regain control. But when he saw Denae and Emma, he froze in place and whirled back on Leo. "Your girl's here! You would've been there if she needed you. I should've been here for Mia!"

Denae's face went flat with annoyance, but even that was replaced with hurt a second later. She leaned into Emma. "He's not himself. Not remotely."

"No." Emma swallowed down a flare of panic that threatened to come up. "Don't take anything he says personally right now."

Leo's gaze darted over to them, his mouth tight and his eyes hooded. He nodded, and Emma shook her head. Beside him, Jacinda took her turn gripping Vance's elbow, trying to anchor him, but Leo remained silent even as tears finally broke from Vance's eyes.

Emma turned away, forcing a deep breath into her lungs. Denae was still frozen beside her, and there was no call to ask why.

Jacinda could do her best to calm Vance down, but the man was in full-on panic mode. And all the agents surrounding him were doing their best to hold it together, to push down just the sort of panic she'd felt threatening moments ago.

But that was easier said than done. Mia was gone.

17

The chick was heavier than I'd expected, even after I relieved her of her vest and gun.

"Gotta get you tied up. You wanna wake up for me, don't ya?"

I jounced her sheet-wrapped body like I was trying to prompt a response, tugging her along, but she didn't even let out a groan as her feet thumped over the ground. Little Miss FBI was down for the count.

I had to reapply the chloroform on the way here, which was no easy trick since she was riding in the trunk. But we switched cars twice as my buddies split off, and that gave me the opportunity to ensure Mia Logan didn't get too comfortable.

She woke up a few times and banged on the lid of the trunk. It was amazing what a person would do when you stuck a gun in their face, especially when you had them tied up and gagged.

I propped her under my arm, angled open the door, and dragged her inside.

One of her feet—boots long gone—caught on the

doorframe. I yanked, and her leg whipped sideways as her foot came free from where it got hung up. That elicited a groan.

I dropped her just inside the door and closed it behind me. After staring at her for a few minutes, I was giddy as a pig in shit about how easily it all went down. With a laugh, I grabbed her feet and hauled her along to a shelf across from our "kitchen."

My brother was in there, hard at work cooking up our next batch.

Once I got Mia settled, I stood up and stretched out the kinks in my back, then I waited for my brother to notice.

Just two years younger than me, he could've been my twin if he hadn't grown soft where I'd grown hard with pure muscle. Now he stood hunched over the table, adjusting some hoses and clamps. I knew the setup was solid already. He just couldn't resist fiddling. Safety-conscious, whiny li'l bitch—that was my brother.

The smell of the lab hung around us, equivalent to paint thinner in a confined space. We always had the windows open when he was in there cooking and had sealed the kitchen off from the rest of the place with a double layer of thick, plastic shower curtains. The stink still spread everywhere, but it didn't make it outside. And honestly, even a few whiffs of that shit couldn't bother me today. I was too high on my fucking success.

"Hey, numb nuts, look up, why don't cha?" I kicked at the Fed's feet, prompting another little groan, and my kid brother finally turned his face my way. He looked like a fucking space alien, standing behind the plastic, especially with that respirator he wore whenever he was cooking.

A muffled word or two filtered through the mask. He peeled one layer of the curtain back, then the next, and stepped out. He tore the mask off, letting it fall to the floor. "What the hell did you do?"

The laugh that escaped me made him turn red, but I couldn't help it. I bent down by the human burrito and pulled the sheet down tight against the floor, showing off her pretty figure for my kid brother.

I tore off her blindfold and ran a hand down her cheek.

My brother's eyes got bigger, mouth gaping, and I patted Mia's boob for emphasis before standing.

"FBI agent in the house." I moved back behind the body, found my handholds under her armpits, and hefted her up again. "Open up the door to the guest accommodations, all right?"

Blinking, my brother just stared at me. "The what now?"

"The back room, you moron. The one that used to be an office?" I started dragging the Fed back there, going just slow enough for my brother the genius to scoot past me.

"Man, who the hell is she? Did anyone see you?" He flung open the door and stepped inside, backing away toward the boarded-over window as I moved in.

I hit the light switch with my elbow, since the fucker hadn't even done that. He was just standing there with his mouth open, like I'd just shown him the inside of Fort Knox.

"Dude, you're acting like an idiot. Close your mouth and help me get her against the wall there." I waved at the metal pipe I'd bolted into the studs in the far corner. Two sets of handcuffs dangled from the chain attached to it.

My dumbass brother just kept staring at me. "What the hell were you thinking?"

"I already told you," I huffed, dropping her down to flop against the wall, beneath the pipe, "the chick's FBI. And I wasn't seen. Nobody saw me at the apartment complex I grabbed her from, and I sprayed over the cameras."

"You did all that by yourself? Somebody had to have seen you."

"No, shithead, I didn't do it alone. I had some of the boys from over the ridge help me."

My stupid brother couldn't seem to get it in his head still. He paced in front of me, picking at his fingernails. "What about those Drivers idiots? Why not have them take the risk?"

"Because, idiot, they're idiots. Like you said. I'm done trusting two-bit street punks. We're moving into the big time, and that means moving up in the company we keep. People around here can be trusted, and you know that for a fact, same as I do."

He settled down enough to stop pacing but kept working at his fingernails. "You sure nobody saw you?"

He always was a nervous jackrabbit.

"Yeah, I'm sure. We used another guy's car to get her out of town, and we switched our cars twice more on the way. We're good."

He dropped his hands finally but stayed by the covered window, looking a lot like Pa had when one of us had screwed the pooch on some new assignment. "But she's FBI? You can't just—"

I whipped her badge out of my back pocket, along with her ID, and displayed both for him. "Agent Mia Logan. Personnel records—"

"Personnel records? How the hell—"

"Shut up." I glared at him until he closed his mouth, then went on as I took a closer look at the badge myself. "Personnel records say she's been with the D.C. Bureau for a few months and was in Richmond before that. Doesn't look old enough for it, but I guess the government knows how to count and take down addresses anyway."

"What about her phone, man? Please tell me you dumped it."

I stared at him like he'd just accused me of wanting to raise taxes. "Shithead, do you think I'm really that stupid? Of course I dumped it. I turned it off and smashed it under the tire for good measure, then chucked it into the river on the way."

I shoved the badge and ID into his hands, then bent by Miss Mia and tugged at the sheet around her head, pulling it loose enough to show her smooth skin and messed-up black hair. I petted it, eliciting another groan. Her lips were a light pink. They looked delicious, but I didn't touch them.

If I had to take a video of her later, let the agents who got it think what they wanted to. That stick she was sleeping with could imagine me painting fresh lip gloss onto her or smearing her lips with mine, and we'd just see where the jerk ended up making his mistakes then.

For now, I angled her head at my brother and let him take her in, gape-mouthed though he was.

She moaned at the pressure of my fingertips on her temple, and I tapped her with my index finger. Hard. Her eyes fluttered before going shut again.

My brother shifted on his feet. "Shit, man. You gotta be kidding with this." He paced to the doorway and then back to the covered window.

I ignored him. Gripped one end of the sheet twisted around the Fed and tugged it out from around her. She rolled out like a dead snake, limp and flopping. Barely groaned when I grabbed her wrist and pulled her back to the pipe on the wall. "Help me out, would you?"

"Shit, man, we're gonna get caught." He stood in the doorframe now, practically hiding behind it. "She's FBI. You can't fuckin' kidnap a FBI agent and not get caught!"

"Meth's making you paranoid, bro." I twisted her arms

behind her, using my boot to shove her hip closer to the wall and get her into place. The handcuffs clipped shut. I moved to her ankles, slid the other cuffs down, snapped 'em on, and we were in the clear. "This bitch isn't going anywhere, and short of that happening, nobody knows who we are or where we are. Let 'em look all they want."

Forcing her into a limp sitting position, I slapped my hand against her cheek. I was wearing kid gloves to do it, but the effect was what I'd hoped. Her eyes blinked open, bleary and dim.

"You with us, Mia, honey? Probably why they have you on the team, huh? You the resident honeypot?"

My brother choked on his air, but the Fed in front of me just blinked. Her mouth opened, and she licked those pretty pink lips. Looked like she tried to talk, too, but no sound came out.

"Man," my brother tapped his foot, peering over my shoulder, "what'd you do to her? She got a brain injury or what?"

"You're the one with the brain injury." I stood straight and took a step back, watching her pull limply at the cuffs and try to get her arms about her. "I gave her some extra chloroform, but she'll come around soon enough. Then we get to have some fun."

She blinked up at us. I grinned at her and winked before I flipped the light off. Let her think about that.

I motioned to my brother, then shut the door on her and led the way back to the kitchen. If there was one thing my brother was good for, it was cooking.

I eyed the little lab we'd set up but focused more on the hooks anchoring it all to the walls nearby. My brother was smart enough to make sure the connections were secure, but I'd seen plenty of setups go south because the simple stuff went ignored.

He'd strapped everything in placc and kept the tubing and ventilation in good order.

I ducked back out between the shower curtains and went to collect the empty cleaner and acetone containers that had piled up. Ignoring my brother, I started stuffing them into a trash bag.

His shadow loomed over me, fidgety and paranoid. "What are you gonna do with her?"

"She's a prisoner of war. Think about it like that. You worry about what our military does with their prisoners of war?"

He chucked himself into a chair that had been worn ragged years ago. "Man, shut up. You know this ain't the same."

"Fuck it isn't." I tied the trash bag shut and tucked the last few empties under my arm before I faced him. "We're at war with the Feds, and if we're gonna win, we need to be able to manipulate the FBI. Just like the fuckin' Feds and the rest of the government's been manipulating the public for so long. You think they don't know what they're doin' with their lies?"

A weak thump sounded from the back room. My brother jumped in his own skin, and I smirked.

"Ignore her. Even when she starts screaming for help. Ain't like anybody's around to hear her."

He shook his head, staring at the wall between us, thinking about the pretty thing I'd caught. "Lies about politics and security aren't kidnapping."

"No? Get a grip and sit back if you don't think so. Wear that mask of yours and keep cooking and leave the rest to me." I hauled the trash bag up over a shoulder. "The government's gonna pay for interfering with our business. And I'm telling you, things are gonna work out in our favor. If anything goes wrong, we got the boys over the ridge on our side. They're all about what we're trying to accomplish and were happy as pigs in shit to be helping out."

Another thump came from the back room, this one with a little jangle of chains to back it up. My brother cringed in his chair but put his mask back on and pushed his way through the curtains and into the kitchen.

"Back to work, my man. Back to work."

I held back a laugh and hauled the trash bag outside, enjoying the warmth and the sunlight that shined down on me. Someday soon I'd know what it felt like to enjoy sunshine pouring down on our property, fully free of any government interference.

That's what it's all about. The freedom to do like I want without sucking up to any damn government bullshit.

They'd learn eventually, but it might mean losing one or two more of their people before they did. That was fine with me. I was perfectly happy to play the teacher in that little lesson.

18

Emma didn't quite crumple into her seat at the conference table, but she came close. Vance had all but imploded with anxiety, pacing around the room while they waited for Jacinda. He finally sat down and resorted to staring at his hands. Emma could tell his head was somewhere else, and it wasn't a good place.

Mia's not dead, Emma girl. Just missing. Gotta remember that.

Across from her, Leo and Denae sat with their chairs close together. They both avoided looking at the pointedly empty chair sitting between Emma and Vance, but Emma couldn't do the same. It ate at the corner of her vision even as Jacinda entered and introduced a petite woman who wore glasses two times too large for her face.

"Everyone, this is Special Agent Anna Kimball." Jacinda waited for some response, got none, and continued. "She's a specialist in geographic profiling—"

Vance glowered at the women heading the table. "She's going to help us how?"

Emma might've kicked him in the shin on another day. Today, she half agreed, but let Jacinda take the response.

"Special Agent Kimball, this is Special Agent Vance Jessup. He is close to our missing agent. Please ignore him."

Kimball stepped up to the table and rested her hands on the back of an empty chair. "I understand what you're going through, though I know you probably don't believe that, Agent Jessup." The middle-aged woman brushed at her bangs and looked around at all of them. "I've dealt with teams who were missing agents before, and I understand the stress you're under. I wouldn't be here if I didn't think I could help, and I won't take any more of your time than necessary."

Emma gave her the service of a small nod. If nothing else, she appreciated that the woman was serious and unsmiling rather than glowing over a presentation. It was amazing how many eggheads really *didn't* know how to read a room when it came to sharing their passion, but this one understood that much.

Good thing, or Vance might have decked her.

"You all know the basics." Kimball tapped a button on her laptop and brought up a map with red dots marking each of their crime scenes. "We use CGT, that's Criminal Geographic Targeting, software to analyze crime scene locations and related data, including timing. The goal is to predict a criminal's home base. Residence, place of business, travel patterns, anything."

Jacinda took her seat and rapped her knuckles on the table. "This will help us find him. That doesn't necessarily mean finding Mia, but it's our best and only way forward."

Emma noted Vance shifting in his seat. She expected more of his bluster, but he kept smartly quiet as Agent Kimball continued.

"You all know the area best, but the more data we have, the more exact CGT can get. Our goal here is going to be to plug in as much information as we can, and I'll use the system to try to home in on where our perpetrator may be keeping Special Agent Logan."

Emma's gut turned over and sparked a flutter of butterflies. She hadn't been prepared to hear Mia's name out of a stranger's mouth as part of a briefing.

Across the table, Denae had her eyes pinched shut in reaction, and Leo's knuckles were white where his hands sat on the table.

Jacinda stood and took an audible breath before speaking. "To that end, we're each taking part of this map and the immediate crime scene. We're going to get Special Agent Kimball everything we can in the way of data related to travel time and local traffic patterns, the time the perpetrator would have to have been on site, witness statements that narrow our timeline corridor, localized street and rapid transit maps, zoning restrictions, and local crime scene statistics and demographics. Understood?"

Silence was the only response, but when it seemed clear that Jacinda awaited more than that, Emma offered a tired thumbs-up and Vance stood up. He muttered something about brewing fresh coffee, but Jacinda pulled him back from leaving.

"Vance, this is how we find her. We use every piece of data we have available. Running out the door to start looking for her won't bring her back. It'll exhaust you and possibly put your life in danger as well. Has it occurred to you that Mia might have been taken specifically because she means so much to you? The perpetrator clearly knows who we are and was observing us yesterday. We have to assume they know about our bonds, both the professional and the personal."

That gave him pause, and Emma was comforted by the look of recognition on his face.

Jacinda seemed to take it as tacit agreement and continued. "We'll do everything in our power to find her and stop the perpetrator from killing anyone else, cop, agent, or civilian. But we do that together, Vance, and we start here."

He calmly retook his seat, placing an arm over the back of the chair Mia normally occupied. "Okay, Jacinda. Okay."

The SSA took that as her cue to assign map quadrants.

Emma met Leo's eyes across the table. *We'll find her*, she mouthed silently.

We have to.

19

Her vision still watery and blurred, Mia tried to focus on the boarded-up window. At least, that was what she assumed it was. A square of stained and splintered plywood had been nailed to a wall in the room.

She could just make out a slim strip of light under the edge of the board. It was the only illumination in the room, other than a similar line of light glowing from beneath the door.

Mia's head drooped awkwardly on her shoulder, and the effort to lift it—even leaning it against the wall the whole time—sent a deep ache through her neck and upper back. Her hands were numb, her arms leaden, and all she could focus on was the boarded-up window, imagining Vance bursting through it on a white horse with a sword in his hand.

A sudden giggle bubbled out of her, quickly turning to a choked sob as she remembered where she was and how she'd come to be there.

I've been here a while.

The scent of chemicals hung in the air, and she had to

fight with her instincts as she breathed in deep. Her tongue and throat could burn, but her lungs needed air one way or another.

She tugged at her wrists, but the cuffs dug into her skin as she shifted. Only the jangle of the chains replied. When she shifted sideways, groaning with the effort, she gazed over her shoulder to see the outline of the metal pipe she'd been chained to.

Sweat dribbled down her face, from the humidity of the room or the drugs she'd been given—and she was certain she'd been given something, because her mind wasn't just reeling, it was making shit up left, right, and center.

Trying to sit straighter, she leaned her head back on the wall. A heaviness fogged her thoughts like a hangover. She found herself staring at the thin strip of light coming in under the door, blinking her way through the disjointed memories from earlier.

Masked men in Nick Doerr's apartment. Nick's body limp on the floor. Murdock collapsing with a syringe in his neck. And then being here, seeing beefy, brown-haired men in duplicate and sometimes in triplicate as she tried to keep her eyes clear, to focus and fight back.

She'd had nightmares that were clearer in her memory than what had actually transpired today.

Or yesterday? I can't have been here that long, though. Right?

When she tested her throat, a squeak of her voice came through. It ached with chemicals. Ammonia, maybe. "Is anyone here?"

Her throat remained achingly dry, and her head hurt with the effort, but she called out again anyway, struggling for volume.

"I need help! Is anyone there? Please!"

Silence.

She yanked her wrists against the chain, the cuffs digging

hard into her skin, but there'd be no help from brute strength. She had none. The cuffs around her ankles seemed much tighter now that she'd fought the ones at her wrists too.

Are those new? I don't remember them cuffing my legs. Shit.

She'd been here for some undetermined span of time, with no idea of where "here" was. Or who she was with. If the barren room she occupied was anything to go by, and the chemical odor that creeped in from beyond the closed door, she'd been captured by meth cookers.

But was it a house or another building, and where was it? Which neighborhood?

Closing her eyes, she tried taking deep breaths, focusing on what she could sense of her surroundings through the haze of whatever drugs she'd been given. No freeway buzz or hum came to her from outside. No clatter of elevated trains or freight lines. Not even the occasional rush of a car to tell her she was in a suburban neighborhood.

Wherever she was, it had to be distant from the city center. She'd been taken from her apartment complex, which might mean the house was somewhere south of D.C., but without more to go on, she had no way of knowing.

Mia shifted again, as best she could, and attempted to catalog herself for any injuries.

Her hands were numb, her back and extremities stiff, and her mind fuzzy. At least nothing felt broken. Still suffering from whatever drug she'd been knocked out with, but not actually injured.

That was something.

Taking a deep breath, her eyes on the door, she set her hopes on the idea that she was in an apartment building where somebody, somewhere, would hear her cries. "Help! Someone! I'm chained up and need help! Help!"

She forced herself to keep screaming, fighting against the

scratchy pain in her throat, as she took stock of the room. A simple concrete floor, bare of anything but a shredded carpet, about ten feet square, on which she was lying. The plywood, which she guessed covered the window. Two doors, both of them closed.

There was no telling whether she was in a basement or even a warehouse or business. She had nothing to go on. But an apartment seemed like a long shot, given what she could tell of her room and the reek of chemicals.

"Help! Help! Someone!" Her voice died on the *someone*, cracking. She was too tired to keep doing this with no response.

But I have to try.

She'd opened her mouth to begin yelling anew, or at least attempting it, when the dull sounds of voices came to her. A loud curse, a thump that might have signaled a fist hitting a wall or a piece of furniture, and then more cursing.

The voices almost sounded the same, but one was more restrained, meek somehow. The other, however, had to be the man who'd kidnapped her. He was loud, angry, and sounded ready to kill.

"You fucking always doubt me. Always!"

The second speaker mumbled something before his voice grew louder, like he'd come closer. Mia could imagine him pacing back and forth out there.

"I'd be more relaxed if you—"

"If I what?"

That was the loud jerk.

"If you didn't leave that knife. They'll trace it…"

"Don't be stupid! They'll trace my left one before they connect that knife to me."

The bits and pieces of dialogue strained and revolved around each other, then faded as both speakers moved farther from the door to her room.

She couldn't make out anything of what the two were saying now. They were arguing still, she knew that much, and damn little else.

Probably the knife Leo found. Where Valerie Lundgren was killed.

That idea gave Mia hope, only because it meant she might be with the person or people who had killed Valerie. If she made it out of there, she could possibly lead her team or MPD directly to Valerie's killers.

They hadn't killed Mia. At least, not yet. That meant she held value for them, and she didn't want to think about what kind.

Whatever their plans might be, she knew they couldn't be good.

The more she struggled to hear them, the more her mind ached.

It was like cotton was being systematically stuffed into her ears and down her throat, pounding out a headache in her skull with each additional thought. She rested the back of her head on the wall behind her, closing her eyes.

One of the voices sounded more scared than the other now.

That's the quiet one. Quiet Jerk.

One of them angrier and always louder than the other.

Loud Jerk.

She'd named her captors. That was a laughable bit of detective work, but her throat was so dry, her tongue so thick with cottonmouth, she couldn't expend the effort to laugh.

They killed Nick and Murdock. Why not me too? They had that rag ready for me instead.

She licked her lips. A hint of chemicals touched her tongue, along with fuzz from the fabric they'd smashed against her face. Rubbing her tongue against her teeth to rid herself of the chemical feel, she willed herself not to throw up. That wouldn't help anything.

Suddenly, she processed the chill that ran all over her upper body. And the cold of the cuffs against her lower back.

They took my jacket. My boots. My phone, ID, and badge.

Glancing down, she noted the outline of her bra against the silk shirt she'd worn that morning. The outfit had felt professional when she'd put it on. Now she felt exposed without her jacket.

Though she'd barely registered the new quiet outside her surroundings with her thoughts shifting back to her immediate circumstances, the arguing had stopped. Footsteps sounded outside the door, and before she could consider whether she ought to pretend to be out again, the door slammed open and the light was flicked on. Mia squeezed her eyes shut against the glare.

"Wakey-wakey, Mia, darling. Time to play telephone."

She forced her eyes open and saw him standing over her. The man was masked now, the requisite black watch cap pulled over his head. He loomed over her, bigger than she remembered, and she found herself shrinking back against the wall despite wanting to show some strength.

"Mia, good to see you awake." He came closer, crouched near her ankles, and she went to bring her legs up, but he slammed one hand down on her calf and held both her legs straight in front of him. He leaned in, pressing them closer to the floor. She whimpered. He grinned, then took his hand away and focused on his phone.

She stared at his phone, focusing on his hands rather than the specter of danger he presented. His fingers were thick, lined with scars and several small scrapes, possibly from a life of manual labor. Mia filed that detail in the back of her mind as she shifted her gaze to meet his. "What do you want?"

Sweat dripped down her back, sticky against the wall and her skin, and she tried to anchor herself in the sensation. She blinked, seeing the man double before her eyes could focus.

He tapped out a call and put it on speaker, then looked at her as he held the phone between them. The camera eye seemed to stare at her, suspicious or accusing, as if daring her to make a move. "You're gonna be very helpful, Agent Logan. Not only will you help me get revenge, but you're going to be part of my empire."

Mia stared at his bright-brown eyes, which practically glowed through the holes of the stocking mask. And then Jacinda's voice burst from his phone.

"Hello? Who is this?"

Mia's mouth fell open as breathing suddenly got harder. Jacinda sounded so close, even though she knew the woman wasn't.

"Supervisory Special Agent Jacinda Hollingsworth, so good of you to pick up. I have Agent Logan with me, and she's alive. You'll do whatever I say, and she'll get to stay that way."

The man grinned down at Mia, rocking on his heels and enjoying himself. Mia's gut clenched. His fingers, sprawling possessively over her calf again, said it all. She wasn't going to get out of this, even if she'd lived this long.

Jacinda's voice came back sounding strangled. "How can we ensure Agent Logan stays alive?"

He scratched at the mask around his lips, betraying his grin. "The government's got its priorities wrong. It's overreaching in every direction. Taking land from people who rightfully own it. Taking taxes for services nobody would need if people would just put in an honest day's work. And the people who do work end up paying those taxes, don't they?"

"Honest people pay taxes too. Have you lost property to eminent domain or another government project?"

"Nice try, Jacinda. But I'm not that dumb."

"Nobody's calling you dumb. We just want to know how to ensure Mia stays alive."

"I'm sure you do. So you'll listen to me now and listen good." He sneered, then rose and kicked at Mia's leg. She gritted her teeth, fighting back tears flooding out of the fog of her head. "The FBI and all other government scum need to get out of Islingtown. This is my land, so you all need to fuck off. We straight?"

Mia stared up at him, finding it harder to breathe. Hatred hung from this man's every word, but he had to know he wasn't being reasonable. Most kidnappers and offenders asked for a million dollars or more. A helicopter. Some random demand that could actually be met even if it needed to cross the right person's desk first.

Leaving Islingtown without government? He might as well have demanded a visit from Puff the Magic Dragon.

Which meant the man was either delusional or had something planned that made his demands a trivial joke. Like a distraction.

Jacinda replied, but her voice betrayed no emotion. "You're concerned about government encroachment on your land?"

"Damn right. My land, my freedom, and my business. So how about it, Jacinda? We have a deal, yeah?"

"Before I *will* do anything, I need proof that you have Agent Logan and that she is alive."

"Of course you do." His sneer bled through in his words, and in another heartbeat, he'd positioned himself beside Mia against the wall.

I didn't see him move. I'm not thinking as clearly as I thought.

He crouched, and she gagged on the odor of him.

Chemicals, cutting and astringent, warred with a fruity scent coming from his breath, something like strawberries.

The prick of a needle at her neck interrupted her thoughts. "Say hello to your boss, Mia. But you don't tell her anything except that you're alive and want her to do what she's told. You got me? Otherwise," he wiggled the needle, and she felt it stab into her neck a little more, "it'll be a very fast end to our relationship."

Mia swallowed, forcing herself to gently nod, even as the motion made the needle move beneath her skin. He held the phone up to her mouth. "Jacinda, it's me. I'm okay. I'm—"

"Shut it." The man knocked the phone against the side of her head as he pulled the needle away and stood up.

Mia cringed, sinking toward the floor. The sting of the hard plastic against her skull added to the pounding fog fuzzing up her thoughts.

"You heard her," the man paced across the room as he spoke, "and you know she's alive. Now you do what I say."

He pressed end, and then dropped the phone into a pocket of his cargo pants as a laugh erupted from his throat. He bent over with his hands on his knees, facing Mia, with the syringe still poking out from between the fingers of his right hand. He gasped for breath as the laughing came faster, louder, and Mia's heart pounded in response.

The guy was deranged. Laughing like a child at a train of clowns tumbling out from a tiny car, with tears leaking from his eyes as he guffawed.

She looked away from him. Staring down, she saw that the humidity of the room and her own nervous sweat had made her blouse all but see-through. Her gaze jerked back up to him, to her kidnapper who'd just been getting himself under control, and the man gave a great guffaw that left him choking for breath when he saw her expression.

Her blood ran cold with terror. Mia knew she looked like nothing less than a victim in wait of torture.

And there was nothing she could do about it.

The meth lab's here. I'll either die in this meth head's explosion or by his hand or from a lethal dose of his drugs, just like Valerie.

The man huffed another laugh, like he could read her thoughts, then he was at the door, sweeping it open and slapping off the light, throwing Mia into darkness again. He laughed once more as he stepped out of the room and slammed the door.

Mia barely got more than a glimpse at the room outside. All she saw were thick plastic curtains. Paint tarps, possibly.

Limp with fear, Mia sagged against the wall. The stench of her ordeal clung to her, the chemical reek of the house and the man's sweat mixed with that sickly sweet strawberry smell. She tugged experimentally at her wrists in their cuffs, wondering if the kidnapper had somehow been addlebrained enough to forget she had small wrists, but the metal cut into her when she tugged harder. She didn't bother with the cuffs on her ankles. There was no way to slip out of those.

A sob broke from her throat, and she knocked her pounding head uselessly back against the wall.

"They'll find me." The whisper sounded weak even to her own ears, particularly bathed in chemicals as it was, but she said it again anyway. And again.

Vance wouldn't give up on her. Neither would the rest of the team. They might even call in Sloan for help.

Sloan. She wanted to spend more time with her. They'd just found their friendship again, even stronger than before Mia's brother, Ned, had died. She'd spent months hating Sloan for breaking Ned's heart and sending him into a spiral of despair that ended in a fatal car crash.

But that was all a lie I told myself. Ned was murdered by drug dealers, and Sloan helped me take them down.

And then there was Vance. Her wonderful, caring, perfectly coiffed Vance who never failed to make her feel loved. Putting her first every chance he got.

He had to be losing his mind with worry, but Leo would hold him together.

And then we'll all be back together. They'll find me.

They have to.

Muffled voices sounded from somewhere in the building, and Mia swallowed down her despair. She took a deep breath, chemically laced as it was, and opened her mouth to scream once more.

"Help! Help me! Someone, help!" She breathed, no longer hearing the voices, and took another breath to scream again. "Help! Help me! I've been kidnapped! I need help!"

Maybe the voices belonged to the psycho kidnapper and whoever his accomplices were, or maybe they didn't. She couldn't take the chance on giving in to fear and remaining silent. If someone had come to save her, or even to investigate this building, she had to make sure they knew she was here.

"Help! Help me! Help!"

Tears leaked from her eyes, burning on their way down, but she kept screaming. She had no choice.

20

Emma drove slowly, patrolling the middle section of their assigned quadrant of Islingtown. Businesses surrounded them on both sides of the street. The area they passed through now was mostly industrial, battered garage doors protecting struggling businesses or factories still hanging on despite the economy.

A garage broke up the landscape between some industrial buildings and run-down housing. Emma crossed through an intersection and landed on a street rife with houses in need of upkeep. Beside her, Denae went back and forth between staring around them and jotting down observations on her iPad.

They'd spent the first part of the day at VCU headquarters, researching and pulling what data they could from established reports and government databases. Then they'd had a brief greasy lunch before heading out in pairs to patrol the map quadrants and see what more they could discover. As of now, just past sundown, it felt like they were doing little more than spinning their wheels.

Denae tapped a fingernail hard against the window. "A

meth lab could be in that house. Or that one. Or that one." She pointed a bitten-down nail out the other window, past Emma's nose. "Mia could be in that house. Or that one. Or that one."

Emma swallowed, tension building in her chest.

"Or behind us." Denae stabbed a thumb over her shoulder. "She could be tied up in that garage we passed. Or passed out unconscious in that closed-down paint factory we saw when we first started patrolling this sector. Or—"

"Stop it!" Emma's shout hung in the air, the two words more than enough to quiet her partner.

Beside her, Denae choked on whatever she'd been about to say and deflated in the seat. She opened her mouth to respond but didn't.

Emma took a deep breath. "I'm sorry. I shouldn't have yelled."

Denae shook her head, curls vibrating as if doing the same. "No. *I'm* sorry. I just can't stand the thought of Mia being by herself right now."

Or, worse, not by herself.

But Emma didn't say that. She didn't need to.

She turned at the end of their sector of the map, crossing down through a long, unbroken alley beside a warehouse to get over to the next street. More industrial buildings lined the road, but these were set farther back from the pavement. Dumpsters, narrow parking lots, and piles of trash littered the surroundings.

But ahead, a dumpster near the road was vomiting plastic. Emma drove closer and she saw it wasn't just any plastic.

Rubber tubing.

Emma slowed, pointing. "That look like medical tubing to you?"

Denae sat straighter, leaning toward the windshield. "And glass! Look at the ground!"

Sure enough, broken glass littered the ground around the dumpster. As their headlights lit the space, Emma glimpsed a trash bag peeking out of the dumpster with the edge of a glass container showing.

Giving the gas pedal a quick burst, Emma pulled over just shy of running the tires over the glass. She was out of the SUV a second later, flashlight in hand as she leaned over the dumpster's rim.

"Acetate containers, Denae. Look." She gestured her light inside, reflecting off emptied containers and broken glass canisters. "The remains of an old meth lab, or the detritus of a working one."

"I'll call Jacinda." It took only a few seconds for Jacinda's voice to come through the speaker, and Denae didn't waste time filling her in.

"Team's on the way. You have a likely location for the lab at your address?" They could hear Jacinda speaking to someone else on her end, but Emma was already forming an answer.

"We're right up next to what looks like an abandoned warehouse. Same address I just sent you. Broken windows, boarded-up doors, and not a car in sight other than ours." Emma shined her light farther up the street, but the closest thing they had to another sign of life was the buzzing of insects around streetlights.

"Don't go inside. Wait." Jacinda hung up a moment later.

Emma handed the light to Denae and donned gloves before pulling herself up the side of the dumpster. "Between the acetate and the tubing, along with the discolored glass in here, this looks like trash from an active lab, not one that's been broken down."

Denae peered into the dumpster, aiming the light around. "You don't see any full containers or leaking chemicals?"

"Nada." Emma pulled a broken umbrella from the nearer

side of the dumpster and used it to poke at an acetate container outside a trash bag. The plastic canister tumbled sideways against the inside of the dumpster at her touch, light as could be, and Emma heard no sign of splashing. "Empty, from what I can see."

Denae grimaced. "Let's suit up and be ready."

They'd come out prepared, just in case, and the cargo space had everything they could need. Already wearing their vests, they used the endless seconds of waiting to don hazmat suits over their vests and adjust gas masks to fit.

By the time the rest of the team arrived, they were suited up and standing at the ready. Leo and Vance sped up in an SUV, trailing an MPD cruiser with Jacinda in the passenger seat and a familiar plainclothes officer at the wheel.

He got out and joined them as everyone who wasn't wearing hazmat gear got suited up. Jacinda introduced him to Leo and Vance.

"This is Detective Barrett. I believe he's already met Emma and Denae."

Both women confirmed it with a nod, and Emma added, "He was at Chuck Reinhardt's house this morning."

The detective sealed up his hazmat suit and waved. "Wish I could say I'm happy to see you again, but under these circumstances, that'd be a lie."

Stepping forward, Leo checked Denae's suit for fit, while Jacinda and Emma checked each other. Vance eyed Barrett and did the same for him. "Glad to have you helping here, but I gotta say, I'm unclear on why you're along for the ride."

"I've been working a case around a pop-up meth lab. This location tracks with some of the details."

That seemed to settle the matter for Vance. He slapped Barrett's shoulder and stood back while Jacinda began a quick briefing.

"No entrances along that street," she pointed in the

direction they'd come, "but we haven't circled the building yet."

Emma pulled gloves on beneath the hazmat suit's sleeves, adjusting them before bothering to pick up her mask.

The others did the same as Jacinda continued. "Detective Barrett," she nodded at the man, "pulled up the schematics. Unless there's been unpermitted construction, we have one door on the other side of the building, near the far corner, and one on this side, just around from this dumpster."

Denae nodded and spoke quickly before pulling on her mask. "Where do you want us, Jacinda?"

"You and I will go around the building to the side door and hold our position until SWAT arrives. Emma, Vance, Leo, the three of you stack at this door. Detective Barrett will signal in SWAT, but I want us monitoring those doors in case someone inside tries to bolt."

Emma shared a quick glance with Leo before turning her focus to the target. There was no need to voice their shared understanding. If anyone came out of that building, they'd be taken down immediately. Any lethal resistance would be met in kind.

Vance was practically vibrating with nerves. He'd replaced his expensive shoes with more appropriate footwear. The raw red of his lips was visible even behind his hazmat face screen. He'd been chewing on them like a kid, where normally he'd have been more likely to lecture the rest of the team on wearing lip balm that had an SPF component.

"Give us sixty seconds to get around the building." On those words, Jacinda took off at a jog, Denae on her heels.

Barrett glanced at his phone, lifting his gas mask just enough to speak. "SWAT says they're ten minutes out. Let's get in position."

Emma steeled herself, ignoring the urge to look for signs of the Other, whether for guidance or warning. The ghosts she'd seen had never been clear with her about their intentions.

Without a glance at either Vance or Leo, she took lead and stalked toward the door, weapon held at compressed ready. Her colleagues followed behind her.

She drew to a stop at the handle side of the door, and the other agents stacked behind her with Vance at her back. Leo brought up the rear. Emma wanted to bang on the door and announce their presence, but SWAT was almost there.

Just hold position, Emma girl. Cavalry's coming, and you'll be moving inside soon enough.

She turned back to give Vance a reassuring nod when the door slammed open away from her, putting her face-to-face with a man who pushed her backward into Vance and Leo. She twisted away from him and brought her weapon up as the man stumbled past her and into the street. A second man sprinted out after him.

Leo and Vance were already tackling the first man to the ground as Emma revised her aim and called for the second suspect to stop.

"FBI! Freeze and get on the ground! Do it!"

The man kept running, and Emma sped after him, dodging around Vance and Leo as they struggled with the first man on the ground.

Emma raced down the street, following the other man, and Barrett joined her, yelling into his radio that they were in pursuit of a suspect.

Running in the hazmat suits was loud, flapping, and awkward. The suit pulled at her waist, and she ripped the gas mask off her head and threw it to the side. Barrett pulled his mask down around his neck and put on a burst of speed.

Luckily, the suspect was no athlete. Whatever speed Emma and Barrett lost to the flapping suits was more than offset by their quarry's awkward sprint.

The police detective lunged forward, shoving the man in the back. He toppled from his own momentum. The man let out a grunt as he fell, but it was too late for him to get up and regain ground. Emma landed on his back, and Barrett grappled with a flailing arm. The man bucked beneath Emma's weight, and Barrett had his arm twisted around in a lock. Emma yanked up the other, and, together, she and the MPD detective got him in cuffs.

The man spluttered beneath Emma, jerking his wrists against her grip. "The Drivers'll come after you for this! Feds don't own this town!"

As soon as Emma got off him, catching her breath from the sprint, Barrett gripped one of the guy's biceps and pulled him up to his knees and then to standing. She stood back while the detective jerked their suspect into a perp walk back toward the warehouse. They got there as Vance was handing his own catch off to Leo and turning back toward the door the men had burst through.

Emma could see what Leo didn't. Their partner was thinking about going in alone. She raced back to where she'd dropped her mask and snatched it off the ground, then spun back around. "Vance! Wait for me!"

He stiffened briefly but was at the warehouse door in two strides. Leo struggled to keep control of his suspect.

Emma had picked up her mask, shoved it back on, checked the seals, and run ahead to join him. "Vance, you need backup. Let me go in with you."

Stopping him wasn't an option, and she couldn't blame him for being anxious enough to ignore protocol. But going in at all, even with backup, could be career-ending or even suicide, depending upon what awaited them.

It's not like you haven't done the same thing yourself, Emma girl. But that doesn't mean you have to let him take the same risks.

"We should wait for Jacinda's word, Vance. They might not be ready yet, and we don't know what's inside."

"Yeah, you do that, Emma. Wait here. It'll be safer. Meanwhile, I'm going in to save Mia."

And then he was gone, rushing through the door. The slap of his feet against concrete faded against the sounds of the two captive men screaming at Leo and Detective Barrett.

Emma could only hope she'd meet up with Denae and Jacinda inside, and that, together, they could talk some sense into Vance.

With one last look back at Leo, she raced after Vance.

The warehouse was packed full of shelving. A narrow path hugged the walls in both directions. Vance stood to the left of a door with his weapon raised and sighting.

Emma examined the shelves just inside the door. They were stacked full of moldering cardboard boxes, mounds of plastic tubing, and endless piles of fabric that could have at one point been curtains or upholstery.

This wasn't right. Even idiots running a meth lab would want a cleaner space than this, just to avoid blowing themselves up, if for no other reason.

"Vance, something's—"

Her words didn't reach him because he was already racing along the wall. He aimed his gun down each canyon of shelves he passed. Emma had to jog to keep up.

With their sight lines effectively blocked by the shelving, her anxiety ratcheted up several notches. She roamed her view up and down the shelves as they progressed, looking for any sign of an approaching threat.

Nothing moved among the towering rows of shelves. They reached the corner, and some part of her expected a figure to jump out at any moment. Instead, a clang rang out from farther down the wall, and Jacinda and Denae appeared through a door.

Jacinda signaled for her and Vance to hold position, but he'd already spun on his heel and was stalking back the way they'd come. Emma wanted to call out, but if anybody was in the warehouse, waiting to attack, all she'd accomplish was revealing their positions. She motioned to Jacinda, who waved for her to follow Vance, then moved off with Denae in the opposite direction.

This isn't good. Not good at all. We're spread out and don't have backup.

She moved as fast as she could in the clumsy hazmat suit until she reached Vance just as he crossed the doorway from which they'd entered.

They had another dozen shelving units between their position and the next corner, but she froze and drew up short by the first set of shelves.

"You hear that?" Vance's weapon faltered, the muzzle dropping. The gun trembled in his grip as he stood there, straining as if listening to something.

Emma came within inches of him and paused. "What are you—"

He took a hand off his gun and held it up between them, begging her to be quiet. His eyes were open wide, as if he'd just gotten the scare of his life.

To their left, more shelving loomed. No obstacles stood between them and the corner if they remained along the wall. Whatever Vance had stopped for, she didn't see or hear—

And then she did. A weak call for help echoed from somewhere deeper into the warehouse and up ahead of their position. It was muted and rough, but definitely Mia.

"Help! Help me! Someone, help! Help! Help me! I've been kidnapped! I need help! *Help! Help me! Help!*"

Sirens wailed in from outside and Vance cursed, swatting at his hazmat suit to pull off the hood.

"It's her. She's in here somewhere."

He stepped forward, past the first set of shelves, and aimed his gun down the aisle before moving again, going to the next aisle, and the next.

All the while, Emma tried to focus on the cry for help she'd heard.

"Help! Help me! Someone, help! Help!"

Between the growing sirens outside and the thundering of her own heart, she could barely hear a thing beyond the sound of Vance's shuffling steps.

Then the cries came again, louder this time, and unmistakable.

"I've been kidnapped! I need help! *Help! Help me! Help!*"

Mia.

Something in Mia's tone felt forced, almost repetitive.

Emma's breath caught as she watched Vance race ahead, down the shelving aisle he'd just passed. "Vance, wait. It might—"

Vance was gone. His footsteps thumped and slapped against the concrete warehouse floor.

Emma took off after him. He whipped around the last set of shelves, pushing through thick plastic curtains that had been hung to conceal the deepest section of the space. Emma cursed and moved through them as well. When she got past the barrier, she saw him crouched behind a shorter set of shelves that were mounded with bundles of rags and sagging cardboard boxes.

"Vance, wait!" She stopped just inside the plastic curtains as she tried to catch her breath in the constricting respirator.

"She's in there, Emma." He aimed a hand over the shelves at a small, boxed-in office that occupied the back of the warehouse space.

Something wasn't right about Mia's cries. Emma listened as Vance moved to go around the smaller shelving unit.

"Help! Help me!"

He was heading into the one corner their team hadn't cleared.

Mia's voice came again. "I've been kidnapped! I need help! *Help! Help me! Help!*"

She said that before. Just like that

"We're coming, Mia!" The desperation in Vance's voice filled the warehouse.

Emma started moving to join Vance, checking where she put her feet as she moved.

A thin wire stretched across her path.

And it was already broken.

Then she heard something else.

Oren's voice nearly rocked her sideways, it echoed so loudly in her ear. "Emma, no! Stop!"

She froze. The broken wire was a trigger, and Vance had walked straight into it.

"Vance!" She cried out, backing into the plastic curtains and pushing frantically to clear a path to safety.

Oren's voice echoed in her ears, only to be overtaken by the howl of a wolf.

Vance waved a hand back at her and kept moving. He was at the end of the low shelves now.

"Vance! Get back!"

He turned to face her.

And the world exploded.

21

The blast flung Emma backward between the shelves, tumbling and sliding across the floor on her ass. The world spun. Her ears pounded, and she convulsed, coughing out dust and blood from where she'd bitten her tongue.

Clouds of detritus and smoke filled the aisle, billowing over and around her. She heard a shout behind her, yelling. Someone calling her and Vance's names. Every sound competed with a deafening ringing that filled her ears.

Emma shook her head, swiped at the debris that covered her legs, and forced herself to stand.

She staggered her way up the aisle, back toward where she'd last seen Vance. All she could see now were mounds of burning rags, chunks of plaster and wood, and an endless sea of cardboard boxes with their contents spilled out in every direction. Most of it was in flames.

The plastic curtains dividing the back area from the rest of the warehouse curled and waved as fire devoured them.

Emma checked the seal on her respirator and looked desperately at the blaze, searching for any sign of Vance as the fire spread.

Jacinda and Denae yelled for her, emerging from the wall of smoke and dust to Emma's left.

Denae ran past her, landing beside a pile of flaming rags. Emma saw an arm poking out from beneath them. She surged forward to help Denae and stumbled.

Jacinda caught her and held her up. "It's okay, Emma. Denae and I will get him out. Are you okay to move on your own?"

Emma did a quick pat-down of her arms and torso, then her legs. She nodded and stumbled back up the aisle as Jacinda moved to help Denae. They had Vance halfway unburied and were patting out flames around his waist. The suits were flame-retardant, but his had been shredded by the blast. She stood there, unable to vacate the building.

Sirens wailed somewhere outside. Every sound still came to Emma muffled, as if she were underwater. Jacinda was shouting as she and Denae fully uncovered Vance.

"Get him up! Now!"

Emma moved toward them to help the other women carry Vance to safety. Jacinda gave her a startled look that quickly turned to one of gratitude as Emma slapped away the flames still licking at Vance's boots.

She gripped his ankles. Jacinda moved to hold him under his right shoulder and stabilize his head. Denae had a hand under his left shoulder and used his belt to grip his midsection. Together, the three of them shuffled along the aisle where Emma had landed after the explosion.

The wolf's howl filled Emma's mind again, and she staggered, nearly tripping over her own feet. Jacinda had her gas mask on still, but Emma could see her eyes zeroing in on her. "Are you good, Emma? We need to move."

Emma straightened up, gripping Vance's ankles, ready to move backward and set the pace. His face was blank, his whole body limp, but she couldn't think about that now.

They had to get him out. Already, the fire had spread and was jumping from boxes to mounds of rags, coming their way. The heat was coating her in sweat.

Jacinda shouted, and then they moved.

Emma set the pace, stepping as fast as she could while being careful. Within a few steps, they were no longer under the threat of burning shelves falling on them. But the units they'd passed through were now engulfed, with thick smoke blooming and swelling into the air above. The ceiling was obscured.

She turned, looking for the doorway she and Vance had used to enter the building. A figure rushed past, and Emma shifted her stance, preparing to drop Vance's ankles and fight off an attacker. She stopped herself as the wolf's howl that had been plaguing her cut out in an instant.

Leo appeared at Denae's side, taking the weight of Vance's shoulder and midsection so she could focus on keeping his head and neck in a neutral position. The four of them shuffled toward the door, moving faster now as even greater clouds of smoke and flame began to surge in their direction.

The warehouse was an inferno.

In that instant, she remembered what had drawn Vance so deeply into the building to begin with.

"Mia!"

Jacinda and Denae stopped, almost dropping Vance as they staggered. The SSA adjusted her grip and urged them on. "Emma! We have to get out. Move!"

We were all supposed to die here. Those assholes set this trap to kill us all at once.

Emma's fury overtook her grief for a moment, but Jacinda continued to yell commands to move and get out. Finally, forcing herself to concentrate on the one colleague she could save, Emma found her feet. She stepped back, pounding her boots against the warehouse floor in a steady, measured pace until they got to the door.

The three of them carried their burden outside, and in the glare of headlights and flashing red emergency signals, Emma could finally see how badly Vance had been injured.

Oh, God. He looks like a ghost already.

She cast her gaze around, looking for his white-eyed figure to appear. She didn't see him. At least, not yet. As they moved away from the burning warehouse and into a cleared portion of the street, paramedics rushed forward with a gurney and helped get Vance onto it.

She took a deep breath of relief that turned to an uncontrollable sob of anguish when an EMT slapped an oxygen mask over Vance's face and called for a tourniquet. In the chaos of getting him out of the warehouse, Emma hadn't even noticed the blood.

But she saw it now, staining the entire right leg of his hazmat suit.

Firefighters had formed a perimeter, with multiple engines hosing down the far side of the building, where the bomb had exploded.

Where Mia had likely died.

Seeing the flames rise higher and the tower of thick smoke pouring from the burning building, Emma knew that nobody could still be alive inside.

Spinning where she stood, she counted faces and bodies in hazmat suits. Leo and Denae were standing together, some distance away. Jacinda and Detective Barrett were near them, monitoring the two suspects who had been inside the building.

They're the ones who set the trap.

Before she could stop herself, Emma was marching forward on a collision course with the two men who sat on the ground, cuffed and with looks of shock on their faces, but still grinning through it all.

They have answers, and you are going to get them, Emma girl. Even if it means one of them is about to become a permanent resident of the Other.

22

Leo grabbed Emma's elbow as she moved past him.

"Don't. Taking it out on them won't help anybody."

She resisted his hold on her arm, but only enough to free herself from his grip. Then she stood there, glaring at the two captive suspects, wishing like hell she could use her boot to wipe the smirks off their faces.

An EMT came over to stand by Jacinda and Barrett. They spoke for a moment before Jacinda finally ripped her mask off and dropped it as if it were on fire. She nodded, then walked over to join Emma, Leo, and Denae.

"He's alive. Significant blood loss and some fractures, likely internal bleeding. They're doing what they can on the way to the hospital." She waved toward an ambulance that was wheeling around, siren on and lights flashing as it sped away.

Jacinda repeated herself. "He's alive."

Emma tore her mask off and slammed it to the ground. Yes, Vance was alive, and so was she and the rest of the team that had gone into the building.

Hell, the two drug-dealing idiots who had set the trap were alive.

But Emma feared the worst had finally come to pass. They'd lost one of their own in that explosion and fire.

"He's alive, but Mia isn't!"

Everyone around her snapped their attention her way. Leo placed a hand on her shoulder, and Jacinda moved to stand right in front of her. "What do you mean, she isn't alive? Was that why you yelled her name in there?"

Emma nearly collapsed, but Leo's grip on her shoulder was like a lifeline. She clapped a hand over it and squeezed, reminding herself that she at least had three colleagues still standing with her.

"That's why Vance went so far in. He heard Mia's voice. I heard it too. She was yelling for help."

Leo's eyes went hard, and then he emitted a choked curse and turned away, pulling his hand from Emma's shoulder so fast she almost went with him.

Their SSA swallowed hard, breathing deeply and shaking with rage or fear. "Maybe you just thought it was Mia. We were all searching for her and hoping. I know you know her voice, but it's possible you imagined it. You could've heard anything."

Emma forced herself to nod even as she continued searching the flame-wreathed night for signs of her friend's ghost. The firefighters were doing their best, but the building was burning to the ground.

Anyone inside it was already dead or would be soon.

Mia's gone, unless I was right. Unless it was a recording. But it sounded so real, so clearly her voice. In pain and crying out for someone to save her.

Jacinda shuffled her over to a police cruiser with the passenger door open, pushing her to take a seat. From there, Emma watched the chaos in the street and tried not to picture the soot and blood that all but covered Vance as he'd been wheeled away on the gurney.

The flames sent waves of heat into the night and remained unaffected by any sudden chill or collapsing cold that would tell Emma a ghost was near.

Mia, if you're out there, please just let me know. Let me know, and I'll be able to sit here instead of running back inside to find you. Because I really want to do that right fucking now.

The flames crackled, and smoke continued to rise into the sky. At some point, an EMT—or maybe it was Leo—handed Emma an oxygen mask.

Minutes and then hours passed.

More firefighters arrived and spelled each other. Denae came to linger by the cruiser with Emma and Leo. Jacinda was off and on her phone, yelling, crying, and cursing, but Emma couldn't tell what she was saying.

Detective Barrett came by at one point.

"Those shitheads we chased down are known felons, both with warrants out."

Leo stood up from where he'd been leaning against the cruiser's fender. "Where are they now?"

"Headed to the hospital, in cuffs. They were both demanding medical care for 'injuries suffered while attempting to flee unlawful persecution' or some shit. They're with the Drivers, so they can tell it to the judge."

With that, Barrett stepped away to his cruiser and called into the precinct.

Jacinda waved the team toward a pair of ambulances, but nobody moved until Emma stood up from the cruiser and went to the SSA. "We need to wait, Jacinda. We need to know if they can find her."

Leo had an arm around her, and Denae was there too. All of them stayed there, clustered together, waiting for a firefighter or cop to ask them to identify Mia's remains.

Emma pulled in her frustration and anger, stepping back from their huddle.

She homed in on the corner of the warehouse that had exploded. Fire crews still circled that part of the structure, but it was just smoking now. The flames had overtaken the rest of the building and were being kept at bay by long streams of water.

One of the firefighters headed their way, holding something in his hand. "SSA Hollingsworth?"

She nodded and hurried to meet him. "Yes, have you found her?"

Emma and the others joined their SSA as the firefighter shook his head and held out the mangled remains of a smartphone and a portable Bluetooth speaker that would have been about the size of a soda can before the fire melted it. "I understand you heard screaming inside before the explosion. It might have come from this. There's no body in there."

Emma blinked. "I heard her voice. Mia's voice, but it sounded off, like it was her just repeating the same thing."

"Uh-uh." The firefighter shook his head again and then he held up the phone and speaker. "Best guess is, you heard a scream coming from this little baby. There is *no body* in there. EOD team will tell us where the bomb was and what type, but based on my first look, it was incendiary, not high explosive. Still packed a punch, of course, but if you heard screaming back there, you were probably hearing a recording."

Jacinda sagged. "Emma was right. It was a trap, and we walked into it. Vance paid the price, but Mia not being in there, after this…that's the only news that could qualify as good."

The firefighter waited while Jacinda put on gloves, then handed her the phone and speaker to be bagged as evidence.

Denae stared at the items. "I don't want to say it, but we can't know for sure, Jacinda. If that was her voice Vance and Emma heard, the explosion might have thrown her deeper into the building. She could still be underneath that mess."

Leo wavered where he stood, but Emma grabbed his arm and helped him stay on his feet. The ghost of Ned Logan had just appeared behind the firefighter, and his somewhat hazy features were as close to a genuine smile as Emma had ever seen on a ghost.

It wasn't proof that his sister was still alive, but it gave Emma more assurance of that fact than any fried phone or speaker ever could. "Mia's still out there, Leo. She's got to be."

She felt his eyes on her and turned from looking at the ghost to meet Leo's gaze. If he'd wanted to ask what gave her so much confidence, she'd come up with an answer, just like she had before.

But instead of demanding answers, he simply wrapped her in a hug and shook.

23

Little Miss FBI was curled into herself. Cuffed ankles up as close to her ass as she could get 'em. Arms still behind her, of course.

We'd heard her jangling the chain, pulling on that metal pipe. Hadn't done her any good. Her screams had done us plenty of good, though.

I walked in there and kicked her in the side, gently, but enough to let her know I meant business. She had her eyes closed, and they opened up blearily. "You there, Mia? You with us?" The drugs I gave her with some water were working for me.

She opened her mouth to answer, licked her lips, and nodded. "I'd like some more water."

"Feeling dehydrated?"

Mia bit her lower lip. Adorable. "What do you really want?" Her words were slurred, but steady. Maybe I'd get her some more laced water after all.

"For now, I just want to tell you something." I grinned and made sure she had her eyes on mine. "Your whole team's dead."

I let that sink in. She didn't believe me, I could tell, and her next words, even slurred as they were, told me I was right.

"Fuck off. You're full of shit." Her head lolled to the side, and for a minute, I worried I gave her too much. Then she stiffened up again and stared at me, like she was daring me to speak.

Well, lucky for her, I had plenty left to say. I got in really close, right in her face. "They're dead, Mia. Your beloved Vance, Leo, Emma, Denae, and that sexy redhead you call a boss. They went into a warehouse that had a bomb in it, and they died trying to save you. Because they thought you were in there."

Her lips opened like a goldfish's. Popped closed again as her eyes went all wet and confused.

I stood up and took my phone from my back pocket. A couple of swipes were all it took, and I was playing her the evidence, nice and loud. Her recorded voice, screaming for help, like a lost little girl in need of her mommy.

"Amazing what you can do with technology when you put your mind to it." I wiggled the phone at her and let it play while I continued. "Here you are, miles from where your friends all died in an explosion and fire, but they thought for sure they heard you screaming for help. Of course they rushed in to save you. Especially that lunkhead boyfriend of yours."

I turned the recording off. The work was done. Our little bitch in bonds was crying her eyes out.

Mia knocked her head back into the wall, once and then again as her eyes streamed tears. Her hair hung in matted drifts around her face as the sweat from the drugs poured out of her.

Not near so pretty as when we'd taken her, truth be told.

"Government isn't so strong and powerful as you

thought, is it?" I stood up and kicked her leg, just enough to make her feel it. She flinched back into the wall.

I couldn't believe how perfectly my plan had worked.

I'd never imagined the agents would follow my clues so quickly, from me telling them to get out of Islingtown to actually finding that warehouse, but I had to give it to them.

They'd tracked the place down fast. I'd been ready to wait weeks for them to find it, figuring they'd have to search high and low, exhausting every resource they had on the hunt for their long-lost Mia Logan.

That would've given me time and space to expand my operation again. Rebuild and find a new distribution network now that the Drivers weren't kings of the hill in D.C. like Rails Foster had promised me. Them and the Powders fell apart after that little pissing contest they had, and with Rails and the Professor both dead, I had nobody I knew well enough in either gang.

Can't trust a gangbanger anyway. He'll just be about getting paid and getting laid. I'm in this business for something a lot bigger.

My rights and my freedom to exercise them in whatever way I see fit.

But it had been a truly simple thing to take an old Drivers' lab site and set up the trap. Even had those two idiots willing to hang out and lure the Feds inside with the promise of some extra money once they got out of jail.

"When they show up, call me. Leave the call open, turn on the speaker, and leave the phone behind, then run the way I told you. That's all you gotta do. Don't have anything in your hands. No weapons or drugs on your person. Run and let 'em take you down."

They'd been worried at first, especially the fat guy. But I reassured them they wouldn't get shot as long as they kept their hands empty and didn't fight back when they got tackled. Worst that would happen is they'd have to spend time in lockup, waiting for me or my brother to post their bail.

Which neither of us would ever do. Those two idiots were as disposable as could be. They might be Drivers, but I knew they wouldn't talk. Worthless tweaker gangbangers.

"Hey, man!" My brother's head peeked into the room. He stared at me, ignoring the FBI agent we'd broken. "Come check out the television."

I gave Mia another look, but she was barely aware. Her next dose would be her last, but I was enjoying watching her space out. Nothing like seeing a Fed helpless.

Good.

Slamming the door hard enough to shake the floor beneath her, I headed out to see what my brother was shrieking about. Some reporter's stupid face was filling the flat-screen TV.

"…agents entered prior to the explosion. They escaped the three-alarm blaze, and I've been told one agent was immediately transported to the hospital. But the other three remained on scene until the early hours of this morning."

The breakfast burrito I'd eaten curdled in my stomach. *How the fuck had any of them escaped?*

Billy wrapped his arms around his chest. "I thought you said this'd be over. They were supposed to be dead."

My backhand caught my brother in the jaw, and he whipped sideways into the wall, holding his hand over his face like a punk. He shrank away from me. Probably wanted me to pull him in for a brotherly hug and tell him it'd be fine, but I was tired of his shit. I did everything, and all he did was ask stupid questions and cook. Not that the cooking wasn't important, but we had a larger mission. He needed to see that.

"Just let me think, all right?" I glared at him, waiting for an answer.

He twitched away from me and headed back into the kitchen.

I stared at the blank television, thinking back to what I'd set up. I got the call from those dummies and started playing the recording. I could hear them rushing out of the office, following the path I told them to take so they wouldn't hit my trip wires.

I'd put enough of them in there that at least one of the damn Feds would have to trip them. It was a risk, but it obviously worked because the bomb went off and the building burned down.

The explosion was supposed to go off a few seconds after they snapped one of the trip wires, and those were all positioned around that little room where the dummies left the phone. That space had been perfect to draw their interest.

It was so damn simple. Look unassuming, give them the recording. Give them just enough evidence to get the team together in the right spot and *kablooie*.

And Mia's cries for help had been the perfect lure.

So how the fuck had they gotten out? Those Drivers idiots couldn't have warned them. They hadn't known about the bomb. But they managed to fuck it up anyway. Well, that would be the last time I made that mistake. Me and the boys over the ridge and our buddies down the road…we knew what had to be done.

It was time for all-out war against the VCU. They might not all be dead yet, but I still had Mia Logan.

24

Emma sat at the conference table feeling little more than numb, just like the morning before. Jacinda typed away at her computer while Leo and Denae got coffee.

Apparently, her long-time friend Keaton was on his way in from the parking garage, which had surprised her at first. He'd moved from their team to the Richmond Behavioral Analysis Unit when Mia and Sloan moved from there to D.C. She guessed they needed every hand they could pull in.

Emma could have guessed at that, after seeing all the typos in his text. She'd had a joke in mind, but it had died on her fingertips. Not even their old banter could lighten the mood today.

It had been one hell of a night.

Two down, four of us left.

Don't think like this, Emma girl.

Two down, four of us left.

All of them had been medically cleared with little more than bruises and some very minor burns. But Vance might not leave the hospital for weeks.

Jacinda shut her laptop and began the morning briefing

with a recap of her conversation with the doctors who'd done their best to keep him alive.

"I spoke with Dr. Mallory very early this morning. She'd just come from surgery. Vance is alive and in critical condition. Second-degree burns to his torso. His left arm is broken above the elbow. He suffered a severe concussion and would probably have been killed by the blast if he hadn't been behind that set of shelves."

That couldn't be the whole story, though. Emma cleared her throat.

"It sounds like there's something unsaid in there, Jacinda. Vance's condition could go from critical to fatal at any moment, couldn't it?"

With a heavy sigh, Jacinda nodded. "Dr. Mallory also says they're monitoring for complications related to traumatic brain injury. His brain is swelling."

They sat around the table in an uncomfortable silence, and Emma could only think of one thing. Oren's voice, yelling to her, commanding her to get to safety.

A voice that Vance could never hear. Why didn't I stay closer to him? I could've pulled him back, forced him to retreat.

She knew that wasn't likely true. Vance was larger and heavier and more convinced that they needed to be in that building to save Mia. If anything, staying closer to him would probably have meant Emma ended up alongside him in the ICU.

Or dead.

Jacinda met her eyes. "Vance is going to be okay, Emma. I can see your head spiraling. He's going to be okay."

She forced herself to nod.

A pair of hands came down on Emma's shoulders. She startled but looked up to see Keaton Holland smiling down at her. He squeezed her shoulders tight.

Without waiting for a response of any kind, he went to the head of the table to confer with Jacinda.

The SSA stood, gesturing to Keaton. "You all know Agent Holland, and I'll get to explanations for his presence in a moment. First, I want to restate what I just told Emma. Vance *is* going to be okay. He's stable, and that's a good thing. And we all survived, too, which is no small thing."

The team all shifted in their seats, Emma sitting up straighter, while Leo and Denae stared at their coffees. Jacinda motioned for Keaton to sit down and continued.

"Keaton has expertise that can help us, just like Agent Kimball did. She's still prepared to assist should we develop leads that relate to geolocating our perpetrator, but for now Keaton will assist in building a profile based on what we know of our perpetrator."

The team stayed silent, and Emma felt for her best friend as he fidgeted with his shirt cuffs. Awkwardness was Keaton Holland's middle name. It was hard for Emma to imagine a more awkward moment for him to arrive at the VCU offices.

Across from her, Denae sipped her coffee and finally turned to face the SSA. "We're sure nobody was killed inside the warehouse?"

"Yes. I've been awake all night and have spoken to the firefighters who responded. At this time, no remains have been found inside the building."

"So Vance and I heard a recording." Emma spoke flatly, painfully aware of the lack of emotion in her own voice. She pulled her coffee closer and tried to focus.

Mia's ghost hadn't showed up to haunt her. That was something.

"That's what we're thinking, yes." Jacinda shifted her gaze to Keaton. "A smartphone and Bluetooth speaker were found near the blast site. We believe it was meant to lure our team in prior to the explosion. Either the detonator's timer was off, the killer miscalculated how fast we'd move, or we just got lucky. One way or another, nobody was killed inside, as he clearly intended."

Leo shifted in his chair, toying with his coffee cup. "And what did they find in the end? Was the lab active? Or just a trap and nothing more?"

Jacinda played her pen back and forth on the table in front of her. "It was a trap. The site had been used as a lab at one time, probably by the Drivers, before they developed their partnership with whoever is providing them crystal clear meth. The warehouse itself was mostly metal shelving and cardboard boxes storing old clothes from what Detective Barrett speculated was a front business."

"Who owns the building?" Emma sipped her coffee, trying to get over the numbness. "Anyone we can talk to? Other than those Drivers we chased down, I mean."

Jacinda shook her head. "The warehouse went into foreclosure years ago. We could talk to some bankers, and we will at some point, but—"

The phone rang. It brought Jacinda's voice to a still, and Emma's coffee cup froze on the way to her mouth.

Carefully, Jacinda accepted the call on speaker.

"Congratulations on surviving." The perpetrator's voice drifted, gruff with annoyance. If he hadn't had Mia, it might have made Emma smile to hear the frustrated emotion.

Jacinda grimaced. "Is that why you're calling? To offer congratulations?"

"You're not out of Islingtown, are you?" The man's voice huffed, and Keaton jotted something down on a notepad as the caller continued. "We're going to try a different tactic. I'll give them Mia Logan, who's still alive."

Suddenly, her screams echoed through the room, but muffled. Emma flinched, but Leo met her gaze across the table. *Recording*, he mouthed. She nodded back. The screams weren't as clear as the voice.

But that didn't mean Mia wasn't still screaming, or that she even remained alive. Jacinda's stiff posture and Denae's downturned eyes meant they were all thinking the same thing.

"Here are my terms." The man paused and seconds ticked by before he continued. "Your task force must be disbanded, and the FBI must *give up* on this corner of D.C. And I mean completely. You have forty-eight hours to comply, and I want the announcement of the unit being disbanded on every news channel and website. I want to see it on your website too."

Jacinda closed her eyes and shook her head, with apparent disgust as much as anything. "Forty-eight hours is a tight window to make all that happen."

"I trust you can get it done, Jacinda, darling. If you don't, I'll be torturing Mia Logan to death, and putting the show online. I guarantee I can find a dark net site willing to host video of an actual Fed getting taken apart piece by piece."

Leo flinched, visibly, and Denae's lips tightened as the caller continued to describe the horrible acts he would commit against Mia.

"But I'm not above grabbing the men on your team. Don't think they're safe. I am *not* afraid of any of you, and I'd say having one agent in the hospital is proof enough of how serious I am. Are we crystal clear?"

The recording of Mia's screaming played again, louder this time, and Emma had to close her eyes even as her mind spun over the words the perpetrator had used.

The killer hung up on the end of another scream, but even in the silence, Mia's pain lingered over the room. Emma sat forward and broke that silence with what felt like the first genuine lead they had on tracking down the killer.

"You all heard it, right? He said 'crystal clear' like it was important. Keaton, back me up here."

Keaton did exactly that, adding his own thoughts. "He believes himself in charge, dominant. And that phrase 'crystal clear' is significant. I'd say we just heard the voice of whoever was supplying the Drivers with their meth."

Emma was grim. "He's targeting us because we killed his operation, and now he wants to kill ours."

25

Even with the new information galvanizing her and her colleagues, Emma's mind couldn't stop replaying Mia's cries for help. They echoed in her mind like the ten-second loop of a horror movie, taunting her.

"We need to find this guy yesterday. Mia was screaming for all she was worth."

Denae stood up and paced behind her and Leo's chairs. "Maybe that wasn't pain we were hearing. They could've been scaring her."

"It could also have been anger." Jacinda's voice was flat, impossible to read until she looked up to reveal a burning rage in her own gaze. "If he told her we were dead. That one of us was injured in the hospital, which he clearly knows. She could've been screaming with rage."

Emma nodded. "There's no reason to believe she's actually hurt. Just taken. Mia's strong. And we're going to find her."

All this time, since the killer had hung up, Keaton had been typing one-handed on his keyboard, hunting and pecking out notes to himself. On the surface, he might have appeared emotionless and cold in the face of those screams. But Emma and Denae had both worked with the man before he moved to Richmond. They knew he could compartmentalize like nobody she'd ever met.

When he looked up and stopped typing, a tiny flare of worry showed in his eyes. Emma had known him too long not to recognize it, but she swallowed the awareness down. Keaton's worry wasn't anything the rest of them didn't feel. He tugged files out of his briefcase even as he broke eye contact with Emma, and then he got the nod from Jacinda to speak.

"I know it's hard to get that phone call out of your heads, but I'm here to help analyze this guy. We can do this. That call supports the profile I've been putting together, and I think we have even more to go on now. We know a few things about him."

Keaton took a breath, giving them seconds to collect themselves, then he went on as Jacinda stood to write notes on the whiteboard behind him.

"First, he's skilled at cooking meth, or he has a skilled cook close at hand. That grants him access to his murder weapon of choice and fits with the trap he set."

Keaton's gaze moved across each of them, and Emma nodded for him to continue.

"Second, he's extremely clever and careful and probably has accomplices. There's no way he'd have been able to grab Mia and take out Officer Murdock single-handedly."

The team shifted in their seats or, in Denae's case, continued pacing the room as Keaton went down his list of conclusions about the perpetrator.

"He likes to play games. The planted evidence pointing to Marcus Foster, the threatening phone calls, and the outrageous demands, which he has to know will never be met even if he's only letting that thought get as far as the back of his mind. He knows he won't get what he's demanding, but he demands it anyway."

Emma chimed in. "He's full of himself, overconfident. These phone calls are about setting up false games, just like that trap he set. He's leading us astray."

Jacinda let out a frustrated grunt but kept writing as Keaton picked up the conversation again.

"Final point, he has a deep-seated hatred of the government or wants us to believe that, and I'm inclined to suggest we take him at face value there."

The SSA paused and looked up at Keaton. "Explain." Jacinda could be intimidating for anyone, but was doubly so for someone like Keaton, who still struggled to make eye contact with most women.

Adjusting her posture, Emma attempted to encourage Keaton to stay his course. "You're on a roll. What's the clue we're missing about this guy?"

"I believe he sees himself as the leader of a cultural movement dead set on defeating the federal government. His actions are extremist in scope. He's setting himself up as a leader of something, firing the first shot, as it were."

Jacinda slapped her marker down. "He's trying to revive the lost cause? Make this into his own Fort Sumter moment?"

"Possibly. But it needn't be connected to reviving the Confederacy. He could be the sort who'd see the State of Jefferson as a refuge from democracy."

Leo turned in his seat to look Keaton in the eye. "State of what now?"

"State of Jefferson. It's an old idea that's gone up and down in popularity over the centuries. People out in Northern California and Southern Oregon still talk about regional autonomy."

"And how does that connect to our killer here?"

"The demands and threats he's made suggest he thinks the government should be abolished. He's also connected to the drug trade, which puts him outside the mainstream in an even more obvious way. Taken together, I'd say we're looking at someone who considers himself a sovereign citizen and probably has a group of people around him with similar attitudes. They might even look to him as a leader. A sovereign statesperson, if you will."

Denae frowned, writing on her iPad. "I've heard about people who call themselves sovereign citizens. Those State of Jefferson types. They don't all hold to ideas of violent revolution, even if they're ready to mention it. How do we know this guy has a following?"

Keaton shrugged. "Because he took action." He gazed around the table, then sat back in his chair, clearly in his element. "People like this don't develop such extreme views in a vacuum. But of all the people whose thoughts are radicalized, how many take action? And how many people take action alone, setting themselves up as the spearhead from the beginning?"

Emma leaned forward, following her friend's line of thinking, finding more focus now that she had something to steal it away from Vance's broken body and Mia's screams. "You're suggesting he took the conspiracy theory against the government into his own hands."

"Right." Keaton nodded, the tiniest of smiles on his lips. "I suspect he got radicalized online, found support for his ideas on anti-government conspiracy boards. I'd say that's our best line of investigation. He mentioned the dark net. We'll need Cyber Division's help, and that might take time. But we can look for anything connecting Islingtown or D.C. with mentions of meth, and especially if those connections are made in congruence with anti-government sentiment."

Leo grimaced. "Every conspiracy board out there that's anti-government is going to talk about D.C."

"True enough. But we can narrow our search to around the time the Drivers started moving in from Baltimore."

"Six months of online content is still millions of data points."

Keaton acknowledged that with a sigh. "It's still a lot better than starting with the first instance of anti-government sentiment posted online. If we're right, and he is the meth supplier for the Drivers, we could narrow our search to focus on the disruption of his distribution network."

Jacinda knocked her marker against the board to grab their attention. "Which is exactly what we'll do, with special focus on mentions of Islingtown. The perpetrator keeps demanding the FBI disappear out of Islingtown specifically, remember? Any questions before I hand out assignments?"

After a beat, Leo nodded. Emma simply waited.

"Leo and Denae will be questioning the captured Drivers being held by MPD," Jacinda cordoned off assignments on the whiteboard as she spoke, "and Emma and I will check out the remains of the latest crime scene. Keaton will work with one of our cybersecurity experts in trying to track down information about the killer on the dark net and other suspicious websites and message boards."

Denae and Leo exited, apparently as anxious to get started as Emma felt. She moved over to Keaton and Jacinda. The SSA picked up her bag and looked back and forth between the two of them before nodding. "I'll give you two a minute."

Offering Keaton a half smile as Jacinda left the room, Emma let him pull her into a fast hug.

Then he leaned back to look her in the eye. "How are you doing?"

"Better than when you last saw me?"

His brow knit, lips tightening up a touch, but then he smiled.

It was the truth, after all. Their last meeting was just two weeks past, when he and Neil Forrester had showed up on her doorstep to pull her out of the pit of grief over Oren's murder.

"I know now isn't the time for a full catch-up session," Emma glanced into the main bullpen, where Jacinda waited for her, "but I want to thank you personally for being here."

Keaton offered an easy grin for the first time since she'd seen him that day. "Where else would I be? Mia's one of our own. I want to help."

She almost didn't ask the next question but couldn't quite stop herself. "You think we'll really be able to find him online?"

Keaton gripped her arm lightly, and the pressure was familiar. Comforting. "*Yes*. Adamantly, absolutely, yes, there's a very real chance. Anti-government nutjobs tend to believe they aren't alone in their perceptions even before sharing their own beliefs. It takes a larger forum to gain the confidence to act on them."

He sounded so confident.

"I hope you're right." She started to turn away but paused. "And Mia? You know more about behavioral analysis than I do. Be real. In your honest opinion, what are the chances Mia survives this?"

Keaton's brow crinkled. He ran one hand back through his hair, then over his brow. Like he wanted to wipe away the question.

Emma wilted. "You don't think she will, do you?"

He caught her before she fled, grabbing her elbow just as she turned. "There's no point in trying to answer that question, Emma. We can't. That'll be wasted time when we really just need to focus on finding her as soon as possible."

Emma swallowed the ball of doubt in her throat and forced a nod, unable to meet his gaze.

"Look, I know you don't like that answer, but we could ask ourselves about the what-ifs forever. They never do any good. Just remember that Mia worked in the Behavioral Analysis Unit for a long time, too, okay? She knows how to figure out bad guys."

Emma looked out into the bullpen at Jacinda. She was on her phone, running a hand through her red hair. The action revealed how nervous she was to anyone who knew her. "I know that. I'm just scared."

Keaton hugged her around the shoulder, watching Jacinda, too, and probably coming to the same conclusion. "I'll tell you this. I think there's a very good chance that Mia will know how to keep herself alive in any bad situation that comes her way. If she has a chance or option of turning the odds in her favor, she will, and that'll buy us more time."

Hugging him back, Emma nodded into his shoulder. "I hope you're right. Thanks."

The words felt empty, but Keaton knew what he was talking about.

"If she has a chance or option of turning the odds in her favor, she will."

That was a big *if*, though, and they both knew it.

26

Leo pulled Denae into an empty conference room, ignoring her whispered protest as he angled them inside and shut the door. "Just talk with me for a second, Denae. Please."

"We don't have time." She leaned against the table at the center of the room and crossed her arms, frowning in frustration. "Suspects, remember? And—"

"Just hold on." He puffed a sigh, shoving bangs out of his face. He'd planned on getting a haircut that day. His weekend plans had involved a haircut, a picnic, a nice walk in the park. Maybe dinner with Denae's parents, at their house or somewhere nice.

It was a Sunday, after all. And here they were, barely breathing, with one colleague missing and one in the ICU.

There was so much he wanted to do with Denae, and circumstances seemed to keep getting in the way. He loved working with her, but a small part of him wished their job didn't make everything so complicated. The work was dangerous, and he'd be lying to himself if he didn't acknowledge he would probably react the same way Vance had if it were Denae in trouble.

But, for now, if all he could get was a moment with her, he would take it.

He stepped closer and took her arm gently, pulling up her sleeve so he could view the snow-white bandages running from her palm up to the middle of her forearm. "Before anything else, can we just take a second and tell each other we're okay?"

A beat passed, and then some of the tension left her. "It's just a second-degree burn. You worried I'll scar? I got news for you, Scruffy. It won't be my first." She leaned into him, lips close to his ear. "But you already know that."

A smile came to his face with the tease, but it didn't lift his spirits. And he still couldn't take his hand from the edge of her bandage. "This has gotta hurt."

"The doctor gave me painkillers—"

"Which you didn't take." He looked her in the eyes, lingering in the darkness there that he so loved to get lost in.

She nodded in confirmation.

"You've gotta take care of yourself, Denae. I need you."

"No, you don't. You may think you do. But either way, you're not getting rid of me anytime soon, so it doesn't matter, okay? We're gonna be fine."

He whispered his fingers over the bandage. Aside from Vance, she got the worst of the burns, while Emma had ended up with a concussion she'd convinced the doctor not to formally record and a bunch of bruises. He'd have bet her ears were still ringing from the blast, too, though the woman wouldn't admit it.

And here was Denae, burned and, in pain or not, bandaged up and back on the job.

"We're going to find Mia and be okay. I just need to know you're okay emotionally as well as physically. That you're okay to keep going."

Denae's eyes softened. "That's a lot of 'okays' for a guy who's usually such a charmer."

"Ha." He pulled her in for a hug, relishing the feel of her leaning into him. He'd needed this, and he was pretty sure she did as well. Her body was warm and solid against him. He inhaled her, catching a faint whiff of coffee. "I get it. I'm just saying, the whole night while we were apart, getting examined, I was worried about you. Scared for all of us. I just needed a minute with you."

He rested his hand on the back of her head, tangling his fingers in her curls.

"I'm glad you took the minute. I needed you too." She leaned against him more heavily, her breath warm on his chest through the cotton of his shirt. "I'm just glad it wasn't Jamaal that came running out of that meth lab. And that you're okay."

"I am. Just give me one more moment."

She relaxed against him, and he closed his eyes and just held her.

Ever since they'd heard Mia's cries for help, he'd been unable to stop the images of Denae being kidnapped, tied up, or hurt. He knew that wasn't healthy. But with Mia being held hostage, the dreadful, intrusive fantasies were hard to escape.

It could have been you, Denae.

"We'll stay strong for each other, Leo." She shifted and stretched, kissing him on the chin, then the lips, before she met his gaze again. "For each other. Okay?"

He nodded. "Okay."

She grinned, finally pulling away to arm's reach and leaving the embrace to head toward the door.

In the interrogation room, the two gang members sat with their hands cuffed to bolts in the table. Both of them twitchy meth addicts, one in a raggedy navy sweatshirt made looser with Leo and Vance's takedown, and the other in a torn grunge-band t-shirt.

It wasn't customary to have both suspects questioned in the same room, but Jacinda had pushed for it, suggesting it might be worth seeing how they acted together before identifying which of them was more likely to have information and be liable to share under pressure.

Leo focused on the taller one in the sweatshirt. He had the bad teeth and searching eyes of an addict. Unlike his friend, he carried some weight on him, but it was unhealthy weight. The kind that came from a slow metabolism and constant stream of junk food running up against a meth addiction that would've taken another man to skin-and-bones territory. "Mike Dervish?"

The guy stared, eyes twitching. He shoved one hand forward so the other could scratch beneath the sleeve of the sweatshirt, probably at an abscess from too many needle injections.

Leo looked to the other one even as Denae opened the file in front of her. "And that makes you Colton Brewer." Unlike his friend, Colton was the classic skinny meth head, but with short, unevenly cut dark hair rather than the bald shine Mike sported. "You two are in a lot of trouble. What can you tell us so we can help make that trouble easier to deal with?"

Colton twitched, shaking his head fast, like he might be pushing off something other than a chill from the meth crash. When Leo raised his eyebrow at him, questioning, the man just looked down at his hands.

"Feeling the need for a fix, aren't you?" Leo brought a sneer to his lips and leaned forward over the men's files. Their criminal records didn't matter as much as what they knew at this moment. "That means you need to help us. Why were you in that warehouse? Were you breaking down the last of the lab? Involved in setting the trap to begin with?"

Mike twitched hard enough that his sweatshirt shifted around his neck. "Fuck off, man. Ain't a crime to run out of a building. We don't know anything about no trap. We were exercising."

Denae barked a laugh that set Colton back hard in his seat, lips opening in surprise to show blackened teeth. "Exercising?" She looked at Leo for effect, shrugging. "He doesn't even know. Talk about clueless."

Colton licked his lips, and Mike tensed before he leaned forward and spoke. "Doesn't matter what you're talkin' about. What you want to believe. You're Feds. You do and believe what you want. We ain't tellin' you anything because there's nothing to tell. We were going out for a jog, and you started pointing guns at us and yelling. Of course we took off."

Leo met his eyes and smiled. Making sure he was honest, and letting Denae take her turn at playtime.

"Your boss sold you boys out." Denae tucked some curls behind her ears. "Why else are you still in police custody? If the boss wanted to bail you out, he could have. Bail can't be that much for fleeing the scene, right? Do we know what it's set at, Agent Ambrose?"

Leo flipped through the paperwork in front of him, pretending to be looking for information he knew wasn't there. Just keeping up appearances and letting the Drivers across the table sweat a bit. The cops out front had already told him, and Denae knew bail was set at $25,000 for each man.

"I believe these upstanding gentlemen are looking at twenty-five grand apiece."

Denae whistled. "I guess I was wrong. That's a pretty high price tag to free a couple of dirtbags, even for a drug dealer pushing crystal clear."

Colton shook his head. "He'll pay it and—"

"Shut it!" Mike seemed to shiver in his chair, glaring at Leo. "You can let Colton ramble all day, but it won't change nothin'. We're not giving you anything, because we have nothing to give. We'll be out soon, and one way or another, we'll be treated like kings."

"Kings." Leo scoffed, his nerves wound tight. This guy spoke like someone following a cult leader, backing up Keaton's guess at their perpetrator having followers. "And what's your kingdom gonna look like?"

Denae leaned forward when both men failed to answer. "You want to be out to enjoy whatever it is you're expecting, you need to talk. It's that simple."

Mike shook his head. Colton took that as his cue to lean back in his chair and stare at the ceiling, swaying a little in his seat as he examined the acoustic tiles above.

"Talk, and you're out by lunch." Leo watched them, considering whether it'd be worth it to start talking about meals and specifics to work their taste buds against them. But they were meth heads. They might not even have taste buds at this point. "Back on the road to being kings, if that's what's coming."

Mike's gaze came back to him, unwavering, and then the man grinned a rotted smile that spoke of years of drug abuse. Probably years of following someone else's promises of a kingdom they'd inherit too.

Which meant they wouldn't get anywhere sitting at this table.

Leo stood and stretched his arms. He might not have been the best actor, but these guys didn't need an Oscar-worthy performance.

Beside him, Denae took the hint and rose to her feet. "I could use some coffee. Yeah?"

Leo offered a dismissive glance to the two men sitting cuffed to the table. "Sounds good."

Outside, Denae closed the door behind them a little more loudly than necessary and gave him a raised eyebrow and the tiniest of frowns. "We weren't in with them that long. What's up?"

"You really think they're going to talk anytime soon? That this isn't wasted time?"

She pursed her lips. "It can't hurt. What else have we got?"

He looked back at the closed door and shook his head. "Neither of them batted an eye when I mentioned the bail figure. They were expecting something that large and are probably expecting it to be paid later today."

"So what's the play?"

"Threaten their safety net."

"And how do you suggest we do that?" Denae crossed her arms, frowning deeper. "Magic? We were bluffing about their leader turning on them, remember?"

"Right. But if we can convince them he's about to get caught, they might be scared enough to talk in order to protect themselves. Work a deal to get out with time served unless we can prove they knew about the bomb or helped plant it." Leo kicked his boot heel into the wall, leaning back against it and staring at the closed door of the interrogation room. "You heard the way they talked. About being 'treated like kings.' I'm thinking that backs up what Keaton was talking about. A leader and online radicalization. Someone with a *following*. I think it's the more likely path to get us to Mia."

Denae looked like she might protest, but then she cocked her head and stared off into the distance, considering. "I don't want to give up on them yet, but I see what you're saying. How about I stay here, and you go off to help Keaton and his Cyber team?"

Leo chewed on the idea. "I guess there's no need for us to stick together inside the Bureau, and those guys are cuffed.

You'll get a uniform to escort you back to the Bureau? Even to get a soda at the corner store?"

Denae chuckled, eyes lighting as she crossed the hallway to peck him on the cheek. "This is D.C. We have chain gas stations and Cokes, not little corner stores and sodas. But, yeah, I take your meaning. I won't go anywhere without backup, Scruffy."

He kissed her forehead, holding her tight for a second, then pulled away and headed back upstairs.

She'd be safe here. And if he could dig something up with Keaton, it might be just the tool they'd need to get these idiots to talk.

27

Emma pulled her badge out alongside Jacinda, displaying it to the lone firefighter who'd met them at the crime scene perimeter. Behind him, the smoking remains of the warehouse loomed beneath the late morning sun. The sides of the building had mostly melted and been eaten through by flames, but some of the tall, metal shelving units still stood like scorched dinosaurs peering over the wreckage.

Sniffing the air, she caught a hint of chemical aftermath, but not as much as she might have expected.

The firefighter led them toward a man in a hazmat suit and respirator just exiting the ruin and introduced them before disappearing. Their new host pushed one gloved hand through his black hair. Crow's-feet spread from his bright-blue eyes when he smiled, giving off a sense of cool confidence.

"SSA Hollingsworth, Agent Last, I'm Agent Alec Martin. With the DEA. Call me Alec. I guess you want to see inside?"

"If we could." Jacinda nodded down at his hazmat suit. "Those still necessary?"

"To be on the safe side." He led them over to a nearby car

and popped the trunk. "Help yourself. Suits, goggles, and respirators, just to be safe. They're outfitted with speakers, so we can talk just fine."

"I thought the lab wasn't active?" Jacinda pulled a suit up over her boots. "We barely saw anything in there but detritus. Empty containers out here, which I'm thinking now were part of the trap. Evidence planted to lure us in."

Alec agreed with her but offered an alternative theory. "You're probably right, but we've found trace evidence that confirms this building had, at one point in time, been used to cook methamphetamine. A lot of chemical residue remained, including around the dumpsters. Those containers might not have been used here, but they still contained small amounts of hazardous substances. Best to be on the safe side."

Just as Jacinda finished getting ready, Emma adjusted the goggles on her face and shifted her gaze back toward the building. "Lead on, Alec."

He moved down the side of the building, and Emma braced herself. They were heading back to the same door she and Vance had entered through the night before. "My area of expertise is meth lab explosions. I've been working on figuring out exactly how the trap worked."

Jacinda hesitated ahead of Emma, near the door, and then seemed to force herself forward with a lurch. Emma doubted she herself looked much more graceful overcoming her memories, but she managed.

Alec's voice came back somewhat muffled through the respirator as he surged ahead of them. He moved toward the corner where the explosion had happened rather than toward the old lab.

"We've scoured the building as best we can, given the limited time we've had. The fumes and chemical remnants of the old meth lab are a big part of what made the smoke and the fire dangerous and caused it to rage as long as it did. But that was all secondary to the explosion."

He turned the same corner around the shelves that Emma had cleared just before hearing Oren's warning call. No wolf howl sounded, and her lungs unclenched just a touch. She froze on seeing the low shelving unit that had served first as Vance's hiding place and then probably saved his life from the blast.

It was a mass of charred planks hanging at sharp angles from blackened metal uprights. The mounds of filthy rags and moldering cardboard that had fallen on Vance still gave off trails of smoke. Across the space, now open to the sky, sunlight cast down on teams of firefighters moving through the ruins and applying retardant foam to hot spots.

Agent Martin directed their attention to the place where Emma and Vance had thought Mia was being held, the little boxed-in office at the edge of the warehouse. It was nothing but a few blackened studs jutting up from the floor now.

"Meth labs usually explode when a high-vapor pressure solvent, like acetone, gets left in an enclosed space for a long amount of time. Just like with a natural gas leak, the flammable substance builds up to a high enough concentration, and all it takes is the tiniest spark and boom."

Emma was sadly too familiar with what he described. It wasn't that long ago her team had been chasing a woman around small-town Virginia as she set off explosions using gas lines and old film nitrate with time-delayed fuses made from light bulbs. Thinking about that put a question in her mind.

"Do we know what set it off? I spotted what looked like a trip wire right before the explosion, but I was so focused on Vance, I couldn't see if the wire was connected to anything, or if it really was a trip wire at all."

Alec came to a stop just a few steps from where they'd

rescued Vance, focused on a mound of smoking debris in the corner ahead of them. "Even with a flame, I doubt the remains of that lab on the other side of the building would've blown up. But look over here."

Jacinda and Emma moved up to stand beside him as he described the scene.

"From what I can gather, you had this fairly small room here. Mostly a storage area or office. Firefighters confirm this room is the point of origin."

Emma scoffed. "I could've told you that."

"Yes, of course. I didn't mean to suggest otherwise. But could you confirm the nature of the blast? From what I've found, it looks like someone poured acetate all over the room and then set up an ignition on the other side of the door. That's probably what was connected to the wire you saw, though we're still looking for evidence to explain exactly how the ignition was tripped. Sadly, the blaze destroyed so much, we may be stuck speculating until a lab can comb over everything we pull out of here."

He pointed back to the area where the office had once stood. "If you're right, and Agent Jessup did snap a trip wire, that probably started a timer, which would've ignited a butane lighter. You were looking at a ten-to-fifteen-second window, if I had to put a number on it. Based on what I'm seeing, and from experience, that feels right to me."

Emma thought back to when she'd been yelling for Vance to come back, to get away from the office while Oren's ghostly voice resounded in her mind against the howling of a wolf. If she had to guess, it could've been anywhere from fifteen to thirty seconds from the time Vance broke the end of the shelving aisle, where she'd seen the trip wire.

Alec moved forward and toed some of the debris near the exploded room. "If anyone had been in this room, they'd have been at the center of the blast area."

Emma nearly choked on her own breath. "And wouldn't have survived."

"Not a chance. The initial blast would have…well, you don't need the details. I'm confident that the phone and speaker found last night were meant to lure you all in here."

Jacinda squatted down and examined a mound of sodden, blackened rags. "We were meant to die here, together. Alec, thank you for your explanation and please extend my thanks to your office." She stood and wiped her gloved hands together. "You'll tell us when you determine the exact nature of the device used to set off the blast?"

"Absolutely. Somewhere in all this mess, I'd be willing to bet you a year's salary we'll find the remains of the ignition source."

Jacinda asked about some chemical staining on the wall, and Alec began explaining, but Emma's focus pulled toward the shelving unit that saved Vance's life by partially shielding him from the force of the blast.

Her skin had gone cold, even within the suit, and sure enough, Officer Drake Murdock's ghost lingered by the half-collapsed racks of debris. Emma glanced toward the SSA and DEA agent, both of whom were focused on the ruined office area.

Keeping her eyes on the ground, Emma pretended to examine the debris as she made her way toward the ghost. Drake drifted closer, and Emma allowed herself to drift with him.

"What can you tell me?" So quiet was her question, she wasn't even sure it could be heard through the respirator. Drake didn't react. Moving closer, though, she realized the ghost was muttering to himself.

Don't take the suit off, Emma girl. No matter how tempted you are.

It was so hard to hear him, and she was tempted, but her

better sense won out. She moved deeper into the cold of the Other, close to him, and strained as best she could to listen.

The only words she could make out were, "I called, but I wasn't fast enough." No matter how close she got, that was all the ghost said, an endless repetition of what were probably Officer Murdock's final thoughts. Then he wandered off.

Minutes passed with her examining the debris along the floor near the ruined shelves, staring at nothing and listening to his repetitive muttering. She was ready to rejoin Jacinda when Drake Murdock's ghost rushed forward, like he'd been blown in her direction.

She watched his shimmering figure skip like a rock on a pond across the burned-out warehouse floor and fly to a stop in front of her face. His eyes met hers, and he let out a pained howl.

Emma stood frozen, face-to-face with the ghost.

His hands swept up and clamped around his ears as he moaned in anguish. "I called. I called but I wasn't fast enough. I couldn't go for him."

She took a risk. "Who was it? Where did he go, Drake?"

"Couldn't go for him. Go for," his white eyes met hers, "go for!"

He'd hollered that same phrase, along with talk about a howling, when Emma saw his ghost outside of Mia's apartment. "Go for what, Drake?"

Before Emma could ask anything else, he vanished.

Emma glanced around, hoping for another glimpse of Drake and some sign that he'd meant for her to look at the area where he'd appeared. But all she saw were the same mounds of debris and the aftermath of the violence from last night. She shook herself and moved over to join Jacinda and Alec, trying to ignore the looming piles of rubble that had been intended as their grave markers.

I hope the folks at HQ are having more luck. Because the ghost that's on our side wasn't much help. But do I really want to see another one ever again?

As much as Emma feared admitting it, the thought still crept in. More than ever, she dreaded the next touch of the Other for one very specific reason.

Mia was still missing. Presumably alive, but they had no way of knowing how long that would remain true.

The perpetrator had killed every other cop and Fed he and his crew had come into contact with. Why would he spare her?

28

Leo found Keaton slurping down an energy drink in a monitor-heavy corner of the Cyber Division's back office. Blank monitors were stacked around haphazardly, but he and another man sat at a small table taken up entirely by four desktop computers. Each of them shifted their focus between two different computers, seemingly doing the work of four men while the rest of the large space buzzed with chatter, machinery, and case updates.

Even one-handed, Keaton was managing two stations. He typed with one hand at one computer and listened to headphones hooked up to the other monitor. It played through a video of an angry man standing atop a pickup and waving a yellow Gadsden flag with its coiled snake and motto.

Glancing back to the rest of the room, Leo took stock of the chaos and wondered whether any of the surrounding agents could lend help, but all of them seemed focused on their own work. Group stations had the focus of various teams, and the men and women located by themselves at isolated desks might as well have been in another world, they were so focused on their own tasks. Over it all, the blue light of monitors cast a tired glow in the slightly too-bright room.

Leo found that he preferred this corner.

He would also have preferred more than two men being tasked with finding Mia, since hunting through websites was apparently their best bet.

Moving around the table so that he could catch the focus of Keaton and the other man, he held up his iPad. "Can I help?"

Keaton slapped his energy drink on the tabletop with a *ding*. "Leo, yeah, I thought you were busy on interviews?"

"Denae's got it." He reached across the table and shook the stranger's hand. "Leo Ambrose, Violent Crime Unit."

"Tom Legosi, Cyber." He lifted one hand from his keyboard and kept typing with the other, not meeting Leo's eyes.

Keaton pulled a clipboard with a printout from where it had been propped beside his monitor and motioned Leo to pull over a seat. "This is a rundown of popular conspiracy websites the FBI has on its radar. We've been searching for every post that mentions the Drivers, the Powders, Islingtown, crystal clear meth, and the FBI within a thirty-day window. Unfortunately, there's too much information to sift through. And that's without even touching social media."

Running his gaze down the list, Leo waited for something—anything—to jump out as relevant. "What about anti-government sentiment?"

Keaton dropped the clipboard with disgust and pointed to a little icon at the bottom of his computer, which showed 12,096 notifications pending review. "Nearly all these sites run rampant with it. It's like searching the FBI. We get so many hits, it's almost useless to sift through without a whole army at our disposal. And the bulk of our hits come from the last two weeks, so narrowing our time frame doesn't really make things easier."

Tom nodded, still not looking up from his computer. "Searching the Powders or Drivers brings up drug-related conspiracies, plenty of mentions of 'crystal clear,' like it's some kind of drug that will change the world. These people are zealous as you can get, but figuring out which user might be our perpetrator is worse than looking for a needle in a haystack. It's more like looking for hay. Any one of these people could be it."

Keaton nodded to the desktop computer directly in front of him. "I have social media pulled up and lists to go with it but haven't had a chance to start in on that yet. You familiar with any of these sites?"

Leo leaned forward. Some of the open browser sites he recognized and some he didn't. "Discord? I thought that was a gaming platform."

"Ha." Keaton grabbed his clipboard again and flipped past a few pages of printouts. He waved it in front of Leo too fast for the sheet to be readable. "Used to be. No more. My girlfriend practically lives in a book club server she found on there, and I'm in a few movie servers myself."

Leo glanced among the monitors, suddenly wondering if the thankless work up here was useless, after all. "I did some searching through Facebook groups and Instagram back when I was in Miami. If you're still working on those," he gestured at some of the open browser windows, "how about I take them off your hands since I'm familiar? More heads and typers, lighter work?"

"Let's hope so. With social media sites updating their user interfaces in real time now, searching them can be a mess, but the big ones are a bit of a crapshoot anyway. I'll give you what I've already got for them, as well as notes on their updated login procedures and terms of service in case we can use those to track this guy."

Keaton scrolled deeper into his clipboard of printouts and pulled free a couple of empty sheets that he handed over. "There's a list of known conspiracy groups and persons on both sites also. Start searching and cross 'em out as you go."

With that, Keaton turned back to the monitor in front of him, and Leo plucked a pen from a repurposed coffee mug near Tom's computer. As he settled his iPad on an open table nearby, he tried to focus only on the first group on his list, rather than taking in the sheer length of the list.

I volunteered for this. Might as well make myself useful.

He sent Jacinda a quick text to let her know where he was and settled in. Within seconds, the tapping of his own screen and the near-audible buzz of his eyes scanning web pages like a hovering drone joined in with the other two men on the case, and time melted away.

Unfortunately, that was exactly how it felt—like they were losing time.

He couldn't help glancing up to the clock as he ticked off groups on the sheet Keaton had given him. They all sounded the same, depending on what search terms he put in, and none of them made any more sense than the last.

The idiots on these sites couldn't even spell, let alone plan an attack on the FBI.

Leo went back up to a post he'd seen about the Drivers being more than a gang. The comments along these lines were so idiotic, treating the gang members almost like they were messengers of a coming revolution instead of the everyday criminals Leo knew them to be. But maybe that was the point? Some attempt at running up a false flag and distracting the FBI from what was really going on in terms of meth distribution?

Sighing, Leo began digging into the users posting similar

comments, following them down rabbit hole after rabbit hole until he'd added a half dozen websites of interest to Keaton's list, but without actually getting anywhere.

When he found himself questioning whether or not a user had a point about Drivers being less violent than other local gangs, despite the meth, he realized he'd gone too far and needed a break. Badly.

He glanced at the corner of his screen. More than two hours had passed, and he'd barely made it halfway down his list. Less than that if he included the sites he'd added as potential false flag hot spots to keep an eye on. Nearby, Keaton and Tom kept typing away, but neither had yet signaled they'd found anything worth reporting.

He stood and stretched. "I'm gonna check in with Denae. You guys need anything?"

"Nah." Tom reached beneath the table and pulled two more energy drinks from the little cooler he'd stored there. "You want one?"

Leo's stomach growled, but he knew better than to accept the offer. "My system isn't built for those things."

"To each his own." Tom waved the chemical concoction in farewell as Leo headed past the ranks of computer stations and into the hall. Every step eased his stiffness but escalated the tension running through his nerves.

By his count, they were coming up on twenty-seven hours since Mia had gone missing, and in the interim, they'd lost another agent on top of her.

He didn't want Denae to hear any touch of despair in his voice, so he forced himself to concentrate on the positives. He, Emma, Jacinda, and Denae were all alive. Keaton had joined them, and he'd proven himself effective at building a profile that could help them net a killer.

They *would* find Mia.

Somehow.

In the relative quiet of the hall, he texted Denae and waited for her to get a second to call him back, figuring it wouldn't be long if she'd kept her promise to stick around the interrogation rooms.

When she did, he hit the receive button before it had finished ringing once. "Hey, how's it going?"

"The same. Colton and Mike are still acting like they're in some kind of time-out."

Leo grimaced and leaned back against the wall. "I wish we knew the endgame. This guy they're following isn't stupid, so he has to know there's no way we can meet his demands."

Denae's sigh trembled in his ear. She sounded exhausted. "What about you? Anything?"

"Not yet." He glanced back into the depths of the Cyber Division, hoping to see Tom or Keaton bouncing up from their computer with excitement, but they remained hunched over their keyboards just like before. "We keep trying different search terms, but everything that looks like a lead just turns out to be a few more heads on the Hydra."

"What's happening with Emma and Jacinda?" Denae cleared her throat, talking to someone in passing before she went on. "They were headed back to the warehouse, right? Couldn't hurt to check in there."

"Yeah, I'll do that." Leo breathed in, counted to three, and breathed out. "Just stay safe, okay?"

Because I can't stop thinking about Mia. And about you being in her place.

"Will do. Talk soon." Denae hung up a second later, and Leo only lingered on her image on his screen for a moment before dialing Emma.

When he'd filled her in on where he was, her voice got a touch more excited than when she'd first picked up.

"Perfect. I was just about to call Keaton. Can you search these conspiracy sites by username?"

"I think they've been doing that but hold on."

"Just get them to search for the phrase 'go for' in conjunction with any of the relevant terms we've already been working with. I found something at the warehouse that makes me think that phrase is important."

The hesitation in her voice raised his hackles. The last thing he needed right now was Emma falling back into her habit of being secretive. "What did you find, Emma? What was it?"

"Later. I'll tell you later. Jacinda and I are about to head out."

She ended the call, leaving Leo with a silent phone in one hand and a head full of questions that he really didn't have time for.

Stepping back into the room with Keaton and Tom, he relayed Emma's request. "Can you search posts and usernames for the words 'crystal' or 'clear' in any combination with the phrase 'go for?' The Drivers were selling meth called 'crystal clear.' Fast-forward to this morning, and the perpetrator used the same phrase when he called us. He said he'd make the truth 'crystal clear to the world.' What if that's part of his online presence, like a website or a username 'go for?'"

Keaton paused with his fingers over the keyboard. "I guess? But why that phrase specifically?"

"Emma called and said she found something at the warehouse that makes her think it's connected. She wants us to look for it alongside relevant terms, like Drivers, Powders, Islingtown."

"We've been trying those, Leo," Keaton said, as he typed away, "and we might as well be typing gibberish for all the useful hits we've had."

"Okay, but what about in conjunction with 'go for?' This is Emma's request. I'm just playing the messenger."

Tom piped up without raising his head again. "I got one hit. A user from a Canadian IP address applauds the Drivers for moving into D.C., and says they were 'going for broke.'"

Leo's heart sank. He'd hoped for a quick solution with the lead Emma helped them develop. "Great, she helped us find a Canadian drug addict, but nothing that might lead us to Mia."

Keaton and Tom went back to their keyboards. Leo dropped into his chair and got back to work on his iPad. Tom messaged him the government watchlist they'd been referencing for groups and messenger boards, and Leo happily took the lower third.

This felt like a lead, finally. And with any luck, it wouldn't be just another Hydra's head.

"Focus on going through different permutations of one word first, then add the second." Tom kept typing, muttering to himself between directions. "It's easier to keep track that way, and you won't miss anything."

Within minutes, Leo had a rhythm.

Crystal. Chrystal. Cristal. Christal. Krystal. Kristal. Clear. Cleer. Klear. Kleer.

Only one combination had to hit pay dirt, and they might have their guy. Try as he might, he couldn't shake the feeling that Emma found something she was convinced had value. He had no real reason to trust her because she'd failed to provide anything concrete, but he honestly didn't have anything better to go on at the moment.

"Hey, look at this." Tom sat back in his chair, and Keaton and Leo hurried to his shoulder. A site called Waking Up had a banner emblazoned with the Gadsden flag at either end.

In the middle of the image, firearms of every type were scattered around a collage of the presidential seal, blue line flag, and various official seals, including the FBI, TSA, and

DEA. Even the National Park System was represented. A large crimson *X* ran across each seal.

"Subtle." Keaton muttered beneath his breath but landed his thumb on what Tom had found a second later. "User *GoForCristalCleer*. I'm seeing what you're seeing."

Keaton refocused on his monitor for a second and googled the username *GoForCristalCleer* at large. "Same username appears on at least a dozen of our watchlist sites. If it's the same person, this is one active anti-government son of a bitch."

Leo leaned closer to the first monitor as Tom pulled up the user's profile page. "Thousands of comments on the site, and he just showed up here a year ago? Cross-reference with 'FBI' and see what happens."

Tom searched within the profile's feed, and they were left with hundreds of remaining comments.

Leo grinned. "One of these posts is gonna lead us right to him."

Keaton nodded, lifting his phone to his ear. "I'm calling in reinforcements. We didn't have anything solid before, not enough to put more than two people on this. With this username now, we have enough to bring in more eyes and try to hunt down an IP address. I'll start working on the warrants, since we can't expect these websites to cooperate through traditional channels. We can get eyes on other websites while we wait on paperwork to come through and get us that IP."

Leo nodded, but his eyes were already working over the list of sites where this username had appeared. The big social media sites and conspiracy sites would absolutely fight to protect their users' privacy.

But the smaller ones with less to lose?

If he'd learned one thing working with Vice

investigations in Miami, it was that small fish could be cracked for information a lot easier than big ones.

Whether they helped out of fear or a desire to avoid a heftier penalty come sentencing, Leo'd taken down small-time drug dealers and pimps that led him to bigger ones.

It'll probably play out the same way here. Go for the smallest operations first and see if they're willing to help out.

And if they weren't, he could always take the step of securing a warrant.

Tom began reading through posts even as Leo took a seat and began searching for site managers for these smaller sites. For the first time in hours, he felt like they had a decent chance, and they owed it to Emma. Whatever it was that inspired her to call with that suggestion of hers.

He just had to hope they would be in time to save Mia.

And that's assuming she's still alive for us to save.

29

Mia shifted against the wall, tugging weakly at the cuffs on her wrists. Her forehead was slimed with new sweat covering the old, and where before she'd had cottonmouth, now it felt as if cotton blanketed every one of her senses.

Her hearing felt off, buzzy and unsure. She blinked away moisture from the constant humidity and tears and sweat. Her tongue was thick with chemical residue. And somehow, her hands and feet felt numb and cold, even though the rest of her burned hotter than a fucking desert.

The kidnapper had been drugging her. She was sure of it now.

But all he offered her was water. She'd die if she didn't drink it. Where did that leave her?

Nowhere good, Mia, darling. Nowhere good.

"Daaaarling. Mia, daaaarling." The overly silly, overaccentuated, drawled-out word she mimicked hung in the air, even with her raspy voice for delivery.

She giggled and knew immediately that wasn't a good sign. "Daaaarling." She tried it on again, and when she pictured Vance saying it back to her, teasing her before kissing her, the latest try at the word bled into a coughed-up sob.

In her most recent nightmare, the kidnapper had been stabbing the syringe into Vance's neck instead of Officer Murdock's, and she'd had to stumble-step over him to get away, leaving Vance behind to die. The nightmare before that had been filled with angry wolves high on meth, chasing her and Emma through a forest of skyscraper-tall syringes while Vance screamed in the background.

The one before that, or maybe a few previous, had a blazing inferno as the backdrop. That one had come right after the killer had shown her the picture of the blasted-apart warehouse and informed her of her teammates' deaths.

Don't believe him, Mia, daaaarling. Do not believe him.

The accent, even imagined, made her smile through her tears. She jiggled the cuffs against the pipe, sinking into the jingle and not allowing herself to talk anymore.

She was dehydrated enough.

A door in the room outside slammed, making her shrink back into the wall. She'd begun imagining how it would feel to have Vance walk in that door, grinning—maybe with a white pie from their favorite pizza place near his apartment—when the sounds of an argument reached her.

Blinking, she tried to focus, but it was still Vance's grinning face, now taking a bite of an éclair, that stumbled through her mind.

I'm practically hallucinating from drugs and hunger. Fuck.

She knocked her head back into the wall, anchoring herself in the pain, and then she did it again. Giving credit to the drugs, the thud of her skull against the wall barely registered as acute and instead hung around her in a haze.

The cottonmouth really wore on her, and she licked her chapped lips. What she wouldn't give for some water.

Not drugged, ideally, but maybe it wasn't drugged. Maybe

this was just the dehydration. Or the hunger. She'd been there a while.

How long, she didn't know.

The argument got louder.

"...throw in the towel!"

Mia blinked, staring at the door and focusing on the man who was speaking. It wasn't Loud Jerk getting worked up again.

It's the other one. Quiet Jerk.

His voice held less confidence. It was higher in pitch. Afraid.

"There's no way! You think the FBI's gonna do that? Dude, get a grip! We're gonna end up in prison for fucking life after this. You kidnapped a Fed!"

The room outside remained silent, still, and Mia kept waiting for the sound of a slap or even a gunshot. The man who'd brought her to this place, Loud Jerk, was anything but patient.

Mia blinked again, expectant and terrified that she was about to hear a man being murdered. Which meant she would likely be next.

Finally, Loud Jerk responded.

His deeper, angrier voice came through the door to Mia's ears like the roar of an engine.

"You're talking bullshit. First, those Drivers idiots think we're going to bail them out, so why would they talk? By the time they figure out we lied, it won't matter. The plan isn't for the demands to be met, you ass. It's to draw them out. Kill 'em. Show the world what true freedom really looks like."

Mia's head pounded, her chest feeling hot. The words echoed in the fog of pain around her. Loud Jerk wanted to kill agents. Draw them out and kill them.

He lied to you, daaaarling. He lied to you.

The air vibrated around her, thickening her tongue even

more, but she smiled and said it out loud. "Daaaarling, he lied."

Quiet Jerk was railing now, stamping around out there. Up and down the hall outside her room, he paced and cursed.

When Loud Jerk spoke again, he sounded close. Close enough that Mia's breath hitched on an inappropriate giggle. Drug-fueled, she widened her eyes as she pushed her heels into the wall and tried to focus.

"If we kill a few Feds, then a few more, nobody on the street's gonna cross us. Every gang will bow to us. We will be kings, Billy. Kings of the land."

Mia blinked. That was idiotic. Gangs fought. They didn't get crowns and rule over kingdoms.

"I don't know, man." Quiet Jerk sounded even more frightened now. "I don't think it's gonna work."

"Shut it, all right? Have some faith." Some shuffling and low voices followed. "Haven't I always taken care of you, Billy? We're fuckin' brothers. Gimme a hug."

"Daaaarling." Mia wished her chest wasn't so hot, her tongue wasn't so thick. "They're brothers, daaa—" She stopped and thought about what the men were saying. It energized her. Using the wall for support and her grip on the pipe she was cuffed to, she maneuvered into a sitting position.

Loud Jerk used Quiet Jerk's name.

Quiet Jerk is Billy. Like a goat. A quiet, little bitty Billy goat.

The air around her buzzed with humidity and pain, but she couldn't control the laughter that bubbled out of her as she imagined a dancing goat outside the door to her room. She glanced up to the ceiling and saw Vance grinning down at her with an ice cream cone in one hand and her favorite hairbrush in the other.

"I know, Vance." Her laughter faded out and became a sob. "I'm a mess."

His image froze in a smile, even after she closed her eyes. She was starting to drift when he began singing to her. No song, but a singsong lullaby all the same. "The brother's the weak spot, Mia, darling. It's the brother that's making me sing."

Daaaarling, he's right. Think of your brother Ned. And his brother the Billy goat.

Mia swallowed. Picturing Ned like he'd been when they were kids, then at the funeral.

Moisture wet her eyes, but she was too dehydrated to produce actual tears. Vance kept singing.

The Billy goat brother is Loud Jerk's weak spot.

Her mind was spiraling, and she only wanted to watch Vance grinning at her from where he sat on the ceiling, singing with ice cream on his lips.

30

Emma answered her phone the instant it started jingling.

"Hey, Leo, you got something?"

"You could say that." He let out a huff of a laugh that Emma recognized as pure stress relief. "Your hunch paid off. We got a username with multiple profiles on conspiracy sites and anti-government message boards. Keaton's called in Cyber reinforcements, and they're working on an IP address and location."

Emma's heart jumped. "That's fantastic. Hold on. Let me tell Jacinda."

She'd hoped "crystal clear" would get the Cyber folks somewhere, but she hadn't believed it. Murdock's ghost had only mentioned the word "clear," but the more she'd thought about it, the more it rang true for her as something to focus on while Jacinda and Alec continued to examine the area where the blast occurred, looking for fragments of a cigarette lighter or some other ignition device.

And thinking about Jacinda had reminded her of the perpetrator's phone call from that morning, when he'd used the full phrase "crystal clear." She hoped Murdock's ghost had given her something useful, even though *"Couldn't go for him. Go for…go for!"* was about as vague as she could imagine.

Not that ghosts had a history of telling her anything useful without wrapping it up in vagueness first.

Frantically, she waved Jacinda over.

The SSA's thin-lipped expression grew more open as Emma explained what Leo and Keaton had discovered. She left out the part about encouraging them based on something a dead cop told her, but Jacinda either didn't catch any hesitancy in her voice or ignored it if she did.

"Put the call on speaker, please."

Emma thumbed her screen and updated Leo. "Jacinda's here. Any luck on the IP address?"

"Nothing yet, but Keaton and the Cyber wizards are hard at it."

The incessant clicking of keyboards rattled through the phone connection even as Jacinda instructed Leo to change course. "I want you back on the interrogation. Get those idiots over to the VCU offices. We'll all sit on them if we have to, but use what you've found and get those Drivers to talk."

Leo's chuckle rumbled through the phone. "Read my mind. I'm already at the elevator. Denae and I will have them here when you arrive."

Emma ended the call as Leo clicked off.

She and Jacinda thanked Agent Martin for his help before making a quick exit from the still smoldering remains of the warehouse and all but sprinting toward their vehicle. Wherever the IP address would take them, things would go quicker and easier if the remaining team members were all in the same place when information came through.

And it wasn't as if Officer Drake Murdock's ghost had reappeared to offer up anything else of use. The warehouse had gone cold with the Other at one point, but it had been a long-dead meth head mourning his own wasted life and making no mention of anything crystal or clear.

Jacinda drove almost as fast as Emma would have but held back from whipping around slower drivers. Emma used their driving time to check in with the hospital, giving Jacinda an update after talking briefly with Dr. Mallory.

"His condition hasn't changed. He's still unconscious, but she's not seeing anything to indicate he's getting worse."

"Or better?"

Emma shook her head. "No. It's a waiting game. His parents are there now and asking about Mia."

"I take it they don't know she's missing."

"We've kept that quiet, for good reason. The doctor said they seemed upset that she wasn't there by his side, but they know she's an agent too."

"Parental concern." Jacinda left it there, and Emma shrugged.

"We'll find her before Vance wakes up."

Jacinda took a left turn fast, without braking, and pulled into the Bureau lot.

Emma was out of the vehicle ahead of her. By the time she got to the door, though, Jacinda was on her heels.

In the elevator, Jacinda texted Denae and Leo that they were in the building. The agents met them outside the doors leading to the interrogation and interview rooms.

Denae's curls were tucked behind her ears, and circles hung beneath her eyes. "I've done my best. They're not saying a word."

Jacinda grimaced. "You told them we have their guy's username? We're tracking him down?"

"They both took it as confirmation we didn't have anything else and laughed." Denae shook her head, rubbing one hand over her brow. "Whatever he's said to them, he's either scared them worse than the threat of prison, or they have rocks for brains."

Emma peered into the room holding the heavyset man she'd chased down last night. They'd been separated back at the precinct, and each had at least a few hours to stew. Mike Dervish had sweated through the collar of his grunge band t-shirt but still sat with a smug expression on his face. "He looks like he's expecting a four-course meal to arrive any minute."

She moved to the next door and examined Colton Brewer, the skinny meth head who Leo and Vance brought down first.

Emma glanced to Jacinda and Denae. "May I?"

The SSA nodded. "See what you can do."

Beside her, Denae twisted her lips as if to say, *Do your best*.

"Which one do you think will crack, Denae?"

"I've been hammering on the big guy, Dervish. Nothing seems to work. The skinny one wouldn't look me in the eye and might have said a few unkind things. Just for that, I'd love to see him fall apart. But I also think he's your best bet."

Emma straightened her jacket, took a breath, and pictured Mia. Her friend had a talent for interrogations. Those young, fey eyes and Hollywood lips. But Emma had her own ways. Her own strengths.

"I'll start with him, then. How about you collect Dervish and tell him something to make him smile as you walk by Brewer's room? Stop in front of the door so he can see Dervish clearly."

Denae started laughing. "Emma Last. Seems you know how to spar after all."

"You still owe me that gym date. After this case is over, we'll put on the gloves together."

"It's a date." Emma slammed open the door to Brewer's room and stalked to the table, yelling before the door clicked shut behind her. "I'm going to be *crystal clear* with you, and if you want to avoid life or possibly a seat on death row, you're going to answer my fucking questions. You understand?"

The guy leaned back in his seat as if Emma had aimed a gun at his chest and pulled the trigger halfway to the pressure point.

Emma grabbed a chair, dropped into it, and waited. Her phone buzzed with a text from Denae.

Getting Dervish out now. Make sure Brewer can see the door.

Standing fast enough to send her chair scooting back, Emma moved to ensure Brewer had a clear line of sight to the window set into the interrogation room door.

A minute later, Denae paraded Mike Dervish by. They paused outside the door, with Dervish's face clearly visible. He was grinning from ear to ear. A moment later, they'd moved out of sight.

Whatever Denae said to him, it worked. Time to crack this egg.

Emma turned back to Brewer and stared into his eyes. "You ready to talk? Your friend's interrogation seems to be over."

The man's mouth dropped open and closed, sputtering.

Emma nearly growled at him. "Speak!"

"Fuck you! Mike wouldn't talk. Lay off, bitch."

"Such language, Colton. My colleague mentioned you liked to use unkind words."

"Y'all can eat shit. I ain't sayin' anything."

Emma crossed her arms over the table and leaned toward him. "Are you aware that persons involved in a conspiracy to commit murder can be charged as accomplices, even if they didn't participate in the act of murder itself? That means you're going down for life, possibly earning a death sentence, if it was shown that you had knowledge of the conspiracy or were instrumental in any way related to the murders, kidnapping, and attempted murder of federal agents."

She let her fists inch across the table toward his cuffed hands. "Dervish was in that warehouse with you, which means he probably knows exactly as much as you do, right? And he just walked down the hall, smiling."

Emma let him sweat a bit, watching his Adam's apple bob up and down as he swallowed.

"Feel like talking now, Colton?"

He swallowed again, Adam's apple rolling under the pasty skin of his neck. But still he stayed silent, glancing around the room, letting his gaze land on anything but her.

"You're screwed, Colton. If you somehow get out, word on the street will be that you and Mike helped us. Your gang isn't going to like you very much after that, and I'm willing to bet they'll be crystal clear in conveying their displeasure. It's possible Mike already made a deal. He might even be getting protective custody. Who knows? What I do know is that you probably have one chance at surviving this, and that's you giving me a name."

Colton swayed in his chair, swallowing so fast that he looked more like a lizard with a bug than a man with an answer. "You said Mike already did. He made a deal."

"Speak!"

Colton jarred in his seat. His knuckles whitened. "Delton Potter. His name's Delton Potter."

Emma was out of her chair in another second, heading for the door. Colton hollered after her about making that deal, but she ignored him.

Jacinda had her phone held out when Emma reached her and Denae. Leo picked up immediately. "Jacinda, I'm here with Keaton. IP address has been identified."

"That's great news, Leo. I believe we have something equally exciting to share. Emma, would you do the honors?"

"Our guy's name is Delton Potter."

Paper rustled on Leo's end of the phone, and then he

spoke fast. "That's awesome, Emma. There's a Potter family with a residence near the IP address location. The killer's in Reginald, Virginia. It's a tiny rural town about an hour and a half away."

"Meet us in the garage, Leo." Jacinda gestured Emma and Denae toward the elevator, and the three of them began speed-walking. "It's time for us to team up and take this guy down. We're bringing an army along for the ride to make sure this ends today." She ended the call and stepped through the elevator doors the instant they opened.

Emma and Denae followed her in, and Emma hit the button for the garage.

"Whatever you said to Dervish, it worked like a charm."

"I went with your idea about a four-course meal and told him we had some refreshments prepared, since we'd kept him and his friend here so long."

"How generous. Can I guess what he got?"

"Bag of peanuts and a candy bar from the vending machine, cup of stale coffee, and an aspirin. Poor man said he had an awful headache."

Jacinda all but cackled behind them. "I can't wait to see how he feels after we bring Delton Potter in to share his interrogation room."

31

Emma vibrated with tension as they drove to the town of Reginald.

A long line of backup followed them, including a bomb squad, SWAT team, and hostage rescue unit. Air support was expected, as well, with the nearest police agency confirming a helicopter was on the way.

"Town of Reginald, here we go." Leo waved his thumb at a tiny *Welcome to Reginald* sign they passed, but Emma scoffed.

"Not much town to speak of. Do they even have the internet out here? Are we sure this is the place?"

Leo was quick to answer. "The website owner gave up Potter's IP address, and Cyber Division confirmed this location."

We'd never have thought to look here, not without a lot more evidence to aim us this way. And it's all thanks to the owner of the nascent Tell Me Your Truth conspiracy site.

Their IP warrant might be hours away, but Leo's hunches on which website was most likely to give up user info at the words "Federal Bureau of Investigation" had paid dividends.

Dilapidated houses and trailers, junked cars, and a landfill were the only signs of occupancy until they reached a turnoff for a tired main street with a single swinging stoplight over an intersection. Crowded around the corners were a bar, a feed store, and a small plaza ringed by weather-beaten and overgrown rose bushes that hadn't yet bloomed for the season.

Emma craned her neck around at a man riding a bike who'd chosen to use the opposite lane on the road. With no cars to fight him for it, he wasn't in any danger of being run down.

Apparently, Denae had noticed him as well. "I'm no longer surprised I've never heard of this place. Who the hell lives here?"

"Nobody." Emma swallowed down nerves, wondering how they'd ever find Mia among a mess of backroads and what had to be abandoned trailers and camping sites. What else would this area exist for, but as a backstop for campers or people who lived on the road?

Jacinda pulled into the parking lot for a tiny sheriff's office, which couldn't have had more square footage than the average D.C. row house. The caravan carrying their backup stayed in the street, engines idling. Only their team got out of their vehicle.

Emma kept to Jacinda's heels as they moved through the glass door, where they found the sheriff staring out the window. He replaced his glasses as he turned to face them, eyes locked in a squint.

Jacinda stuck her hand out, and he accepted it with a tired nod.

"Some group you got with you. SSA Jacinda Hollingsworth, I'm guessing?"

She nodded. "Sheriff Johnson?"

"Call me Ricky." He moved back behind his desk and picked up some files, riffling through them before he looked back up at the team. "We've had a meth problem for decades, but it's been gettin' worse over the last couple years. Figured out somebody's supplying high-quality product, but I always assumed it was being brought in from elsewhere."

Jacinda accepted the files and passed them to Leo, who began paging through them while listening. "And why's that?"

Ricky shrugged, shifting on his feet and leaning back against some file cabinets that tilted from decades of paperwork. "You need some know-how to make meth and not kill yourself in the process. Folks around here mostly strive to graduate high school, if they stay past the age of sixteen. The ones that do go to college tend to stay gone. Brain drain, they call it."

"And you've never found out where the meth's coming from?"

"We've caught a few people with it on 'em, but they won't say where they got it. Every one of 'em was ready to serve time before giving up a name."

"So they're scared." Denae traded looks with Emma, lips pursed. "More scared of whoever's in charge than the law. That tracks with what we're dealing with, but we got a name."

The sheriff's eyes went a touch wider.

Emma glanced to Jacinda, who nodded for her to go ahead. "Does the name Delton Potter mean anything to you?"

He nodded. "Whole Potter family used to live here, but the home's been abandoned for a while." He tugged at his beard, frowning past Emma's shoulder as if focusing on something else. "Delton's the older of their two boys. Botha them gotta be in their mid-twenties now. Their parents died five years ago, maybe. Or six. Parents were big-time users, but they died in an old-fashioned car accident. Driving too fast in heavy rain on the mountain roads. Always thought it was ironic that they were actually clean when they caught that curve."

"And Delton's still in town?" Emma glanced at Leo, who shook his head. Nothing in the files before him about the Potters, then.

The sheriff shrugged. "He could be, I guess, but I assumed the boys moved on after their parents' deaths. Billy's the younger brother. Think he was supposed to go to college. Woulda been the first of Reginald's sons to do that for as long as I can remember, but I don't know if he actually went through with it."

"When was the last time you spoke to either of them?"

"I haven't seen the boys since shortly after the parents died."

Leo closed the files he'd been looking through and passed them back to the sheriff. "Where's the family home?"

"I can save you all the trouble of checking. I pass by it several times a week. That place is long unoccupied or I'm a squirrel's uncle. Roof fell in during the last snowstorms."

Emma stomped her foot and turned to face the door as the others kept talking about the old Potter property. Outside, the convoy of SWAT trucks and police cruisers rumbled in the street, their engines still idling. That guy they'd passed on the bicycle was coming back down the street, still using the center of the lane instead of staying to the right edge.

He flipped a finger at each vehicle as he passed by, earning him a few waves in return until he reached the back bumper of the last cruiser. The officer in the driver's seat opened her door and stepped out, forcing the cyclist to put both hands on his bike and swerve aside. He flipped her off over his shoulder as he passed, and she waved at him with a grin on her face before getting back into the vehicle.

Thinking about the guy's behavior, Emma turned back to the conversation. "Sheriff?"

"Ricky." He smiled. "What can I do you for?"

"Have you ever run into anti-government groups around town? I mean, more than just someone angry about paying their taxes. Militia types, sovereign citizens, that kind of thing."

He nodded. "Yeah, we have them out here."

Jacinda opened her notes app on her phone, ready for more. "Do they have a place they like to meet or convene? A compound, maybe?"

Ricky nodded again, his face showing a grimness that hadn't been there when they'd walked in.

Jacinda held her phone up, finger poised to type in the information. "Where?"

"Well, it's just land, so far as I know. I can get you directions." He dropped into his desk chair and began scribbling a map on a blank sheet of paper. "If Delton and Billy are involved in this, I guess I'd have heard stranger things in my day."

He put aside his pen, gave the map another once-over, then added some short notes to it. "I don't know what you'll find out there. I just know of it because you can't help but hear about where those militia types spend their time. I get calls now and then about illegal hunting or gunshots at all hours of the night. Never manage to catch anybody doing anything, of course. They're always packed up and gone before I get there."

Jacinda stepped in. "Are there any structures on the land? Anything you're aware of that might present armed individuals an opportunity to mount an ambush or fighting positions to resist law enforcement?"

He shook his head and picked up the map, holding it across the table for Jacinda to take. "Nothing like that, unless you count trees. I've never gone too far in because it's private land."

Jacinda glanced at the map and gestured to a nearby copier. "You mind making a few copies?"

He shook his head and moved over to the machine. "Not a bit."

Jacinda turned back to Emma and the others while the sheriff fought with the decades-old copier. "Emma, Denae, take the Bureau vehicle and lead the way. Leo and I will ride with SWAT so they can get firsthand access to the map and know what we're about. We'll focus on this land parcel while the cops who came with us check out the old Potter property."

Emma reached for the first map in the sheriff's stack and gave it a look. She tapped at the map, indicating a square he'd marked as a "blue barn." "Down Main Street and out of town 'til we hit this barn, then we take a right at the first paved road and a left at the old church?"

He nodded. "You'll know it when you see it. Church burned down last year and still looks like a horror movie set, but the steeple stands. Tell you what, though, if you're gonna roll down that road with all that cavalry out there, you want to be ready for some resistance. Lotsa folks out here pride themselves on being free to do as they please."

"What type of resistance should we expect?"

"The locals have a tendency to run in packs. And they didn't grow up playing kick the can 'til they got called in for family dinner. More like shoot the can to smithereens from two hundred yards away."

Emma gripped the map tighter and nodded her thanks. Denae had already turned for the door.

Armed resistance or not, it was time to go get their friend.

32

Mia, daaaarling, I do believe those are steps outside.

Blinking away the sweet, Southern voice that had become her only friend, Mia tried to focus through the haze. Her vision wobbled, and at first, she wasn't sure whether the door was actually opening, but then Quiet Jerk, the stockier, nicer of the two, stood peering in at her. He picked at some acne on his chin as he stared.

It's a Quiet Jerk, the Billy goat, daaaarling.

Mia giggled. She tried to hold her head up, but it lolled, flopping to the side. "I could use the bathroom." She tried licking at her lips but found she couldn't and attempted one more word. "Pleeese, please."

The man raised one arm and scratched at his already mussed hair. "I don't know. I came in to see if you want some more water. My brother told me to see if you'd need some if he was gone this long."

Mia blinked at him. He couldn't be past his twenties. His face made her eyes hurt, and she had to fight the accent down before she replied. "Just really need the bathroom. Please."

Her bladder ached. Any more water and she'd pee herself. Not that her pants weren't already soaked through with sweat, but with the burning in her body getting worse and the humidity only seeming to mount, she imagined that the stink of pee would soon lend itself to the list of smells in the room.

Maybe vomit would follow it.

I'll die, daaaarling, I'll just die.

He stepped into the room a little more, looking at her with concern pulling his mouth into a frown. "You sure?"

"Yeth!" She swallowed. Trying to hold her gaze steady on the man. This was the nice one. The quiet one who maybe wasn't a jerk after all.

The Billy goat!

She just had to use that knowledge to get herself free after she got to the bathroom. She'd used it, what, twice since they'd had her? Dehydrated or not, that wasn't enough. "Yes. Bathroom. Please."

He lumbered over to her, and she couldn't help but flinch out of his shadow. She'd asked for it, yes, but every time one of the men came near her, she was reminded of her soaked, see-through blouse and the *humidity and sweat soaked* trousers that clung to her legs. The heat in her body feeling like it practically radiated off her bones didn't help.

Rather than eyeing her like his brother did or touching her, though, Billy crouched beside her. He pulled a pair of cuffs from his pocket, then leveraged her shoulder away from the pipe. The new pair of cuffs went onto her wrists, above the first pair.

Par for the course.

He undid the cuffs entwined with the pipe, then unlocked one side of the pair holding her ankles together. The man's hand landed on her bicep. Through the slick of her blouse, his fingers felt like hard tentacles pulling her up.

With her feet asleep, Mia fell against him, then thudded back into the wall when she tried to overcorrect and get some distance.

He grimaced at her.

"Don't judge. It's your brother. Giving me drugs. He's a bad goat."

She giggled, but rather than asking what she meant, Billy tightened his grip on her bicep and muscled her away from the wall. She couldn't focus, the room moved so fast, and she tripped as he pushed her forward, barely keeping herself from thudding her head into the doorframe as she fumbled ahead of him, propelled too fast.

"I can walk." She stumbled, the whole hallway wobbling around her, and Billy caught her again with a grunt.

They were at the little bathroom down the creaky-floored hall in seconds. He didn't push her inside like his brother had done earlier when she'd needed to pee, but she fell against the vanity, anyway, and leaned there heavily. Abdomen against the porcelain, sweat-soaked clothes clinging to her, hands still cuffed behind her back.

She avoided looking up into the mirror, having made that mistake once already. The memory of her sweaty skeleton of a face and matted hair would live with her as much as her drugged-up imagination would. "Could you take the cuffs off?"

At least, that was what she thought she asked. Billy only muttered something, reached out and undid the button on her pants, then backed away and slammed the door.

"Kick the door when you're done! You got five minutes, max!"

Mia shifted so her hip rested against the vanity and looked down. The grungy toilet, lid up, had urine stains around the rim and the base. Not that she'd expected them to clean it since last she saw it.

Swallowing, trying not to breathe through her nose, she lifted one foot to try to put down the lid. Her balance said goodbye within seconds, and her foot nearly landed in the disgusting well of water before she stumbled backward to lean against the vanity again.

She cringed, turned around, and backed up. Finding the seat with her hands, she dropped it.

Don't even think about your hands being sticky, daaaarling. Don't dare.

Her tears wetted her eyes, from the smell or the humidity or the fear. From the back, she pulled and tugged at the waistband of her pants, using the edge of the vanity to get them down to her knees.

At least he helped you get your pants off, Mia, daaaarling.

Mia's next thought almost had her wishing she'd just peed in her pants instead, but she'd come this far and wouldn't waste the opportunity.

Hovering over the toilet seat wasn't an option. She didn't have the balance, so she plopped down.

The release made her cry a few real tears. To be so thankful for this little bit of dignity that was itself rimmed with grime and derision.

There was no toilet paper. She sat for a second, swallowing down the dread of pulling up her filthy panties and pants, but then squatted in front of the toilet, fishing around behind her until she grabbed the waistband of her underwear. She struggled, tugging them up, then did the same with her pants.

Finally, Mia stood and leaned over the vanity. She leaned all the way over and nudged the handle with her chin until clear water came out. She'd tried to drink it previously, but the sink was too shallow, so she'd learned better. Instead, she simply turned around, strained her muscles past pain, and rinsed her hands as best she could. She couldn't lift her cuffed hands high enough to turn the water back off, so she turned back around and leaned over.

Leaving the water on during her first trip in had led Loud Jerk to backhand her so hard she'd fallen against the wall and nearly brained herself on the empty towel rack. She doubted Billy would do the same, but she wouldn't take any chances.

"I'm done!" She kicked at the door.

Billy slammed open the door, visibly annoyed. He left her pants unbuttoned and pulled her into the hall. She stumbled back toward the room with the pipe in the wall and the covered-over window, empty of any fighting energy. Even if she could pull away, she'd never manage to take him down or make it more than a dozen feet before he reached her.

She was cuffed, drugged, dehydrated, and starving.

Mia swallowed hard, feeling her throat grow tight. But her mind was clearing a bit. Moving and peeing had helped bring her back into her body, out of the drug haze she'd spent the past who knew how many hours enduring.

She wasn't clearheaded by any stretch of the imagination, but she was coming down from whatever high she'd been forced to experience. Billy dragged her into the room, and she did her best to make it easy for him, forcing her limbs to obey as they moved toward the pipe. She thumped to the floor obediently when he pulled her wrists down.

Billy focused on his work, reconnecting her hands to the pipe before removing the extra cuffs he'd put on her, then turning to her ankles. His hands trembled against her skin, fumbling at the metal even though he only had to click them shut.

Tweaking. He's tweaking. And I'm not anymore. At least, not as much.

He must've hit the pipe while she'd been in the bathroom, and her nose was just too chemical-burned from her surroundings to have smelled it before now. But if he was an addict, that meant he was vulnerable.

She might be drugged, but she was still smarter than the average meth head. At least, she thought she must be.

Her voice cracked, and she licked her chapped lips, trying to focus on speaking slow and steady. "Have you tried to convince him?"

"Convince who?"

"Your brother. It won't work. His plans are cuh-razy."

"You can't even talk, lady. Shut up."

"It's not me. It's his drugs." She pressed herself against the wall, reserving her energy to focus rather than to try and kick his hands away from replacing the cuffs on her ankles. "You were dragged into this." She almost smiled as he stopped with his hands on her ankles, one cuff still not fully closed.

"Yeah? You think you know shit about me?"

Mia nodded slowly, making sure her head didn't flop to the side again. He needed to believe her, as much as she needed to believe herself. "You got forced. Just like me. By your brother, right? You didn't choose to join him."

He tightened the cuff too tight around her ankle, then slapped her calf for effect before standing and staring down at her. "Shows what you know. This is the family business, lady. My brother knows what he's doing, and I've been with him from the beginning. You'll behave if you know what's good for you."

But even as he spoke, he twitched. Shifted on his feet and looked around the room as if he expected someone to barge in.

To barge in and arrest him, if she was reading his skittish eyes right.

"No. You don't get it." Her voice was rough, not even recognizable as her own now, and her tongue felt twice the size it should be, but she kept going. "This is waaaay bigger than your meth op. You and him are in over your heads."

"And I could say the same thing about you."

"Or you could let me go. You might avoid prison."

He grimaced, sneering down at her. "Like that's even possible anymore. You think I'm dumb? You're FBI. You could be the worst FBI agent in the world, the government would still be coming down on us. Fuck off."

She stared up at him. If she let him stare back, maybe he'd talk himself into helping her, even as humidity clung to every filthy inch of her and she suffocated on the chemicals wafting throughout the house.

"Let me go. Please."

He shook his head. "Maybe I do want out, but it's not happening. And whether my brother's off his rocker or not, it's too late. We gotta see this through to the end. And you're not going anywhere."

Mia opened her mouth to protest, but a door slammed in another room.

In a moment, her door swung shut, too, and Billy was gone.

She'd used every last spark of energy for that mindless conversation, and it had ended exactly as Billy had said it would.

Nowhere.

And that was where she'd stay until Billy's brother decided to "see this through to the end." Mia thought about what that meant for her if the team didn't find her soon. And she was left with a burning throat, blurry eyes, and a curtain of fuzziness enshrouding her skull again. She had no answers.

33

Emma drove slower than she would've liked—within the speed limit by just a hair—only because they had to catch the landmarks on the map. Denae kept an eye out since they had no address, clenching it in one fist as if their lives depended on it.

Mia's does.

"Leo was supposed to be meeting my family this weekend." Denae rubbed the map between her fingers. "We were talking this week about me maybe going out to meet his grandmother and brothers this summer."

Emma forced herself to remain focused on the road. The quiet in Denae's voice seemed almost mournful. Uncomfortably close to dejection. "We're gonna—"

"Don't say it." Denae coughed on a breath of air, then waved the map at Emma in what looked like a fast burst of anger. "Don't say we'll find her. I know you want to believe that. I know we all do. But I'm *terrified* it's too late. I've been so worried about Jamaal with all this shit already."

Emma thought of Oren telling her to breathe deep and center herself. Telling her to go slow and steady, and she'd be okay. "One thing at a time, Denae, okay? That's all we can do."

"Things have been going so well with Leo." Denae's voice was almost a whisper now, and Emma strained to hear her. "But this case is such a reminder, you know? Of how much danger we all put ourselves in every day. One tiny mistake, and things are over forever."

Emma couldn't help it. She glanced in the rearview mirror, clocking the caravan behind them. Their friends and colleagues and a shit ton of backup that might or might not make a difference, just depending on how cocky or suicidal Delton Potter might choose to be.

At the moment, her only real hope was to find a way to save Mia and avoid losing anyone else. But she did have faith Mia was still alive.

She would've come to find me from the Other if not.

"Don't be so sure it's forever." Emma could almost feel the shock in the car, Denae breathed in so suddenly. She didn't need to glance sideways to recognize the surprise the other woman felt. "Death is a natural part of life, and the risk we take every day is worth it, considering how many lives we save. If or when *any* of us die doing important work, today or next week or ten years from now, we'll have an eternity to feel proud of the lives we led."

Denae shifted her back toward the passenger door, staring. "I didn't know you were so religious. You got any more surprises for me?"

Emma chuckled, then she glimpsed their next landmark and put on her turn signal. "I prefer the term *spiritual*. You ask me, religion's got it all wrong."

Denae pushed some curls behind her head before looking back down at the map. "I don't even know what to say to that."

Nodding, Emma simply kept driving. Denae might be lost for words, but she sounded reassured.

Considering what they were driving into and how many unknowns there were, that was about all Emma could ask for. If Denae could take some comfort in anything Emma had said, maybe her so-called gift was finally something she was learning to live with.

Maybe it was something they'd all live better and longer with, too, if they had any luck at all.

First, though, they had to find Mia. And they had to get her back alive.

34

Mia drowsed against the wall, finally feeling some semblance of her awareness returning. Billy had been the last one to bring her water, and whatever he'd told his brother, she didn't think he drugged it. Vance's face no longer interrupted her thoughts every few seconds, nor did his voice with that bizarre accent.

Her punishment, she guessed, for bothering Vance into watching the whole of *My Fair Lady* with her the night before their team's world had gone sideways again. That had been their last night of peace together.

She stretched her wrists within the cuffs, which felt tighter than ever now that she was approaching something akin to sobriety. She remained foggy, sure, but she was no longer hallucinating.

Heat still pounded through her body, making the presence of the drugs known, and her nose burned from the chemicals that leaked into the room from the air outside. The hallway was worse, telling her the meth lab in the home was close to where she was being kept.

At least I haven't blown up. On top of no longer seeing Vance on the ceiling, that practically makes me lucky.

But she doubted she'd gotten through to either man in any way that mattered. Loud Jerk's threats and his pipe dream of blackmailing the federal government were sure signs of unhinged thinking. The man was off his rocker.

Maybe he didn't use his own drugs—he didn't have the look or the sweats that his brother Billy did—but Loud Jerk's mind was full of conspiracies and self-aggrandizing bullshit.

Getting through to him was a lost cause.

The team had to be searching for her. She knew that. But how close were they?

Do they even know who these guys are and where they live?

She sucked in a breath, determined not to waste any more of her body's deficient water supply on tears. The main kidnapper acted like a pro, which meant her team could be right outside, and he'd still present an invincible front.

Billy might crack under pressure, though, and she'd use that to her advantage if she could.

Sweat continued to drip down her back, and the thudding in her head escalated with every passing minute. These signs were not inspiring confidence.

Still, if these could be the final hours of her life, she wasn't about to take it peacefully.

Mia bit her cracked lip hard enough to draw blood and tasted it, anchoring herself in the slick, coppery taste.

As long as she was alive, she had a chance.

Especially if she was coming down from the high. She couldn't help considering ways she might escape as footsteps sounded in the hall again.

The door flung open, hitting the wall behind it.

The man who'd taken her from Nick's apartment and dragged her into his meth lab had on the same cargo pants and dirty button-down, just like the last time she'd seen him. No mask, but she wouldn't think about what that meant.

Making an effort to keep her eyes dazed and unfocused, she forced herself to peer over his shoulder with lazy, unfocused eyes, rather than directly at him. His sneer still registered, but he didn't seem to process that his brother hadn't given her an additional dose of drugs.

When he crouched in front of her and played his hands along the top of one of her socked feet, she couldn't help but twitch, though. At that, he ran his hand up her wet trouser leg, clamped down on her kneecap, and squeezed until she whimpered and looked at him.

"Looks like your colleagues just don't care much about you after all. Guess the FBI's willing to chalk you up as a casualty."

Mia's stomach twisted.

I might really be out of time.

His hand remained on her knee, clenching and unclenching, making her leg shift unwillingly with the pain. Mia wondered how much pressure it would take for him to dislocate her kneecap—and if that was his ultimate plan.

"I don't think I'm gonna get what I want from your pals. You know that means I need to kill you."

She licked her lips, tasting the coagulated blood, and stared down at his hand on her knee. "No, you don't have to. You have a choice."

"Voice is clearer today, huh?" He squeezed tighter.

She shut her eyes against the pain. *Fuck.*

"Guess my brother forgot to drug you up, but that's okay. Means you get to know you're being killed. Know what your friends are looking forward to—"

"*Delton, there's someone outside!*" Billy charged in on the heels of his words, eyes wide. His hair stood out all over his head like he'd been running his hands through it, and a mask hung around his face, indicating his cooking had just been interrupted.

"You used my fuckin' name?"

Her kidnapper—Delton—dropped Mia's knee and stood as the words registered. He moved to the boarded-over window and listened, like that might tell him something. Then he raced for the door a moment later, shoving past Billy as he went.

Billy ran after his brother, leaving the door ajar, and seconds later, Mia heard Delton, the asshole who'd just threatened her life, yell.

"Get the boys over the ridge *ASAP*! Now!"

Mia's whole body went cold. She thought their only enemies were these two lone brothers, drugged up and dealing. But now there were others, and whatever was being planned, the confident threat in Delton's voice told her the team might be walking right into it.

She considered screaming, but if her team was outside, that might make things worse. The sound of those recorded screams Delton had played for her echoed in her memory. Maybe he hadn't succeeded in killing them, but he'd tried. And he'd used her as a decoy to do it. She'd be damned if she'd act as bait for him now.

Instead, she clamped her lips shut, ignoring the taste of blood.

And she waited.

35

Emma's nerves ran hotter and hotter as they approached the final landmark the sheriff had marked on the map. Despite having comforted Denae just minutes earlier, she felt every tick of the speedometer heighten the tension in the vehicle.

If they were wrong about this, it was over for Mia. Because at the very least, Delton Potter would find out they'd been trying to come for him rather than back off and wait for his next trap.

When they got to the "winding dirt road on the right," Emma turned in as quietly as she could. A half mile up, with thick stands of trees on either side, they found another little turnoff, just as Sheriff Ricky had notated, that led over a short rise.

Emma stopped the SUV, and she and Denae got out. The caravan came in behind her, and Jacinda waved for her attention.

When Emma headed over, the SSA explained the plan. "Air support is five minutes out, but SWAT's sending up aerial drones for recon as we speak. The old Potter property checked out as abandoned. Those officers will join us as soon as they can, and we'll hold position until they arrive."

Emma couldn't believe her ears. "Hold position? Mia could be in there dying right now."

"And we're no help to her in that case. If she's still alive and can be rescued, we'll be no help to her if we charge into a potentially armed and fortified area without at least a little reconnaissance first."

Emma burned with frustration but acknowledged Jacinda's point as she stood next to the SSA's vehicle, Denae beside her.

A pair of SWAT officers prepared their reconnaissance drones a few feet away. One of them motioned Emma over to the laptops they'd be displaying the drone feeds on. "We should be able to see any structures or fortifications and hopefully get a visual on Agent Logan's location."

The drones went up moments later, humming into the air as the operators guided them over the rise in the gravel road and into the area beyond.

Emma watched the screen, with Denae, Leo, and Jacinda all huddled around her. The camera view from the first drone revealed the gravel road they'd been following. It crested the rise and led down a short slope to a longer stretch. Trees stood along the right side of the road, but the left was exposed to an open grassy area.

Where the road terminated at the far edge of the clearing, a small house sat waiting for them, tucked into withering trees and patches of dying brush.

The first drone operator held his craft's position, hovering with the camera focused on the building. "Looks like it's about fifty yards away. Maybe sixty. Not much cover here to there. We'll probably want to approach along the periphery. I'll maintain position here in case we see any movement."

Beside him, the second drone operator acknowledged the comment. "Going in for a closer view of the structures."

Her drone was closing in on the building, bringing more detail to the grainy image. Old and scratch-built with mismatched siding and corrugated tin roofing, the house stood amid a ring of thin trees, most of them dead. The dying brush and tree stumps gave the area a haunted and ghastly appearance.

Emma held in a shudder. "Those stumps look like broken teeth." She half expected an army of ghosts to appear. Goose bumps rose beneath her sleeves. Normally, she wasn't one to feel a sense of foreboding, but this place felt *unwelcoming*.

Beside her, Denae huffed. "Fitting, considering what's going on inside the house."

To the left of the front door, Emma saw two mounds or stacks of some material under tarps.

A carport sat to the right of the house, at the end of a gravel drive leading up from the road. Two beat-up sedans were beneath the covering structure beside bags upon bags of trash.

"Leo, do either of those cars look like the one from the liquor store?"

"The one on the right. Same make and model, an older Chrysler."

"What about those tarps?" Emma aimed a finger at the screen and asked the operator to get closer.

"I'll see what I can do, but any lower, and he'll hear the drone for sure. He probably knows we're here already."

Emma spotted a shape that looked like a small, square roof, tucked into the tree line at the perimeter of the property. "Is that an old building or maybe a makeshift structure?"

The drone operator brought her craft down lower. They all startled as a human figure emerged from the brush and grasses piled up around the square object. The long barrel of a rifle was visible for a moment, then the air was split by two shots that crashed through the sky.

Both drone feeds cut out simultaneously. The operators cursed and set down their controllers. Jacinda let out a string of profanity too.

"I guess that answers our question." One operator squinted his eyes, but that was the only hint at emotion he showed. "They're armed, they know we're here, and they have sharpshooters in concealed positions."

Emma remembered what the sheriff had told them.

"...they didn't grow up playing kick the can till they got called in for family dinner. More like shoot the can to smithereens from two hundred yards away."

She was ready to suggest they begin moving around the periphery, as the SWAT officers had proposed, when Jacinda's phone began ringing.

The SSA went to her vehicle and retrieved it from the dashboard mount. She answered the call and put it on speaker, mouthing, *Guess who.*

"Jacinda, we've been through this before. You do as I say, and Mia lives. Since you've decided not to do that, I guess that means she dies."

"I'm glad to hear Mia's still alive, Mr. Potter."

"Figured out who I am, huh? I bet you're really proud of yourselves, using all your government overreach to pry into the lives of sovereign citizens."

That verifies who's helping Potter. Locals born with shotguns in their hands.

"Government overreach isn't why we're here. We just want Agent Logan returned to us."

"Well, see, that's where we have a little problem. Because I don't think you're just going to go away once you get her back. Are you?"

"We'd like nothing more than to leave this place behind, with Mia."

"If you're serious about leaving with her, then you and Agents Ambrose, Monroe, and Last will approach with your hands raised. Alone. None of your backup. I see a single SWAT uniform, and Mia gets the best and last high of her life."

Jacinda met Emma's gaze and those of the others.

SWAT officers were assembling, checking body armor, helmets, and weapons.

"Mr. Potter, we're serious about leaving with Mia. And we don't want anyone getting injured or dosed with anything."

"So come on down the road, Jacinda. No armored vehicles, no riot shields. Just the four of you. And no SWAT bodies in the mix."

The call dropped, and Jacinda stared at her phone before tossing it onto the front seat of the SUV.

"Okay, team. We do as he says. The four of us enter, hands raised. Helmets on and check your vests. If they're planning to pick us off, the best we can do is protect ourselves and hope SWAT's able to neutralize the threat before it emerges."

Leo motioned to the sky with a finger. Emma looked up and caught the telltale chop of a helicopter's rotor. "Just in time. We got a location for at least one of their shooters. They'll be able to identify where any others are hiding, and SWAT can take them out."

Air support is here. Mia, just hang on. We're coming to get you.

Behind the two drone operators, who now held M4 carbines, Sergeant Harsey, the SWAT team leader, signaled for his people to circle up and addressed Jacinda.

"We'll move along the periphery in both directions from this road, staying to the tree line. With air support, we'll spot their sharpshooters, even if they've moved since firing." He motioned at two pairs of officers near the back of his formation. "Our sharpshooter teams will move out with us and provide counter-sniping support from locations along our route. We'll radio you once they've completed infil maneuvers and are in position. Then you can begin your approach."

36

SWAT team members were moving out even as Emma and her team followed Jacinda up the rise to the trees. They kept below the crest of the rise, just in case any sharpshooters had visuals on their location already.

The SSA met their gazes in turn. "Remember, we want to avoid any shooting if we can. We have to assume Mia's inside and therefore in the line of fire. When Sergeant Harsey gives us the all clear, we approach as instructed, hands raised."

Emma stood behind a tree near the top of the rise in the road leading to their objective. The SWAT teams had begun stalking through the tree lines, building the perimeter that would encircle Delton Potter's hideout.

Moments later, Jacinda's radio crackled with Sergeant Harsey's voice. "Air support is scanning with their IR camera. So far, nothing. We know they have at least one sharpshooter on the perimeter somewhere. That person could be in motion and concealed."

"We heard two shots though. Does anyone have a sense of where the second shot came from?"

"Possibly from the house or somewhere behind it."

"Are we good to approach?"

"We have sight lines on the gravel road leading in. Stay to the right side. If anyone starts shooting, go for the trees and take cover. We'll work with the bird to identify the shooter's location."

Jacinda confirmed, then met the team's gaze one by one. "We ready to move?"

The plan was bold. Emma admired Jacinda's guts. She and the SSA might butt heads occasionally, but Emma had never doubted Jacinda's leadership. Neither did the rest of the team. In this moment, all of them would step into a minefield to save Mia. So if Jacinda wanted bold, they would be bold.

Emma adjusted her vest and nodded. Leo and Denae did the same, and the SSA radioed Sergeant Harsey that they were moving out.

"When we get closer, Denae and I will approach from the left. Emma and Leo will be on the right. If any shooting starts, they'll head for the carport. And Denae and I will look for cover by the firewood in front of the house."

"Good copy, Agent Hollingsworth. Let's get your agent back."

Emma stepped up the gravel road and looked back at Leo and the others. "I'll lead with Leo." Not waiting for Jacinda's confirmation, she moved up along the side of the dirt drive, using the trees for cover where possible, for whatever good that did. Even in neutral-toned clothes, their team and their backup would've caught the attention of a toddler engrossed in their favorite cartoon, let alone a drug dealer-turned-kidnapper with a posse of born and bred snipers.

Before she could set one foot over the rise to start their approach, a gunshot cracked from her right, then another from beyond Denae and Jacinda's location across the road. Everyone dropped to a prone position, sliding down the gravel rise as a flurry of automatic weapons fire rattled out in both directions.

Sergeant Harsey's shouting came from Jacinda's radio. "Multiple hostile units engaged. Looks like they planned on putting you in a kill box. We have one of their sharpshooters down. No idea how many more could be out there."

"How did they hide from the IR camera?"

"I've seen ghillie suits, and it looks like they have some makeshift cover built up out here, probably with a radiant barrier of some kind. Stay put for now."

Jacinda replied that they would hold position, but Emma only half heard the SSA's words. She was already on her feet and charging up the rise, staying to the trees as best she could.

Mia's in that house, and SWAT shut down their kill-box idea. This is our chance.

Leo came up to Emma's shoulder as Jacinda and Denae formed up beside a tree on his left. The SSA wasted no time in ordering them all to stand down, focusing her gaze on Emma as she did.

"We wait until SWAT confirms it's safe. Nobody's rushing out there alone."

"How long do we wait? What if they're killing Mia right now or running to some other location?"

Jacinda's eyes never wavered from Emma's. "We wait. When it's safe, we'll move in and pursue if we have to. Air support will let us know if they start moving."

Seconds later, Jacinda's radio crackled again. "Three bodies moving away from the house, going deeper into the woods. Multiple suspects fleeing to either side as well. We're flushing them out."

Dancing from foot to foot, Emma was ready to run straight for the house. "I say we head to the carport. Follow the road, staying to the tree line, and take cover by the vehicles. SWAT will tell us which direction they're going with Mia."

Jacinda nodded and told Sergeant Harsey the plan, then motioned for them to move out. Emma was already stepping over the rise and heading down the other side before the other three had started moving.

With Leo and the others at her six, Emma pressed on, aiming for the first of the two sedans under the carport. She slid to a stop beside the right rear fender, and Leo joined her seconds later.

Jacinda and Denae were there soon after.

The only sounds, other than their rapid breathing, were the echoing voices of SWAT agents calling out for suspects to disarm and put their hands up. A few stray gunshots rattled out from across the grassy area. Jacinda checked with Sergeant Harsey if they were still safe to move.

"Good to go, Jacinda. We have three suspects in custody. Two wounded and another confirmed dead. Air support confirms the three that fled the house are among those we've picked up."

"So Mia might still be inside the house."

"Possibly, yeah. We can't get visual on the interior, and they must have a radiant barrier inside, because the IR isn't picking anything up."

Emma inched around the sedan's rear bumper, and a slip of movement caught her eye. She froze, focused on the front window, which was mostly covered with plywood. But one vertical band was left clear, probably for ventilation if they were cooking meth inside.

A lumbering shadow moved by, and then another one. Neither could possibly have been Mia—not unless they'd disguised her as a man and somehow convinced her to play along, which seemed unlikely.

"They're inside, Jacinda. Somebody's in there. At least two people."

Thumbing her radio, Jacinda relayed the news to Sergeant Harsey. "We have at least two persons inside the house. We're going to approach. Stay back unless I call you in."

"He could still be planning to gun you down on his own."

"I understand that. We're wearing vests, and it sounds like his support left him high and dry. I'm going to negotiate with him." Jacinda stayed concealed behind the sedan and called out. "Delton Potter! We're here, and there are no SWAT officers with us. We want to talk."

Emma counted the seconds. Thirty-seven of them passed before a head appeared at the window, just taking a peek. There and then gone, but clear enough that Emma had glimpsed the fury in the flat line of his mouth and angry brow.

Their target was behind that door.

37

Staring out the back kitchen window, I saw blood. Blood from my backup who'd run off like cowards the minute that helicopter showed up. I only got one of them in the back, dropping him on the ground while his buddies scattered like rats from a sinking ship.

And that was what I was standing on, a sinking fucking ship. I knew it and knew there was no way out of this mess except dying.

I bet my sharpshooters ran off too. They took out those damn drones, then bailed, just like the fuckers who were supposed to have my back here.

I looked at the body out there, sprawled on the ground behind the house, legs sticking out from behind some bushes. I spit on the floor, wishing I could spit on the dead coward's face.

The shooting had stopped, and the Feds were at my front door now. I could still hear Jacinda Hollingsworth telling me she wanted to talk.

My brother came up behind me, and I almost spun around and shot him for it.

"Delton, man, we're fucked. We're so fucked. This ain't funny anymore, man. We gotta give up. Just go out and—"

I smacked him sideways into the curtains hanging outside the kitchen. "You a coward, too, Billy boy? Like that piece of shit in the dirt out there?"

He held a hand to his face, and I wanted so badly to just kick him in the teeth and keep kicking. A tear streaked down his cheek.

Crying like a baby. I knew you were only good for one thing. Cooking in the kitchen.

"You're useless. And you disgust me. Get the fuck out of my sight."

Billy shifted on his feet, eyes finally coming to me.

I grinned at him, channeling all the rage I'd been building up over these long years of suffering under the government's thumb. I had one play left. "Time to make a last stand, Billy. Time to prove you deserve to wear the Potter family name."

Without waiting for him to catch on, I stepped around my brother and slammed open the door to the room where I kept our pet Fed. She was lying flat on the floor, as flat as she could get while being chained to the pipe.

A few bullets had come through the plywood covering the window, but nothing hit her. Some splinters were stuck to her blouse.

She looked like any other addict with the sweats, working herself toward death in her own little hole of depression.

Billy hovered behind me, wringing his hands like Mom might've if she'd still been around. "Delton, man, what are we doing?"

"Trust me. Follow along. You're gonna be fine. Piss me off, and I might just shoot you myself. Save the government the trouble of spending taxpayer dollars on a bullet for your useless ass."

I tucked the gun into the back of my pants, then squatted

down and undid my prisoner's wrists from around the pipe. I re-cuffed her and undid her ankles so she could walk, then yanked her up to standing. Even without the cuffs around her ankles, she stumbled, favoring the knee I'd been playing with earlier.

I shoved her past Billy and into the living room.

He stopped behind me. Jacinda was yelling again about wanting to talk.

"Billy, help me with her."

He shook his head and sank down to sit on his ass right by the plastic curtains closing off the kitchen. I almost shot him right then and there but just spit at him in disgust instead.

"Fuck you, then. I'll tell them it was all your idea." I turned away and all but carried my prisoner to the door. Limp-limbed, she whimpered some nonsense about changing my mind, but she didn't pull away.

Probably knows what's still in my pocket.

I opened the door just a touch and brought her tight to my chest, then shifted her so that her head hung out the door. I held it up by grabbing hold of her hair with my free hand. "We're gonna do an old-fashioned trade! SWAT and their helicopter need to fuck off! Then we talk!"

My little bargaining chip twitched in my grip.

I heard someone yell, "It'll be okay, Mia!" and my whole body went hot with annoyance. I pressed her into the wall between me and the door, using my weight and a knee against her legs to hold her up while I dug in my pocket for the syringe. I got it out, pulled the cap off with my teeth, and stuck my arm out the door enough so they could all see what I was holding.

"No fucking games! See?" I placed the needle to her neck.

A high-pitched whimper bled up out of her throat. "Please."

"Shut it." I tented her skin with the needle, drawing blood without pressing down the plunger. "This is for the revolution, and you've earned it."

Panicked shouts erupted outside, proving they'd seen the needle.

I yanked the bitch back inside and landed her against the wall in front of me even as I slammed the door closed with my foot.

"Delton!" Billy called from where he still sat on his ass by the kitchen. "Man, you're gonna get us killed! We gotta surrender."

I took the syringe away from her neck and held it between my teeth, freeing up my hand to reach for the Desert Eagle at the small of my back. I drew it and aimed at my brother, holding it on him until he paled. Maybe that would get through to him.

"Don't even fucking think about it."

38

When the door cracked open and Mia's ragged face appeared, a surge of relief rushed through Emma. Seeing her friend's face was the greatest proof of life she could've received. She looked like absolute hell, but she was alive, and that meant they had a chance to get her back.

As long as Mia stayed alive, everything would be okay.

A pair of SWAT officers had arrived at the opposite side of the house. They circled around the back to ensure nobody fled from that direction. Two additional pairs of officers were converging from their positions on the periphery but were keeping as hidden as possible. And six members of the SWAT team made a show of departing from the property, in response to Delton Potter's demands that they do so.

The helicopter had moved away, as well, but maintained visual contact with the site.

Paramedics were en route with additional law enforcement.

It'll be okay. It'll be okay.

Emma didn't know if she one hundred percent believed herself. The only thing she knew for certain was that she wanted to handle the negotiations with the dirtbag. "Let me do the talking, Jacinda. He'll underestimate an underling, especially a woman, and that could give us a shot at getting Mia out of there safely."

Leo grunted, still staring at the door where they'd seen a loaded syringe at Mia's throat. "This asshole doesn't seem primed to listen to anyone but himself."

Jacinda squinted at Emma. "Talk me through your approach."

"He's already taken down Mia. He'll expect another woman to be just as easy to defeat, and he's challenged you every time you've talked with him."

"True enough, but he's also given us information each time we've spoken."

"But he knows you're the leader. You're in charge. He's going to keep challenging you and might be more likely to hurt Mia in the process, to prove his dominance."

The SSA sat quietly for a moment and finally nodded. "Okay, Emma, you're it. We'll keep out of sight as much as we can and will back you up from here."

Holding her gun up as if in surrender, Emma stepped partially out from behind the stack of firewood and aimed her focus at the front of the house, remaining on alert for any movement from the window. "Delton, this is Agent Emma Last!"

"Fuck off!" he yelled through the cracked door. "I want your SWAT assholes off my land, and that shit bird in the sky needs to leave! We get that, or you get nothing!"

"You want the SWAT assholes to leave, I hear you. SWAT's already leaving, Delton."

"Get rid of the shit bird!"

"And the helicopter is just observing from a safe distance. See? All we're asking for in exchange for your requests is Agent Logan, alive. Let's talk about a peaceful resolution."

"You don't have the power to make deals when I've killed a cop! I'm not stupid!"

"You're not stupid. You know how things work."

"Damn right I do!"

Emma kept her tone smooth and soothing. This was the hard part about hostage negotiations—keeping the hostage taker calm and reasonable when all you wanted to do was shoot him in the head. Emma held her gun higher, to where Delton would have to see it away from her body if he looked out.

"We can make a deal, Delton. You have a hostage. Since you know how things work, you know that if you kill her, you are done. We won't be willing to negotiate. You take a deal, you and your brother get out of here alive. This can still end with nobody else dying."

For an agonizing second, he didn't answer, and then the door was pulled open again. Delton stepped out with Mia in front of him. He hunched behind her, using her as cover.

Emma's throat nearly closed, and Leo groaned beside her. Mia's clothes clung to her body indecently, and her mouth was opened wide in pain. The syringe Delton had threatened her with before was already inserted into her neck—though he hadn't pushed in the plunger.

Mia was suffering, but alive.

She seemed to rally even as Delton clutched her tightly to him.

"I'm okay. Everybody, I'm okay."

Delton hissed something in her ear, and she flinched. His hand holding the syringe wavered a bit, and Emma could see the needle sliding deeper into her neck.

Mia let out a high-pitched yelp that was drowned out by the monstrously loud howl of a wolf in Emma's head.

Instinctively, she brought her gun down as she covered her ears.

Before Delton could react to her movement, his brother appeared behind him, pushing past with his hands raised, running forward and falling to his knees. "Don't shoot! I want to negotiate!"

Sirens wailed from behind them, announcing the arrival of paramedics and more cops. Delton stiffened and cursed.

"He's gonna—" Leo was cut off by a shout as Jacinda and Denae raced forward to collect Delton's brother from where he'd flattened himself on the ground.

Delton backed against the doorway, sinking to a crouch and holding Mia against him with his left arm.

The syringe was hanging out the side of her neck as he dropped his right hand behind his back and quickly brought up a huge handgun that he aimed in Jacinda and Denae's direction. His left hand crawled up Mia's chest to her collar to grip the syringe clumsily. He held it with his fingers over the plunger, and he could still drive it down before anybody could stop him, even with his nondominant hand.

Emma lifted her gun high in the air, showing Delton she meant him no harm.

Mia sagged back against him as he shifted, trying to retreat into the house. With her eyes closed, she looked half dead.

Waving off her fellow agents, Emma took a tentative step forward. In her periphery, she could see Jacinda cuffing a whimpering Billy Potter while Denae and Leo aimed their weapons at Delton.

The older of the two brothers spit more venomous insults at them all. "You fucking parasites. Federal bullshit investigators! Take one more step, and she dies!"

Emma heard the threat in his voice. He was at his last resort, with absolutely nothing to lose. If he saw anyone take one more step, he would press the plunger.

But he couldn't watch all of them at once.

He was focused on Leo and Denae, who hadn't lowered their weapons or stood down. They were an imminent threat, so Delton Potter didn't see Emma as she took a delicate step forward, and then another.

Two more steps, and she'd be close enough to rush in and stop him.

But Delton was done negotiating.

The fingers of his left hand curled in and brought the plunger down as he opened fire.

"No!" Emma yelled.

Mia crumpled against him, her mouth shooting open in reaction to the overdose of meth. Delton continued to fire, aiming wildly now.

Emma sprinted toward him, her gun up.

She was done negotiating too.

Mia slid down the man's body, falling to the dirt in front of the house, and Emma took her shot.

She hit Delton square in the forehead and toppled him backward through his own front door, where he thudded on the floor.

As Emma reached Mia, desperation forced her to ignore everything else around her. She clutched at her friend's convulsing form and began yelling for medical help. Emma held Mia and carefully removed the syringe from her neck. She smoothed down her friend's matted hair as EMTs swarmed them.

39

In the chaos, Emma fell back as the EMTs gathered Mia onto a gurney. She watched them haul her friend and colleague into the ambulance, but she couldn't hear the wail of the sirens.

The wolf howl was too loud. High pitched and ululating, the cry made her head ring. She pressed her hands against her ears, but the gesture didn't help. The sound was *angry*.

Emma stood in the open space between the house and the stacked firewood, her hands over her ears like a child. She turned away from the cabin and saw another EMT team surrounding someone on the ground.

Thinking about the wild shots fired, Emma's heart thudded in her chest. She'd been so focused on Mia, she hadn't seen anyone else go down.

Immediately, she started counting up her team and everyone was accounted for. Leo and Jacinda were administering first aid with the EMTs, who were pulling out more equipment than Mia's team had. Denae stood over the whole group, watching.

Whoever was on the ground was in bad shape.

Emma stepped forward, the howling growing louder and louder in her ears. She gritted her teeth against it.

Then it felt like she was buried in ice.

Denae faced her, white eyes staring straight into her soul.

"No," Emma whispered, and she didn't hear her own voice. She ran to the group around the person on the ground and recognized Denae's body.

Leo was bent over Denae, putting pressure on her armpit, begging her to come back.

Emma looked at the body on the ground. Shredded fibers from the edge of her vest, beneath her left arm, told Emma what had happened.

In his wild firing, Delton Potter had struck Denae in the armpit. He'd probably hit her heart. There was blood all over the grass, soaking into the dirt. One of the EMTs was packing the wound, which slowed the bleeding. But Emma didn't know if that was due to the EMT's efforts or because the heart Leo was so desperately trying to revive had stopped beating.

Behind Leo, Jacinda stood with one hand on his shoulder, trying to pull him back to let the EMTs in there to help. But Leo wasn't listening.

Denae's ghost stood looming over Leo, even as he begged and pleaded for her to come back to him.

"Come on, Denae, dammit!"

She's gone, Leo. I can see her.

Maybe Emma could do something. She'd been warned about trying to interact with the Other, about trying to talk to the ghosts of people she was close to, especially her mother.

But what good was this so-called gift if she couldn't use it to help the people she cared about most in the world? She fell to her knees beside Leo, but she addressed the ghost standing over them rather than the woman on the ground.

Putting as much authority as she could muster into her voice, which she could barely hear over the howling, she looked straight at the ghost. "Denae, come back." She steadied her gaze on Denae's blank face. "Denae, you heard me. I said come back. Right now!"

The wolf howl crescendoed. She never knew a sound could be so loud.

Beside her, Leo startled, looking up, focusing all the while on his grim task. Then his eyes shot back down to the woman he loved. "You have to come back, Denae. Please. Please."

Emma could see plainly that the ghost was listening. "Denae, please. Please, please, please. We need you. Come back."

Denae's ghost spoke softly. "Tell Scruffy I'll keep the wolf quiet for a while."

Leo pressed Denae's chest beside her, muttering his own demands to no avail.

Emma was so tired of ghosts' cryptic bullshit. Why couldn't they ever give her a fucking straight answer? "What do you mean, tell Scruffy you'll keep the wolf quiet? What do you *mean*? You tell him! Come back right now!"

Leo's gaze went briefly to hers. "What the fuck are you talking about? Emma? What the hell—"

"Denae said…" Emma couldn't finish the sentence. It was too much to explain. Too big. "I'll tell you later, I'll tell you everything, I promise but—"

Denae's form shimmered, faded, and finally disappeared from view.

The howling, the cursed howling, stopped.

Panicked, Emma hollered into the space where Denae's ghost had been a split second before. "Denae Monroe, you get back here *right the fuck now*!"

Leo screamed something unintelligible.

Jacinda was suddenly behind Emma, gripping her shoulders and shouting with…joy?

She hauled Emma back. And Leo moved aside too, finally. Denae, the Denae on the ground, was surrounded by EMTs now. One of the EMTs held her wrist in his hands and nodded while the others took over compressions and prepped her for travel.

The one holding her arm cracked a weak smile. "It's faint, but she's with us."

Emma and Leo stood as the EMTs lifted Denae onto a gurney.

"Let's get her in. It's going to be touch and go."

As if in response to the EMT's doubt, Denae's ghost was across from Emma now, flickering in and out of sight beside Leo.

"Tell Scruffy—"

"Tell him yourself, Denae." Emma shook Jacinda's hands from her shoulders. "We're saving your ass right now, so you tell him yourself!"

Leo swooped back in beside Denae on the gurney, but his eyes, swimming with a million questions, remained trained on Emma.

No matter how this played out, Emma would have some serious explaining to do. She shook her head and stepped past him and the EMTs.

"Denae, come back here!"

Her friend's ghost floated away and vanished again.

The End
To be continued…

Thank you for reading.
All of Emma Last series books can be found on Amazon.

ACKNOWLEDGMENTS

The past few years have been a whirlwind of change, both personally and professionally, and I find myself at a loss for the right words to express my profound gratitude to those who have supported me on this remarkable journey. Yet, I am compelled to try.

To my sons, whose unwavering support has been my bedrock, granting me the time and energy to transform my darkest thoughts into words on paper. Your steadfast belief in me has never faltered, and watching each of you grow, welcoming the wonderful daughters you've brought into our family, has been a source of immense pride and joy.

Embarking on the dual role of both author and publisher has been an exhilarating, albeit challenging, adventure. Transitioning from the solitude of writing to the dynamic world of publishing has opened new horizons for me, and I'm deeply grateful for the opportunity to share my work directly with you, the readers.

I extend my heartfelt thanks to the entire team at Mary Stone Publishing, the same dedicated group who first recognized my potential as an indie author years ago. Your collective efforts, from the editors whose skillful hands have polished my words to the designers, marketers, and support staff who breathe life into these books, have been instrumental in resonating deeply with our readers. Each of you plays a crucial role in this journey, not only nurturing my growth but also ensuring that every story reaches its full potential. Your dedication, creativity, and finesse have been nothing short of invaluable.

However, my deepest gratitude is reserved for you, my beloved readers. You ventured off the beaten path of traditional publishing to embrace my work, investing your most precious asset—your time. It is my sincerest hope that this book has enriched that time, leaving you with memories that linger long after the last page is turned.

With all my love and heartfelt appreciation,
Mary

ABOUT THE AUTHOR

Mary Stone

Nestled in the serene Blue Ridge Mountains of East Tennessee, Mary Stone crafts her stories surrounded by the natural beauty that inspires her. What was once a home filled with the lively energy of her sons has now become a peaceful writer's retreat, shared with cherished pets and the vivid characters of her imagination.

As her sons grew and welcomed wonderful daughters-in-law into the family, Mary's life entered a quieter phase, rich with opportunities for deep creative focus. In this tranquil environment, she weaves tales of courage, resilience, and intrigue, each story a testament to her evolving journey as a writer.

From childhood fears of shadowy figures under the bed to a profound understanding of humanity's real-life villains, Mary's style has been shaped by the realization that the most complex antagonists often hide in plain sight. Her writing is characterized by strong, multifaceted heroines who defy traditional roles, standing as equals among their peers in a world of suspense and danger.

Mary's career has blossomed from being a solitary author to establishing her own publishing house—a significant milestone that marks her growth in the literary world. This expansion is not just a personal achievement but a reflection of her commitment to bring thrilling and thought-provoking stories to a wider audience. As an author and publisher, Mary continues to challenge the conventions of the thriller genre, inviting readers into gripping tales filled with serial killers, astute FBI agents, and intrepid heroines who confront peril with unflinching bravery.

Each new story from Mary's pen—or her publishing house—is a pledge to captivate, thrill, and inspire, continuing the legacy of the imaginative little girl who once found wonder and mystery in the shadows.

Connect with Mary online

- facebook.com/authormarystone
- x.com/MaryStoneAuthor
- goodreads.com/AuthorMaryStone
- bookbub.com/profile/3378576590
- pinterest.com/MaryStoneAuthor
- instagram.com/marystoneauthor
- tiktok.com/@authormarystone

Printed in Great Britain
by Amazon